That
Far Away
Look

That Far Away Look

Michael G. Moran

Autumn Harbor Press

Atlanta, GA

That Far Away Look

Autumn Harbor Press

October 2009

ISBN 978-0-9825732-1-1

For more information about Autumn Harbor books,
please visit our website @ www.autumnharbor.com

To Alison and Molly

Chapter 1

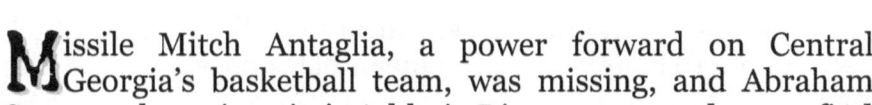

Missile Mitch Antaglia, a power forward on Central Georgia's basketball team, was missing, and Abraham Seamer, the university's Athletic Director, wanted me to find him.

It was close to November, near the beginning of college basketball season, and I was driving north from Atlanta to Ithaca to meet Seamer. I had no trouble finding the huge sparkling glass building that he had told me to look for over to the right of Marshall Avenue. That was the new athletic complex that housed the athletic offices, ticket sales, and Central's athletic hall of fame. It looked more like a place of worship, a cathedral or an ornate masonic temple, than a modern campus building. It certainly did not look like traditional athletic architecture, a coliseum or a gymnasium. I followed Seamer's directions to the visitors parking lot and found myself at a small wooden structure that housed a guard.

"Got a pass, sir?" a tall black man in uniform inquired,

scrutinizing me and perusing my car inside and out. He looked like a former athlete who had gone to seed, a bit puffy in the belly, walking with the slight limp due to an old ankle or knee injury.

"I have an appointment to see Abraham Seamer," I replied.

"Your name?"

"Stirling, Nick Stirling. He's expecting me."

The guard scanned a list on a clipboard.

"Certainly, Mr. Stirling. Just park down at the end of the lot at the right. The door you take is across from your spot."

I took a stab in the dark and asked, "What can you tell me about Mitchell Antaglia?"

The guard looked at me carefully, as if he were weighing his options. "You mean Missile Mitch Antaglia, the great white hope for Central basketball?" he said mockingly. He looked tall enough to have played college ball himself.

"That's the one," I replied.

"The only scuttlebutt I hear around is that young Mitch went home to daddy when the mean black coach treated him bad."

"You don't say, Clarence," I said, after looking at his name tag. "You think Mitch took off because he didn't like the head coach?"

"The new *blaaack* coach."

Another car pulled up behind me to enter the lot, and I had to move on.

"If I take this job, I'm supposed to find the Missile," I said as I eased my Accord into the lot. Glancing into the rear view mirror, I saw Clarence giving me a friendly salute.

I entered the door Clarence had pointed out, walked up the stairs, and found myself in a huge hexagon of a rotunda that had the feel of a museum. The floors were white marble, speckled with black veins, and the walls were painted in black and red patterns, the color of the Georgia Central Lions. Along the walls were various glass cases with gleaming trophies. From the ceiling hung colorful banners celebrating Central's championships, most of them for football, golf, and tennis. Not many for basketball, I noticed. Several lines of people, mostly dressed in the school colors, inched to a two-windowed ticket kiosk in the middle of the floor to buy football tickets.

"But I was told I could buy four extras, not just two," one white-haired alumnus whined to the ticket seller as I walked by. "I paid my $10,000 and expect better treatment than this!"

"Next!" the ticket agent barked.

I found the elevator and took it to the third floor, where I had no trouble locating the Athletic Director's office. The matronly secretary seated in the outer office was busy talking to a huge lineman with a moon face and a cast on his ankle. "And once it's healed it will be better than new," she said as I walked up. The name plate on her desk said Candy Saddleford. When she noticed me, she winked at the athlete, who glanced at me, teetered on his new crutches, and lumbered away.

She smiled at me and shook her head. "That's one of the best freshman defensive guards in the nation, just recruited last year. And now the poor thing's hurt and won't be able to play against Tech in a few weeks and in the bowl game this December. He feels like his world is coming to an end."

"It's hard to remember that many of these huge guys are just teenagers," I said, remembering my own football days as a half back in high school.

"You're right, hon," she said with friendly brightness. "How may I help you?"

"Nick Stirling, Candy" I said. "I have a 10:00 with Mr. Seamer."

She looked me up and down. "You're the detective from Atlanta?"

"That's right."

"You look younger than I expected," she said.

"Forty is the new twenty," I joked.

She smiled and said, "I'm glad you're here. He's expecting you."

She picked up her phone, pushed a button, and whispered into a mouth piece. "O.K., I will," she murmured.

"Coach Seamer said to go right in," she informed me, pointing to a door to the right.

When I entered the office, Seamer walked toward me, holding out his hand. He was dressed in a red polo shirt that emphasized his pot belly, a pair of chinos, and athletic shoes with the ubiquitous Nike swoosh on the sides. He had the nervous demeanor of a man with too many responsibilities and too little time and talent to meet them. His eyes darted uncomfortably around the room to avoid mine. Then he glanced at his watch as he moved me toward a pair of divans, making it clear I was on the clock.

As he returned to his desk for a file, I eyed his spacious office. Everything was in school colors, including the rug, which was bright red, the same color as his knit shirt. The walls were painted black, and on them hung photographs of Seamer at various ages. In one, he was a college running back with a flat top and a Georgia Central uniform, jumping slightly and giving an invisible opponent a straight arm. In another, he was an assistant coach, standing to the right of a football team that looked like it was from the 70's, given the hair styles and side burns. In yet another he was being carried on the shoulders of two madly grinning linemen celebrating an important victory. In more recent photos, he was shaking hands with various dignitaries, including Jimmy Carter, who smiled toothily in the direction of the camera rather than at Seamer. In all of them, the old coach looked pleased with himself and was a good deal slimmer than he was now.

"Thank you for driving all this way, Mr. Stirling," he said as he sat down across from me. "You come highly recommended, especially for your confidentiality, by my old friend Lawrence Kimble, the DA in Fulton Country."

I nodded in response to the compliment. I would have to remember to thank Lew for the recommendation.

After a bit of small talk, during which it was established that my former wife graduated from Central and I had attended a few football games near the end of his coaching career, Seamer got down to business.

"As I mentioned over the phone, we're missing one of our basketball players, a youngster named Mitchell Antaglia. He seems to have disappeared about two weeks or so ago, and we're trying to locate him before basketball season starts in December."

"I understand that you mean Missile Mitch," I said.

He looked at me sharply and said, "Yes. That's his popular designation. The athletic program is not so happy with that name. It was given to him by his father, who was a former coach here. Then the media picked it up. The father played a very minor role in our program, years ago coaching various freshman teams up through about 1995. Then he retired, much to everyone's delight."

"Why delight?" I asked.

"Antaglia was an embarrassment," he explained. "He had some odd ideas from the past, before modern methods had taught us how to effectively coach. For instance, when he coached our freshman football team in the scorching Geogia summers, he wouldn't give his players water breaks. Thought it toughened them up." Seamer frowned. "Lucky the SOB didn't kill some kid." He looked like he had law suits on his mind.

"I understand from what you said on the phone that the father is playing an important role in the search for Mitch."

Seamer explained that he was. Though a minor coach, Antaglia had married a younger woman, some sort of German heiress of all things, later in life, about twenty years ago. "Nobody understood the attraction," he said snidely. But Antaglia, Seamer said, also now had money from another source. He had recently published a book called *Coaching Genius* that for over a year had been on the best seller list. "The book is similar to Earl Woods' book on raising Tiger Woods—how to raise a great athlete, a great basketball player in this case," Seamer continued.

"I've seen it in book stores," I said.

"It's not a very good book, in my opinion, but it's been popular. Tells how to feed a young athlete, how to prepare him mentally, how to make him dedicated to his sport, the fundamentals—stuff like that. Half the fathers in the nation with a son now want to make him into a basketball star by following the book's guidelines. Coach Antaglia therefore is suddenly wealthy, thinks he's important, and he's putting pressure on us to find Mitchell for him," Seamer said. "Says Mitch was fine until he got here." He paused. "And by the way, if you take this job, I don't want you to contact Antaglia or his wife. They think all their problems grow out of our mistreatment of Mitch. They've threatened to sue the university's Athletic Program."

"I understand that your basketball program has had some problems and at least some of them did revolve around Mitch," I said. When he looked at me quizzically, I mentioned that I had gotten this information from the Atlanta papers, which had been playing up the inability of the basketball coach to keep his star players happy. One columnist had written that the coach, not the Missile, should be ditched.

Seamer explained that there were indeed problems, serious problems, in the basketball program. The previous coach, a man named Fletcher, had been fired two years ago, after recruiting Mitchell and a few other players of his type. Fletcher had come to Central well recommended for his run-and-gun style of fast break basketball. This was a perfect style for Mitch, who was a fast break player who usually scored on the run. The problems started when Fletcher was fired over a recruiting scandal and was replaced by his assistant coach, Marcus Brown, who introduced a much slower game based on ball control and zone defense. Mitch suddenly no longer fit the game plan, couldn't adjust, lost playing time, and began talking of transferring to another university. "In fact," Seamer said, "one theory was that Mitchell had left on a recruiting trip to another college, but he's been missing too long for that."

"How do you know he's missing?" I asked.

He explained that Mitchell hadn't been back to his dorm room or his parents' house here in town for over two weeks.

"Have you called the police?" I asked, and he said he had discussed the case with Captain Terrence Madison of the Ithaca police, who had said it was too early to worry about a college kid being missing. He said they often take off on a lark only to return in two or three weeks. "You should talk to Madison," he said. "I'd like him involved every step of the way." I nodded that I would.

"Does Mitch have any siblings I should contact?" I asked.

"None living," Seamer responded. "He had a younger sister, Christa, but she died many years ago in a drowning accident."

"A drowning accident where?"

"In the family's backyard pool," he said.

This family has had its share of tragedy with children, I thought. A dead daughter and a missing son.

"Any chance Mitchell's case is a kidnaping for money?" I asked.

"Could be. At least that's what that old fool Antaglia thinks is going on." Seamer paused. "One reason I question the kidnapping is because Mitch faked a kidnapping before, when he was a freshman in high school."

"What happened?" I asked.

"From what I remember, he ran off to Atlanta with a girlfriend of his, and the two of them tried to scam his parents for a sum of money," Seamer said.

"Was this event well known?" I asked.

"No," Seamer responded. "The Antaglias managed to keep it quiet. I only knew about it because I had been Antaglia's boss at one time. But it's something you should check out."

"I'll do that," I assured him.

"And Antaglia now has the gall to blame Mitchell's current disappearance on me and the Athletic Program, for not keeping our most important athlete under lock and key," Seamer said, disdainfully.

"Any truth to that?"

"No, of course not. It's true that Central is a football school, and we traditionally don't do as well in basketball, but we've treated Mitch like any other athlete." He made a sour face. "Given him everything he could expect," Seamer muttered.

"Have there been any recent changes in Mitch's life—new friends, a breakup with a girlfriend, fights with a roommate? I've found that kids Mitch's age often are thrown off track by changes like this."

Seamer thought for a moment. "Don't know, Mr. Stirling. You'll have to ask Coach Brown about that. He's responsible for keeping track of his players. His office is on the second floor," Seamer said, pointing down as if to indicate a region of lesser importance. Then he looked at me nervously and said, "This is an awkward time for us, Stirling. Coach Brown has been fired. It happened late yesterday, and I haven't released the information to the papers yet. Coach Schuster, Brown's assistant, will take over as head coach until we hire someone permanently." He ran his fingers through his hair as if he was tired of dealing with such problems. "Please be discreet and keep the firing under your hat for the time being."

"Certainly," I replied.

"Good," Seamer said and shifted his weight on the divan to indicate that our time was up. We agreed on a fee, and he wrote me a check on an Athletic Program account and shuffled me to the door. He poked his head out to ask Ms. Saddleford to show me to Coach Brown's office.

"Keep in touch, Mr. Stirling, and please don't contact Antaglia," he reminded me as he shook my hand. "If you need anything, get in touch with me." He handed me his card. "And see Captain Madison."

"Will do," I said, turning away. "Oh, there is one more thing," I added. "A recent picture of Mitch. Do you have one? I've only seen a few black and whites in the newspapers."

"See Brown about that," he said, as he firmly closed the door. He gave the impression he was just going through the motions of finding Missile Mitch.

Chapter 2

D id you take the job, hon?" Candy asked as we walked into the stairwell and headed down.

"I did," I replied, and she stopped on the second floor landing, looking at me intently. "Good. I always felt sorry for Mitchell."

"Did you know him well?"

"I guess I get to know most of our athletes. A lot of them are looking for a mother when they get here, and I'm often the woman they talk to about their problems, the personal ones, that is. And Mitch seemed to have his share of those."

"What were those?"

"His main issues were with his father," she said.

"What were the nature of these issues?" I asked.

"I'm not an expert in psychology," she responded, "but I got the impression that he deeply resented his father. I knew Coach Antaglia a little—he retired soon after I started here in about 1995—and I found him, well, a bit taken with himself— you know, a braggart. He always put down the other coaches for being soft on the athletes—he liked to work his boys hard."

"Like not giving them water in the summer heat," I said.

"You heard about that, huh? But that's not the only thing he did." She looked around and lowered her voice. "People around here don't like me talking about our problems, but Coach Antaglia, in my opinion, mistreated his boys. He tried to make his players aggressive. He encouraged them to fight each other. His JV players always seemed to be in trouble— you know, fighting in bars, being picked up for DUIs, thrown in jail for stealing from other students, those kinds of things. I think he kinda raised Mitch that way."

"To fight and drink and steal, you mean?"

"Yes. Well, maybe not to steal. But to fight, yes. The worse part was that Mitch was not an aggressive young man. His real nature was to be sweet, but his father had tried to raise him to be mean. And I think he succeeded. Just a few weeks ago Mitch was in a bar brawl in which a number of students were badly hurt. Mitch himself was banged up, too, but he almost killed two frat boys. It made the local paper even though Coach Antaglia tried to keep it out."

"Well, college athletes tend to be aggressive," I remarked to keep her talking.

"But not all coaches emphasize that kind of personal aggression," she said. A lot of the young men she knew were "sweetie pies," she said, and needed, in her opinion, to be handled differently.

"Like Mitch?"

"I think so," Candy said. "You know what he did last summer?" she asked, dreamily. "He wrote me a poem."

"A poem!?" I said, trying unsuccessfully to keep the surprise out of my voice.

"You don't believe me, do you? Well, a lot of our boys have good hearts if they're only given a chance to show them. Mitch has been taking courses in poetry writing in the English department. I think he's got talent," she said, looking at me with a mother's pride. I noticed she didn't have a wedding ring. "We'd better get going before Coach Brown wonders what happened to us."

She led me through a maze of hallways past offices with the names of various coaches and their sports. We stopped at an office at the end of a hall, and she tapped on the door and went in, beckoning me to follow. We entered a small outer office almost entirely taken up by the secretary's desk.

"Deborah must be on break," Candy said with a hint of disapproval. "I'll introduce you to Coach Brown. He's a sweetie-pie," she said as she opened the door. Apparently, he was not aggressive.

Coach Brown lived in a different world from Seamer. The office was smaller and shabbier. It had a lived-in look with a worn carpet and chipped paint. The office looked particularly bad because the walls were bare from the pictures having been removed. Liquor boxes filled with what looked like pictures and other office material were piled in the corner. Brown was already on his way out.

The coach himself was at his desk, his head bent over a pile of papers on which he appeared to be making notes. He didn't notice for a moment that we had entered, but when he did he stood up and smiled. He was tall, 6' 6" or so, and wore a tailored grey sports jacket with black pants and a tie with a bright African print. His hair was cut conservatively close to the scalp. I had seen him a few times coaching on TV, and he looked slimmer in person.

After Candy had made a brief introduction and left, Brown waved me to a chair in front of his desk, sat down, and looked at me with penetrating eyes.

"So you're here about Mitch Antaglia," he said.

"That's right. Coach Seamer has asked me to look into his disappearance," I said, returning his stare.

"Disappearance? Hah!" he exclaimed.

"I take it you don't think he disappeared," I responded.

"No, I don't, Mr. Stirling. From what I've been able to

figure out, by talking to some of the few players he still confides in, Mitch has decided to transfer to another school."

"Why is that?" I asked.

Brown moved his big body in his chair and looked up at the ceiling as if he saw a cockroach crawling above his head. "Let me give you a little bit of history about Mitch," he said as he settled in.

Mitch, he explained, was a holdover from the old head coach, Fletcher, who had brought Brown himself to Central as his assistant to coach primarily defense, his speciality. Fletcher ran a fast break offense, and Mitch had been recruited for that style of play. He was fast as a nuclear missile—hence his nickname—with an almost perfect style to play power forward. When Fletcher was accused of recruiting violations and fired, Brown himself was hired temporarily as head coach and then, under some controversy, was hired permanently. He coached a different kind of game that was based on ball control, setting up shots, and defense, all skills that Mitch had never developed as a player.

"He played more of a street game, fast and loose," Brown concluded. "Fast break, fast shots, aggressive penetration—that was the game Mitch had learned from his father."

"Do you know Coach Antaglia?"

Brown said he had met him briefly at various events and had had a confrontation with him when he brought in his new system. "Antaglia didn't like it from the start and complained that Mitch wasn't getting enough playing time and wouldn't be noticed by the pro scouts that he claimed were interested in his son."

"Claimed?"

"Yes, claimed. Mitch has some talent, but he's not on the level Antaglia claims he is."

"So what happened?"

"Well, after a while, I asked him to leave my office, especially when he made some racial references."

"What'd he say?"

"It wasn't so much what he said but what he implied," he continued. "His specific words were something about 'you people are good players but you need direction'—direction from white people like him. In other words, we can play but can't coach."

"You must have been angry," I said.

"Not so much angry as disgusted. My wife and I had discussed coming to the South from Chicago, where we had grown up and I had begun my coaching career. It was a good opportunity for me to be Fletcher's assistant, and he told me that the South had changed." He straightened his tie. "Not sure it has that much, especially when you look at how few African-American coaches run basketball programs at southern schools compared to the number of players who are black."

"So what do you think has happened to Mitch?" I asked.

"I think he's withdrawn from Central and intends to transfer to another school," he said. "In fact, I helped him make contact with Warner College, a small private school in South Carolina with a good basketball program where he'd be happy. In our last conversation, Mitch claimed he was interested."

"So you don't think he's been kidnapped or murdered?"

He seemed shocked by the word "murdered." "Don't think so. He seemed ready to begin a new future."

"And that was fine with you?" I asked.

He stared at me with those intense eyes. "Yes, it was. Mitch and his father were trouble for me, and I was glad to see them go."

"Did Mitch and his father have anything to do with your firing?"

"Maybe," he said. "Mitch wasn't the greatest player, but he was a white who played city ball, if you know what I mean. His father had enrolled him in an AAU league supported by Nike in Atlanta. He didn't learn the kind of fundamentals he needed to be a good player but he learned all the moves of the city kids—acrobatic spins and fancy dunks. Just the kind of things I discourage. But a lot of people, especially white people, around the state like Mitch's brand of ball and like to see a white boy play black. When he stopped getting playing time, people who matter began complaining."

And it didn't help that you lost most of your conference games last year, I thought.

"Is there anyone else in the program I can talk to about Mitch?"

He said I could talk to his assistant coach, Ronald Shuster, who was just finishing overseeing the team's morning practice at the Schmeling-Wilder Center.

"Smelling Wilder Center?" I asked, chuckling.

"Yeah, kind of a strange name. Apparently part of the money for the building was given by two families, the Schmelings and the Wilders. The Schmelings provided more funds if their name went first," Brown said, smiling.

"Of course, Wilder-Schmeling wouldn't have been much better," I responded.

Brown laughed. "The building has some serious workout facilities for non-athletes, and a lot of male students say they'll be 'smelling wilder' to mean they'll be working out."

I asked him how to get to the athletic center, and he recommended that I take the East-West campus bus that would pick me up right outside and drop me in front of the center. He said he'd call over to have someone meet me and take me to the practice courts. As I left the office, he was busy making notes on the sheets of paper on his desk. By the time the bus had picked me up and was half way across campus, I realized I had forgotten to ask for a picture of Mitch.

The Schmeling-Wilder Center was a huge, new brick building that covered an entire block. The bus let me off on a great circle at the front door. When I exited, a tall young man dressed in long shorts and a tee shirt who was clearly a basketball player came up and asked if my name was Stirling.

I admitted as much. He led me into the building, and we passed various check points through winding halls until we arrived at a series of six basketball courts side by side. Young men, most of them tall and black, were practicing various plays under the direction of young assistant coaches. In the center was a short, bald white man with a whistle who was clearly running the show. He wore a pair of brown shorts that revealed his stubby bowed legs and a tee shirt that didn't fully cover his round stomach. He was balding with short cropped hair and wore a pair of spectacles that made him look like an accountant rather than a coach. My guide glanced at me and, pointing his chin, said, "That be Coach Shuster," and ambled away to join a group of players practicing foul shots.

"Mr. Stirling," Shuster said when he saw me. "I've been expecting you." We shook hands, and he led me off the courts to a small office with a desk and a few chairs.

"Congratulations on your new job," I said as I sat down.

"Thanks," he said, looking at me with hound dog eyes. "This is not the way I had hoped to become a head coach," he continued. "I've been Coach Brown's assistant for ten years, all through the high school years and at Harrison College in Chicago. He's a good man and a great coach. Just didn't catch any breaks in recruiting."

"I understand that some of the players didn't like his coaching style," I responded, "including Mitch Antaglia."

Shuster gave me a sharp look. "I understand you want to know more about Mitchell," he said, pouring me a cup of coffee in a large Central mug.

"I do. He appears to be missing," I said, taking a sip.

Shuster paused, looking into his coffee cup. He seemed to be deciding how much he was going to tell me.

"Mitchell has been a thorn in our side since Coach Brown and I took over from Coach Flecher. He was taught to play what I call street ball and wanted to be noticed by the pro scouts for his quick, aggressive play. The last thing he wanted to do was slow down and play our game based on ball control and defense."

Shuster paused and looked at me. "Do you know much about basketball?" he asked.

"Not much," I admitted. "My team sport was football."

"Well, basketball is a team sport, too. If all five of the players on the floor are not on the same page, the whole team goes to the dogs." He paused and squinted at me. "When a new coach comes into a program and introduces a different strategy, not all players can make the necessary adjustments to pull their weight. Mitchell was a good player of a certain type. He was fast and aggressive, but he couldn't play defense to save his ass."

"Was he angry about the new system?"

"I think he was," Shuster said, pushing his glasses up on his nose. "I shouldn't be talking out of school too much, but Mitchell did a lot to undermine Coach Brown's authority."

"How so?"

"Well, he got the other players angry about the new system, and encouraged them to be insubordinate. You might say that he attempted to lead an insurrection."

Shuster hesitated, and then continued. "In my opinion, Mitchell intentionally lost some games last year. He just refused to give up the run-and-gun style. Coach eventually had to bench Mitchell. This was bad for everyone. A few of the other players supported Mitchell and didn't support Coach. Many of the fans liked Mitchell's swagger on the court and began booing Coach for his slower style. They came to see Missile Mitch and didn't understand the elegance of Coach's style."

Shuster was clearly getting angry, and his eyes began to glisten. He obviously remained loyal to Coach Brown.

"Do you have any insight into what might have happened to Mitch?" I asked.

"I have no inside information," he responded. "I got to know Mitchell fairly well because I tried to counsel him—

bring him back into the fold, if you will."

"Did he have any friends that might know something about where he's gone?" I asked.

Shuster told me that Mitch had few friends on the team, and he understood that Mitch had a girlfriend, but he didn't know much about her. He recommended that I talk with one of Mitchell's former teammates, Jineral Jackson.

"The Stonewall, right?" I had heard of Jineral, who was famous for his defense. He had a knack for standing in front of a fast break like a stone wall, forcing the opposing player to either back off or charge.

"Yeah, except the real general'd roll over in his grave to know that an African-American kid now had at least part his name," Shuster said. "Jineral is gone, of course. When Fletcher got fired and Brown took over, Jineral transferred to Kansas, a real basketball school. He didn't even have to sit out a year because he cut a deal with the NCAA to testify against Fletcher."

"What did Fletcher do to get into trouble?"

"A lot of things, but mostly he promised the top players cars. He'd have rich alumni lease cars and loan them to the kids. Jineral was good enough to play anywhere but came here because he got a mustang convertible, canary yellow. His favorite song was 'Mustang Sally.'"

"Why didn't Mitch transfer if he was so unhappy."

Shuster scratched his neck. "My opinion is that he wasn't good enough. He tried to go to Kansas with Jineral but Kansas wasn't interested. Besides, his father wanted him to stay here, close to the fold."

Shuster started to get up but stopped and sat back down when I asked him about Coach Antaglia.

"I don't know him well," he said, "and I do my best to stay away from him. The man considers himself a coach, and has even written a book..."

"*Coaching Genius*," I interrupted.

"That's it. A terrible book. Antaglia claims that he raised

Mitchell using the principles stated in there. But I don't think you could successfully raise a pig following those guidelines. They made Mitchell a selfish, inflexible player who couldn't adapt to a new, more sophisticated offense. And he's pitiful on defense."

Shuster took a deep breath and looked at his watch, then at me. He said he had to get back to practice and led me out. I thanked him for his information and said I might get in touch later. He gave me his cell number as we walked out to the courts. I left him, a pigmy surrounded by giants.

It was time that I checked in with the police.

Chapter 3

I took the bus back to the athletic complex, walked over to Clarence's shelter, and tapped on the door. Clarence poked his head out and smiled in recognition. I asked him how to get to Ithaca's police station.

Clarence's directions took me to the station. It was a large brick building on the west side of town with police cars parked out front. After parking the Accord in the lot, I went in, and got to see Captain Terrence Madison immediately after mentioning Seamer's name.

Madison was a large stern black man in a starched white shirt and black tie. I showed him my license, which he looked at carefully. Then his face lit up.

"I've heard of you, Stirling!" he practically shouted. "Weren't you the private dick who solved the Parker murder in Atlanta a few years ago?"

"Yes," I admitted.

"All my colleagues in Atlanta said that you cut some corners in that investigation. They complained that you didn't keep them in the loop."

"I kept in touch with the Atlanta police as much as possible," I explained. "But the case broke quickly, and I had to work fast to save a couple of lives."

Madison listened carefully. "I think I know why you're here, to work on the so-called Missile Mitch disappearance."

"That's correct."

"Well, I have some thoughts on this issue. I talked to Seamer a week ago, and he said that Coach Antaglia thinks his son was kidnapped. One of my detectives looked into this and concluded that there was no evidence of a kidnapping. She thinks Mitch just left town. Not at all uncommon for college students to do that. They get a wild hare up their butt and take off after a girl or just go on a bender."

"My initial investigation might support that point of view," I admitted.

"But the other thing I want to make clear is that I don't want you running roughshod over me and my department. I'll give you my cooperation, but I expect you to keep in touch so I know what's going on."

I agreed to but decided to play some things close to my vest. My impression of Madison was that he was a bit impulsive, the type of cop who might overreact to new information.

"Anything else, Stirling?" Madison asked.

"One more thing, Chief. I understand that Mitchell got in a fight downtown about three weeks ago and was arrested. Could you give me the lowdown on that?"

"It was a straightforward college-kid drunken brawl, from what I understand. I read the report written by Detective Brett Snow. According to that, some fraternity boys were drinking in the Sherman's March bar downtown when Mitch came in with his girlfriend. He was pretty drunk already. When a couple of the boys made fun of his time on the bench last season, he blew his top and beat two of the boys senseless. Snow arrested him and brought him in; his girlfriend came along and called his father, who came down and bailed him out."

"Sounds like Mitch has problems controlling his anger," I said.

"You might be right. And this is not the first time he's been in trouble for fighting. Not too long before that, he got in a fight with several football players at another bar."

Madison thought a moment and told me that since he was several men short due to the recession, he could use my help, and he in turn would assist me any way he could, as long as I kept him in the loop. He suggested that I use Detective Snow as a contact person. "In fact, Snow is just coming in from the first half of a double shift. I'd like you two to meet."

Madison spoke into his speaker phone and asked someone to send Detective Snow into his office. I was sitting with my back to the door when I heard footsteps and turned around to find Detective Brett Snow standing before me. She was a cool blonde in a tailored navy blue pants suit that showed that all her curves were in the right places. Police work was sure different than it had been in my day. Madison was clearly enjoying the look on my face as Snow seated herself in the chair next to mine.

The captain gave her a quick summary of what my interests were and ordered her to help me on the case as much as she could. She and I spoke briefly and exchanged numbers. I entered her two in my cell under Snow just as Madison let it be known that the meeting was over. As I got up to leave, he told Snow to keep him informed on developments.

"Have a minute, Detective Snow?" I asked in the hallway.

"Certainly, Mr. Stirling."

"Call me Nick," I said.

She took me to the staff room to the right, and we sat down at a table in the corner. I reviewed the events that had taken place at Sherman's March three weeks ago, and she confirmed that they were accurate.

"I didn't get to the scene until after the rumble was over," she said, "so there's not much to add."

"Did you get the girlfriend's name?" I asked.

She said she had: Rachel Stone. Snow said she had the girl's number in her notes and got up to get them. As she walked away, I appreciated the view.

When she got back with the number, we chatted a few minutes before she had to begin her second shift, and she left me wondering if she had any interest in me. I certainly did in her.

Before leaving the police station, I looked up the number for Sherman's March and put it in my cell before calling the bar. A young woman answered with a breathless "Sherman's March." I told her who I was and what I wanted to know. When I asked who had been working the night of the fight, she said that the owner, Mark Sherman, had been there. She gave me his number, and I called him. On the phone, he told me he knew Mitch well. "My son Jason grew up with him. I've known Mitch all his life and am sorry to hear that he's in even more trouble than he was three weeks ago." He agreed to meet me at the bar in twenty minutes.

Ithaca's downtown area consisted of about twenty blocks across from campus filled with student bars and a few other establishments, such as clothing stores and restaurants. The plan was obviously to put the bars close to the students so they didn't have to walk far from campus to get drunk. It took me only a few moments to reach the area but almost twenty minutes to find a parking space. By the time I located one and walked to the Sherman's March, Sherman himself was there waiting for me at the end of the bar near the door. He was a tall, well-built man in middle age. His hair was dark but greying on the temples. When I introduced myself, he gave me a firm handshake and a booming "Glad to know ya, Stirling!"

Sherman's March was a typical student beer bar. Along the left side of the main room were ten booths, which were filling up with early student drinkers. In the middle of the room were about fifteen tables that could be shoved together for larger parties. Along the right was the bar, which was made of a slab of lacquered wood with tall leather-covered stools along its expanse. The back room contained two pool tables and some video games. A group of male students was playing pool and drinking beer.

Sherman led me to his small office off the back room and pointed to a chair in front of his desk.

"Like a beer?" he asked.

"No thanks. A bit early for me."

He opened a small refrigerator behind his desk and took out a brand of ale I had never seen before. It had a picture of a turtle on it.

"Occupational hazard," he said, as he popped the cap and took a swig. "What do you want to know about the fight?" he asked.

"The facts of the fight are clear to me," I responded. "But I would like to learn more about Mitch himself. I've talked to his coaches and the AD at Central, but I don't yet know what kind of kid Mitch is. Can you tell me?"

"Mitch was a nice kid," Sherman began, "until his father decided to make him into a star basketball player."

"What's wrong with that?" I asked.

"Mostly that he tried to make Mitch one-dimensional, with no interests outside of the game. And Antaglia was very different from the other parents of good basketball players in Ithaca in this regard. We all wanted our kids to enjoy the sport, but Antaglia wanted to force his son into the jock mold. Most of us weren't interested in that."

"Can you give me an example of how he did that?"

Sherman thought for a moment. "Well, one example is

how he tried to start an AAU basketball team in Ithaca, called the Ithaca Rebels."

"What's the AAU?" I asked, remembering that Coach Brown had mentioned it, too.

"It stands for the Amateur Athletic Union, and it's an organization that oversees youth teams, including basketball teams, around the nation," he said. "Local squads can then compete with teams from other parts of the country."

"Sounds wholesome," I responded.

"Not really," he said. "Many think that the AAU operates as a kind of front for the athletic shoe companies—you know, Addidas and Nike—who supply these teams with their shoes and other equipment. They also give the coaches money for team travel plus a salary."

"Why do the shoe companies do that?"

"Their goal is to identify the next great NBA player—the next Michael Jordan or Kobe Bryant—early, like in junior high school, and get him in the shoe company's fold. Then, when he becomes a star in the NBA, he'll endorse the company's shoes and other products."

"You make it sound like the kids are participating in a kind of semi-pro league," I said.

"That's what most parents came to think," Sherman said. "Antaglia tried to make our kids give up their entire summers to travel around the country to play basketball. Most of us parents didn't like that idea and neither did the kids. Antaglia soon found himself without enough good players to field a team, and he was furious. In one of the final parent meetings, he yelled at us for not encouraging our kids to be ambitious."

"What did he do when the Ithaca Rebels fell apart?" I asked.

"He had Mitch play for AAU teams in Atlanta," he said. "From about thirteen on, Mitch had no life outside of basketball. Mitch played on teams that traveled the nation, and when he got bigger and better, he played on various all-star teams. My son used to be his best friend, but Jason never saw Mitch during the summers. Even when he was home, Antaglia coached him one-on-one on the court that he built in his backyard. Mitch had no time off."

"He built a basketball court in his backyard?" I asked.

"A lighted one so that Mitch could practice at night," he said.

Sherman had given me a good idea of what Antaglia had been up to. As I got up to leave the office, Sherman put his hand up to stop me. "I have something you might be interested in," he said, as he walked over to the corner. He reached down and scooped up a blue backpack.

"What's that?" I inquired.

"This is Mitch's backpack," he said, placing it on his desk and knocking his empty beer bottle to the floor. "He left it here the night of the fight when the police arrested him."

"Why didn't the police take it?" I asked.

"Nobody knew where it was," he explained. "It was left in the corner near his table, and wasn't found until the cleaning staff came in."

"Are you sure it's Mitch's?"

He pointed to the initials stitched into the fabric, MMA. "Stands for Missile Mitch Antaglia," he said.

"Can I take a look at it?"

He said he wasn't sure what to do with the pack but offered to give it to me if I promised to take it to Mitch's parents. "I intend to see Mr. and Mrs. Antaglia tomorrow," I said.

On returning to the Accord, I sat in the front seat, looked through Mitch's backpack, and found material for his courses that semester. Since Candy had mentioned Mitch's poetry, the syllabus for Writing the Self Through Poetry, taught by a Professor Elaine Connolly, interested me.

Connolly was familiar to me because she had won some big poetry prize that the Atlanta papers had made much of. The syllabus indicated that the professor had an office hour that afternoon at 3:30. It was now 2:37. I decided to grab a quick lunch and then head over to 132 Miller Hall to see what Professor Connolly could tell me about Mitch.

While eating a turkey sandwich in a shop a few blocks from Sherman's March, I went through Mitch's backpack more carefully. In one of the small outer pockets was a worn slip of paper with the name, address, and phone number of Rachel Stone, written in a woman's hand. I copied the address into my notebook and checked the phone number against the one Snow had given me. It matched. Turning the slip over, I found another note, written in the same hand that wrote Mitch's class notes. It was a reminder to himself that said: "Need help! Call Irving Kaufman ASAP" with a phone number. I keyed the name and number into my cell. In another pocket was a key to room 32 in the Lions Den, a rundown motel on the outskirts of town. I pocketed the key. The rest of the material in the pack consisted of textbooks, notebooks, and pens and pencils. I put all the material back except for the key and the slip of paper, zipped up the pack, and put it in the trunk of the Honda.

By the time I found Connolly's room in Miller Hall it was 3:25. The office was dark, so I sat down across from it on a bench and waited. A few minutes later a shapely grey-haired woman carrying a large cloth book bag turned the corner and stopped in front of the office. She fumbled for her key, and almost dropped her bag when it slipped off her shoulder. Jumping up, I caught it before it fell. Professor Connolly looked at me appreciatively.

"Thank you, kind sir," she said with a smile as I took the bag off her arm. "Are you always so chivalrous?"

"Only to ladies in distress," I responded.

"Like Lancelot of old," she said, with a merry laugh.

"Is there a King Arthur I should worry about?" I joked.

"Alas, no, but the position is open to the appropriate applicant," she said, looking me over.

By this time, we were both in the office. She took her bag from me, placed it on her desk, and hung her coat on a rack.

"Are you here to see me or do you just go around helping women with their bags?" she asked, sitting down.

Her office was not spacious, but it was well appointed. It had several dim lights that illuminated the corners of the room. It had built-in book shelves on all four walls. Most of the books were slim volumes of contemporary poetry. Above the shelves were posters of women writers, some of whom I recognized, such as Eudora Welty and Virginia Woolf. Others I couldn't place. Some looked more like men than women. Her desk was piled with student poems.

Assuming my most nonthreatening smile, I said, "I'm here to see you about one of your students, Professor Connolly," giving her my name, occupation, and current assignment working on a missing person case.

"Who's missing?" she asked.

"Mitchell Antaglia," I responded.

She looked at me sharply. "You know I'm not allowed by law to give out information about my students," she said. "They have a right to privacy."

"I understand that," I responded, "but Mitch might be in real trouble, and I'm trying to find him before he gets hurt or hurts someone else."

Her expression softened. "I guess I can help," she said. "I haven't seen Mitch for almost three weeks and assumed that he had dropped the course. I expected to get the paperwork on him but none has come."

"I especially need a better sense of what he was like as a person," I explained.

"Well, he's one of my most unusual poetry students," she said. "I first taught him in a freshman creative writing class. He apparently took it because it fit his schedule. That first day I thought he was going to jump up and run out of the room when I spoke about writing poetry as a way to explore your feelings and your past."

"What do you think he was afraid of?" I asked.

"At first I thought he was just a big, dumb jock who thought feelings were for girls," she said. "But as I got to know Mitch better, I realized that he had feelings, all right, but they were feelings that frightened him. There was something dark in Mitch."

"Did he write well?" I asked.

"Not at first. He seemed to be blocked, as if he had something important to say but couldn't get it on the page. He didn't even write the first few assignments." She paused as if trying to remember something. "It wasn't until I gave the assignment to write a poem on one of his parents or relatives that Mitch suddenly came alive. It was as if the assignment was a razor that opened one of his veins and all his creative blood began to flow." I winced at the metaphor.

She suddenly stopped talking and looked into the distance. In a surprisingly deep voice she recited the following:

"My father minted me, a coin,
With heads or tails,
And made me join
The team of whales

I couldn't follow
Through the oceans deep
Into a world as hollow
As a timeless sleep.

My father minted me, a coin,
In his pocket placed
With others joined
But no truth faced."

When she finished, she looked as if she saw something beyond this world that she barely recognized. She caught herself, shook her head, and turned to me with a half smile.

"Is that Mitch's poem?" I asked.

"It is," she said. When she first read it, she continued, she thought that he had copied it from some other student, but the more she read it the more she saw its weaknesses and decided that it had to be Mitch's. From that point on Mitch became one of her favorite students, and she worked with him closely in several courses and had great hopes for him.

"What does the reference to whales mean?" I asked, perplexed.

She thought for a moment. "When you think of whales, you think of blue whales, the singers of the deep. So the whales represent poets who sing to each other, like we do in our workshops."

"The poem expresses resentment toward his father," I said.

"Yes, that theme is hard to miss, and it is typical of his work. I don't know if you've read Sylvia Plath," she said looking at me as if giving a test.

"'Daddy'?" I asked.

Her blue eyes sparkled. "Yes, Mitch's work reminds me of Plath's poem 'Daddy.' I'm not a licensed psychologist, but I've read my Freud and Lacan, and I'm convinced that Mitch has been abused by his father in some way. He has deep resentment. He's never been fully integrated into the symbolic order."

"Symbolic order?"

"Yes. According to the French psychoanalyst Jacques Lacan," she explained, her tone shifting slightly into lecture mode, "we all must enter a second phase or order of development, the symbolic order. This order is dominated by the father, and in it we learn language—or are mastered by language. Language speaks us, according to Lacan, not the reverse. Any poet knows that." As she warmed to her subject, my attention began to wander. "We also learn that the father represents the law and cultural rules of behavior. I don't think Mitch's father ever allowed him to enter the symbolic order because he controlled him so aggressively."

"Have you ever met the older Antaglia?" I asked, happy she had returned to Earth.

"I've only seen him around town. Don't really know him, except through Mitch's poetry."

"What kind of kid do you think Mitch is?" I asked.

"I know Mitch mostly through his poetry," she said, looking at me intently. "I don't know him personally that well, even though this is his third class with me. He's a loner and he's a jock, a type of student I don't see much of. But his poems have told me two things about him. One is that he is a very sad young man who has been forced to be something he doesn't want to be."

"What do you mean?" I asked.

"Well, I don't think Mitch wants to be a basketball player. From what I can put together—and Mitch has never said this to me directly—he wants to be a writer and a teacher, not an athlete. He's a very bright young man, but he has never been allowed to develop his intellect or his artistic side. He's been encouraged to be an aggressive jock," she said with a hint of bitterness.

"And the other thing you know?"

"That Mitch is extremely angry and aggressive," she said.

This was not the first time I had heard this assertion.

"What evidence do you have of that?" I asked.

"I edit a literary magazine called the *Ithaca Review*," she said. "It is mostly a small, local affair that I use to publish some of the best poetry of my students. I require them to submit five poems for consideration, and I select the best to print. Space is limited, so I mostly publish the poems of seniors, those with whom I have worked for several years."

"What has this got to do with Mitch?" I asked.

She hesitated. "I rejected Mitch's poems, including 'My

Father's Coin,' and he got furious."

"What did he do, exactly?"

"He stayed after class and told me I was like everyone else in his life who was using him for their own purposes," she said.

"Like his father?" I asked.

"I think so," she responded. "I saw a side of Mitch that disturbed me. He was so angry that I thought he was capable of hurting me."

"My advice is to report the incident to the campus police and to not see Mitch alone either on or off campus," I told her.

We heard a tap on the door and a girl stuck her head in.

Professor Connolly said "Hello, Milly, I'll be with you in a moment" and turned back to me. "We'll have to stop here. Milly has an appointment. But I'd like to continue this discussion. In fact, Mitch recently gave me a very rough draft of one of his poems that I think you should read. It explains the nature of his strange relationship with his father—and his mother. It might be the key to why he took off and where he is. Could you come to my house tonight, at 8:30, for drinks and dinner, Nick? I'm a good cook."

I checked my watch. It was 4:15. I still had to interview Rachel Stone, Mitch's girlfriend, make an appointment with and interview Irving Kaufman, and drop by the Lions Den to check on room 32.

"I think I can make it then, but I still have a lot of foot work to do on the Antaglia case if I hope to find him," I said.

"Do I sense a lack of interest?" she asked, shooting for a light tone that she just missed.

"I'll call if I'm going to be late," I promised. I wanted to read Mitch's poem but wasn't as interested in the rest of her offer. She was a sweet woman but poetry was not one of my burning interests.

"That'll work," she said, and handed me a printed sheet from her desk drawer with her phone number, address, and directions to her house. I guess she invited a lot of forty-somethings over for drinks and dinner.

As I walked out the door and nodded to Milly, I asked the professor if she knew Irving Kaufman.

"Sure," she said. "Everyone in Ithaca knows Irv. He's one of the guidance counselors at Ithaca High."

She smiled at me and then looked at Milly. Walking down the hall, I heard her tell Milly that she had read her revised poem on her mother and thought it had possibilities.

Chapter 4

By the time I arrived at the station house, it was almost 5:00. I parked and took the backpack in to present as possible evidence in the fight incident. I could have taken it to Mitch's parents but wanted to remain in the good graces of the local police. Entering the front door, I practically ran into Officer Snow, looking as attractive as she had earlier in the day.

"Well, look who's back," she said with a friendly smile.

"Are you on duty 24 hours a day, Officer Snow?" I responded.

She said that she would be on duty until after midnight tonight because one of her colleagues was out with the swine flu. After making some more small talk, I turned the backpack over to her, explaining briefly who it belonged to and how I had come into possession of it. I didn't mention the phone numbers and the key to the Lions Den in my pocket. She thanked me with just a hint of embarrassment that she had missed it in Sherman's March, and took it back to the evidence room to check it in.

"If I can help you with anything else, Nick, just let me know," she said, looking back as she walked away. I liked the way she walked.

"I certainly will."

Outside the station house I sat down on a bench and set up two appointments. First, I called Irv Kaufman. The phone rang a dozen times before his wife answered, and I asked to speak with Kaufman. She said he was not at home but at the WYCA, where he tutored junior high students. "He can't stop helping kids even though he's retired," she said. "I'd like to talk to him about Mitchell Antaglia," I explained.

"I'm certain Irv will want to talk to you about Mitch," she said. "My husband's been very concerned about him ever since he was arrested for fighting downtown. It was all over the papers."

"Thanks," I said and called the number she gave me. When I spoke to Kaufman, he agreed to see me later at his home and gave me directions.

The next appointment was with Rachel Stone, who might be able to give me the most information on Mitch. When I called her on my cell, a young woman answered. When I asked for Rachel, the woman identified herself as Rachel's roommate, Britney Rosenthal. After telling her I was working on a missing person case that might be of interest to Ms. Stone, Britney asked if the case had anything to do with Mitchell Antaglia. I said it did, and she said that didn't surprise her.

"When's the last time you saw Mitch?" I asked.

"Not for several weeks, and, to tell you the truth, that's a good thing," she said.

"Why is that?"

"Mitch isn't any good for Rachel," she said, hesitated, and

then continued. "Mitch is an abusive person."

"Does he abuse Rachel physically?"

"Not so much physically," she said, "but he does emotionally. And he practically attacked his poetry professor recently for not publishing some of his poems in her magazine."

"All the more reason for me to talk to Rachel," I said. "I want to find Mitchell so that he doesn't hurt anyone. Does Rachel have a cell phone?"

She said she did and gave me the number after my repeated assurances that I would protect her from Mitch.

When I got Rachel on the phone and identified myself as a detective looking for Mitchell Antaglia, she was clearly upset.

"Do you have any idea where Mitchell is?" she asked in a voice thick with emotion.

"No," I said. "I've only been working on the case for about seven hours. I've learned a lot about Mitch but would like to learn more from you."

"I'd like to help," she said. "But I haven't heard from Mitch in more than two weeks, since after he was arrested in Sherman's March for fighting."

I wanted to meet her alone in a place she felt comfortable, preferably away from Britney, who clearly didn't like Mitch. She recommended a coffee shop called Café All Day just on the edge of campus. I agreed to meet her there in ten minutes. "I'll be in a dark gray business suit with a red tie," I said, thinking that would distinguish me in Ithaca, where most people dressed casually.

I arrived before her and was momentarily afraid she wouldn't show. Then I saw a slim dark-haired girl walk into the shop. Her long hair framed a slender face with large dark eyes that had circles under them. She was wearing a red cloche hat with a retro pea coat and jeans. She carried a large backpack that weighed her down. She saw me, waved, and made her way among the small round tables filled with young men and women writing on laptops, older people reading, and professor types grading papers.

"Mr. Stirling, I presume," she said, smiling prettily at her joke.

"Yes, but call me Nick," I said, standing up and pulling a chair back for her.

When she was settled, I asked if she wanted coffee, and she said she did since she had a long night of studying ahead of her. "A sociology exam," she said, making a face. "My worst subject."

While ordering the coffee at the counter, I looked over at Rachel. She saw me and smiled. She looked young and vulnerable, on the verge of tears, and I wondered what kind of connection she had with Missile Mitch. It turned out to be a poetic one.

When I returned to the table, she told her story. She and Mitch had grown up together in Ithaca, she said. Her father was a math professor and her mother taught in the English department as an instructor. Rachel had taken after her mother and loved literature. In high school, she had worked on the school paper and edited both the yearbook and the school literary magazine. She knew Mitch a bit, but he ran in different circles, mostly in athletic ones. He was the most dedicated basketball player on the team and got a lot of attention. Because Rachel was involved in most school activities, she went to all the home games, and she saw Mitch play. Even she recognized that he was a basketball talent.

"When did you get to know Mitch better?"

"I knew he got an athletic scholarship to Central, but I never saw him much my—our—first semester freshman year," she said. "I took English classes and he took classes in whatever athletes take classes in—I think he told me he was majoring in coaching basketball, but that doesn't sound right."

It did, I thought, considering all the bad press the athletic program was getting on graduation rates, which were among the lowest in the nation.

"Mitch and I didn't get to know each other until we both took a creative writing class with Professor Connolly in the spring semester of our freshman year," Rachel said. "I was shocked to see him in class the first day—he was so tall that he could barely fit in one of the desks on the outskirts of the seminar table. Professor Connolly—she's really great—tried to make everyone feel comfortable and move up around the table, but Mitch didn't want to and stayed on the edges."

"Did you talk to him early on?" I asked.

"Not right away, and when we started to talk it was about Ithaca High and basketball and stuff," she said. She was clearly remembering these early conversations fondly. "When we began talking about the class, he made it clear that he was in it only because it fit his schedule—he didn't really want to write. I was shocked. The only thing I wanted was to write."

She took a sip of her coffee. "At first I thought he was an idiot," she continued. "He'd sit in class with his eyes half closed because he was exhausted from his daily workouts. And he never read any of his poems to the workshop."

Rachel saw I was a little confused and explained: "Professor Connolly believes that no one should be forced to read their work until they're ready. You just have to read five poems during the semester to pass. She's really a great professor," she exclaimed. "Then one day, out of the blue, Mitch decided to read one of his poems, one about his father treating him like a coin that he threw in his pocket with other coins and didn't even love."

She looked at me intensely. "It was a beautiful poem, just lovely, and the whole class thought so, you could tell by the way they critiqued it, like it was a real work of art."

"I think Professor Connolly liked it, too," I said. "She

recited it to me this afternoon."

"She did?" Rachel exclaimed, clearly proud of Mitch's accomplishment.

"What did Mitch think about Dr. Connolly?" I asked.

"He adored her," she said. "He told everyone this year that she was his spiritual mother. I think most of her students felt that way about her."

"Did he tell his parents about his feelings for Professor Connolly?" I asked.

"I assume he did," she said. "He told everyone else."

I wondered how Antaglia responded to Mitch's new interests in poetry.

"When did you and Mitch get close?" I asked.

"Well, we got closer by the end of freshman year," she explained. "But Mitch was a star basketball player, and he had a lot of girls after him. So it took a while for us to become a couple." She used that word proudly, as if she had accomplished something great with Mitch. "We read each other's poetry and critiqued it and planned to put out a chapbook of our work. It was going to consist of our poems that answered each other."

I got a pretty clear idea of the development of this relationship. Mitch, a typical jock, realized that he had a talent for poetry and met a whole new group of friends, including Rachel, who opened an unknown world for him.

"How did Mitch's new interests in poetry affect his basketball?" I asked.

"It had a major impact," she said. "He wasn't happy with the new coach, who made him sit on the bench a lot and didn't let him play his game anymore," she explained, using Mitch's language. "So Mitch began doing something he called 'dogging it,'" which she thought meant that he gave up on the game.

"How'd his father take it?" I asked.

"Not very well," she said. "Mr. Antaglia only wanted Mitch to play basketball. He didn't want him to study. Mitch said that his father wanted him to be in the NPA and make a fortune."

"Do you mean the NBA, the National Basketball Association?" I asked.

"That's right," she said, blushing at her slip. "Almost all of Mitch's poems were about his father, how much his father forced him to play basketball and do nothing else, not even his school work. Mitch is smart, but his father didn't even want him to study, just play basketball with him every spare moment."

"What about his mother?" I asked.

"I think she's an odd lady," Rachel said. "One of the first things I heard about her was a rumor that she killed her daughter."

"Killed her daughter?" I asked, remembering that Seamer had mentioned something about the daughter drowning.

"That's what some people in town thought. She was never convicted or anything, but I remember her daughter, Christa, drowned in the Antaglias' swimming pool when only Mrs. Antaglia was home," Rachel said.

Have to check up on that, I thought.

We paused a moment, both looking into our cups.

"Where do you think Mitch is?" I asked, turning back to my main topic.

"I don't know," Rachel responded. "I'm so confused," she said, beginning to cry. "We saw each other or talked on the phone every day, even during away games. I haven't talked to him for two, almost three weeks. I miss him so much. And the worst thing is I think Mitch has a new girlfriend," she sobbed. I waited for her to continue. When she didn't, I asked, "How do you know?"

"I saw them together, walking downtown, arm in arm, like lovers."

Unable to continue, she put her face down in her arms. Her shoulders heaved as she cried. I started to put my hand on her right shoulder but hesitated. Instead, I asked:

"What did this woman look like?"

Rachel straightened up, and took a tissue out of her pocket. She gave me a sad smile and said she always carried tissues these days for when she thinks about Mitch. After wiping her eyes and blowing her nose, she looked at me intently. "I didn't get a real good look at her because they were half a block away. Plus she was wearing a floppy grey felt hat and sunglasses—those big Jackie Kennedy dark glasses. But she was very tall, model tall. I'd guess almost 6 feet, maybe a little more."

"What made you think they were a couple?" I asked.

"Well, they were kind of intimate together, in deep conversation as they walked. They acted as if nobody else in the world existed except for them. They acted like Mitch and I acted...when we fell in love freshman year," she said, sobbing.

People around us were looking at her and wondering what I was doing to upset her. One girl with short hair gave me an angry look. I thought it best to leave the Café All Day.

When we got outside, I asked Rachel if she needed a ride back to her dorm. She said she wasn't going there but back to the library to study for her sociology exam. She would walk.

She looked up at me with forlorn eyes that were still damp.

"Where do *you* think Mitch is?" she asked.

"I don't know, Rachel. But I think the woman you saw him with has something to do with his leaving."

"Do you think I'm stupid to love him, even though she's now in his life?" she asked. "My father thinks I am. He hates Mitch and wants me to dump him. Do *you* think I'm stupid?" she repeated.

"Don't think so," I said. "It sounds to me that Mitch is a good but troubled young man who has been forced to live a life he doesn't want playing basketball."

Rachel looked at me with a deep appreciation. "Why couldn't my dad be understanding like you?" she asked.

I smiled at her wryly. I had never had children and that was probably a good thing, given my crazy work hours.

Handing her my card with my cell number, I told her to call me if anything else occurred to her or if she wanted to talk some more. She started to walk away when it occurred to me I needed a picture of Mitch. Did she have one to give me? She opened her purse and took out a photo and handed it to me. She and Mitch were standing together in front of a lake. He was a full foot or so taller than she was. He smiled into the camera, clearly happy, his arm around her. I thanked her. She smiled and left, looking back once to wave.

She was a sweet kid, and I couldn't imagine that Mitch would want to hurt her. She made me determined to find her boyfriend.

One of my few leads was the key to room 32 of the Lions Den. It was now 5:30, three hours before I was due at Professor Connolly's house. That gave me time to run by the motel to see who was renting room 32.

The Lions Den was a '50s-era motel that sat on what had once been a major road into Ithaca. With the development of the highway system around the town, that road had become less traveled and the motel had begun to deteriorate. When I used to come to Ithaca for football games, it was still used by fans, but it now had a rundown look that suggested few people took rooms there. It looked like a haunt for prostitutes and drug dealers. A big sign out front said "Rooms rented daily and weekly." Few vehicles were in the parking area, only a large tractor trailer on a long haul and a couple of beat-up pickups with out-of-state plates.

The spot in front of 32 was empty. I pulled the Accord in half way, got out, and kneeled where a parked car's engine would have been. The gravel had fresh oil on it. I touched it with my finger. The oil was warm, suggesting that a vehicle had recently been parked there and left.

"Cen I hep you, cowboy?" a man said as he walked toward me from the main office. He was short, no more than 5'4", wearing a dirty white shirt with a black plastic bow tie and a pair of grey pants with the left pocket ripped open.

"I'm looking for the person in 32," I said, standing up. "Can you tell me who's renting it?"

"Now why would I tell yew thet?" he asked.

"I'm a private detective working with the Ithaca police on a missing person case," I explained, "and I think the person who rented 32 might have some important information."

"Cum back with a search werrent if'n yew want to look in thet room," he said, turning away.

Just then the door to 31, the room next door, opened and a Latino wearing a straw cowboy hat came out. His blue jeans and yellow work boots were covered with dried mud, and he wore a tightly-fitting white tee shirt that emphasized his biceps. He headed for one of the pickups. A girl stuck her head out the door and said, "Hey Jules—if'n that guy's waiting for me, send him in in a few minutes after I've warshed up." She looked at me and smiled. "It'll be nice to do someone who speaks English for a change."

Looking at Jules, I said, "I think the Ithaca police would be interested in knowing what's going on here. Should I give them a call, Jules?" I pulled out my cell and flipped it open.

He said no and asked me what I wanted to know as he led me into the office, which consisted of a desk with a cash register on it and a couple of wobbly chairs. I sat in one as he shuffled behind the desk.

"Who rents 32 and how long has he been here?" I asked.

"Not just a he. It's a Mr. and Mrs. Smith from Atlanta," he said, looking at the ground as if he had found something of interest there.

"When did they arrive?"

"'Bout two weeks ago," he responded. He was trying not to be helpful.

"What do the Smiths look like?"

"Both tall," he said.

I took out my cell phone.

"What you doin'?"

"Calling the police," I said. "Maybe they can get some information out of you."

"O.K., O.K. Put it away," he said, and began describing the Smiths. She was tall, over 6 feet, but he never got a good look at her face because she always wore a wide-brimmed hat and sun glasses. Her husband—"If'n he was her husband"— was tall, too, about three or four inches taller than her.

"How old are they?"

"Couldn't tell 'bout her, but he looked like the other side of forty," he said.

"Anything distinctive about him?" I asked.

"Come agin?" Jules said.

"Did he look odd in any way?"

"He was bald headed and had one eye cocked to the side," he said. "I noticed it when he paid his rent last week."

"What kind of car did they drive?" I asked.

"Old Cadillac, a 1971 black Eldorado."

"What was the license plate number?"

"Don't know," he said.

"By law you're supposed to record that," I pointed out.

He looked at me dully. "Baldy didn't put it down, and I didn't ask," Jules said.

"When do you expect them back?" I asked.

"How'n god's name do you 'pect me to know thet?" he exploded. "They jest com'n go. Sometimes they gone for a couple of days, sometimes they stay here like they waiting on something. They pay their rent, and I don't ask no questions."

I reached into my back pocket and pulled out my wallet. His ferret eyes followed my hand and then stared at the ten dollar bill in it. "I'll give you ten dollars now and ten dollars more if you call me when the Smiths return," I said.

Jules reached greedily for the bill, and I gave it to him along with my card with my cell phone number. He took the bill, folded it twice, and put it in his shirt pocket. He left the card on the desk.

"One more thing," I said, taking out the picture of Mitch that Rachel had given me. "Have you ever seen this young man with the Smiths?"

He took the picture and held it up about four inches from his face.

"Yep, I seen him. He's that basketball player they call the Missile, ain't he?" Jules asked.

"That's right. When was he here?"

"It was him who first rented the room for the Smiths. He give me fifty dollar for the first two days," he said.

I thanked Jules for his help, reminded him to call me, and left the office at 6:15. A couple of hours remained before I would meet Connolly, so I went over to 31 and tapped on the door.

"That you, Jules?" a voice asked.

"Yes," I said, and the blonde opened the door. She was wearing a Japanese silk robe that looked the worse for wear and started to shut the door when she recognized me. I slipped my foot between the door and a jamb. "You're not Jules," she said. "I don't take nobody that ain't come through Jules, so scram, Sam."

"I just want to ask you a few questions," I said, trying to appear non-threatening.

"What're you, a cop?" she demanded.

"Not the kind you think. I'm a private detective working with the Ithaca police department on a missing person case," I explained. "I want to see if you know anything about the couple who rent 32, the room next to you."

By the time I had worked my way into her room, the girl had sat on the bed. The room was painted red and had a large heart-shaped bed in the middle that had not been made up since the last client. A large mirror was attached to the ceiling. Soft rock emanated from a CD player in the corner. She noticed me looking around and said, with some pride, "I decorated it myself. Like it?"

"Nice," I lied. She smiled appreciatively.

"What's your name?" I asked.

"Robin," she said. "I call this place the Robin's Nest. Jules hepped me move everything in and set it up, but the ideas was all mine. I got some of them from Atlanta. I used to work down there but decided to come back home."

Apparently she didn't get all of her clients through Jules, because she smiled at me and stretched out on the bed, letting her robe fall open. "Would you like to make love?" she asked. "I can give you a special price. The English-speakin' price."

"It's tempting," I said, "but I'm on a job now. Maybe some other time."

"O.K., but you're missing the best ride in Ithaca," she bragged.

Trying to get her back on track, I asked if she could tell me anything about the couple next door.

"I just know them to say hey," she said. "I only saw the woman's face once, when I walked by when the man was leaving."

"What'd she look like?"

"She was kinda like deformed or something. Like she had been a boxer—you know, beaten up bad. She had a big brow and high cheek bones, like a red Indian. I could tell, though, that she used to be pretty. Women cen tell things like thet."

"Did you ever hear them talking?"

"I did hear them fighting some—you know, like yelling at each other. I thought maybe they was drunk. They sounded like Jules and my mother when they tied one on."

"Jules is your father?" I asked, trying to hide my

surprise.

"Step-dad," she said. "That's why he lets me use this place without paying much rent at all."

I made her the same offer I had made my father, giving her ten dollars now and promising her ten more if she called me when the Smiths returned.

"For that much you could have had me," she said as I closed the door. I thought about checking into a motel and taking a shower, but decided I didn't have time. Irv Kaufman was next on my list.

Chapter 5

Kaufman's house was located in one of the many subdivisions of Ithaca, Cherry Park. Kaufman's elaborate directions led me to his driveway. His house was a modest brick ranch that was carefully maintained.

When I rang the doorbell, Kaufman opened the door and invited me in. He had a long face with short gray hair and a sharp nose. He reached out and shook my hand. His wife came out from the back of the house and greeted me like an old friend. "We're both glad to see you, Mr. Stirling," she said. "As I said on the phone, Irv is concerned about Mitch. I am, too."

We sat down over sweet tea with enough sugar to cause diabetes. Mrs. Kaufman passed around a plate of cookies I refused on the grounds I had a dinner to attend soon.

"How can we help you?" Kaufman asked, looking at me intently.

"I'm interested in learning more about Mitchell Antaglia," I explained. "As I told your wife on the phone,

Central's Athletic Program has hired me to find him."

"So he's disappeared?" Mrs. Kaufman asked.

"By some reports, he has," I said.

Kaufman slumped over and put his head in his hands, clearly disturbed by the news of the disappearance.

"As you can imagine, Stirling, I'm in a tough spot," he said, looking up. "I was Mitch's guidance counselor, but I was more than that. I also talked to him extensively about his personal problems, which were legion. Legally, anything Mitch told me is privileged information."

"I understand your position," I said. "I'm not after any details about his personal discussions with you or your diagnoses of him but would like some background information on Mitch that might help me locate him."

"Fair enough, Stirling," he said. "What would you like to know?"

"Well, first of all, was Mitch a happy kid?" I asked.

"I don't think so," Kaufman said.

"Can you tell me the cause of his unhappiness?" I asked.

"I can't tell you all that I know," he said, "but I can tell you that Mitch was convinced that he was adopted."

"Was he?" I asked.

"I never found any evidence of that in his school file," he said. "And I asked his parents once if he had been, and they both said absolutely not. Mitch was their natural child."

"Why did Mitch think he was adopted?" I asked.

"He told me that he was in touch with his biological mother," he said. "She supposedly lived somewhere in Kansas."

"Do you think that was the case?" I asked.

"I didn't think so," Kaufman said. "Mitch was prone to striking poses with me. He claimed, for instance, that he had a basketball shoe contract with Nike, a claim I knew was not true."

"Was Mitch a good student?" I asked.

Kaufman thought for a moment or two. "No, he wasn't,"

he said.

"Was he unintelligent?"

"By no means," he said, a bit defensive. "I didn't mean to give you that impression. Mitch was actually quite intelligent. His IQ, I remember distinctly, was well above average."

"Why then was he a poor student?" I asked.

"This is awkward for me to say," he responded. "Mitch was smart enough to do well, but he did not apply himself to his work. I talked to many of his teachers," he continued, "and they all said the same thing. Mitch would try to participate in class. He would try to answer questions. But he never seemed to know anything. It was like he never did his reading and other work. Consequently, his grades were low. I feel partly responsible for Mitch's academic problems because my job was to help him be a better student."

"Did Mitch give you a reason for his poor work?" I asked. "It seems sort of odd to me. Isn't it true that athletes have to attend study hall to keep their grades up?"

"That's true, Mr. Stirling, but it didn't seem to help Mitch much. The only thing he told me is that he was determined to be the best basketball player of his generation so he spent all of his time working on his game. He expected to go to the pros."

"That's strange," I said, "given that his college coaches both told me that Mitch was a good college player but not good enough for the pros. I wonder who told him he was going to be great."

Mr. Kaufman thought for another moment then said: "I probably shouldn't tell you this, but I think Mitch had problems with his father. He was a coach and seemed to use Mitch as a kind of experiment to prove that his methods, whatever they were, worked."

"I know something about those methods and have some questions about them," I responded.

Mrs. Kaufman offered some more tea and filled my glass.

"Is there anything else you can tell me about Mitch?" I

asked, taking a sip.

"I hesitate to bring this up," he said. He looked at his wife, who looked back and encouraged him to talk. "Mitch seemed to me to be very aggressive," he continued. "One of the reasons I saw him so often was he got into arguments and even some fights with other Ithaca High students."

"Were these fist fights?" I asked.

"Occasionally they were," he said. "But most were just shouting matches. He could be set off by the smallest thing. Another student looking at him. Or a teacher asking him to stop talking during a lecture. When he got to my office, he was easy enough to calm down, but in class he was a tinder box ready to catch fire."

"Do you have any explanation for this aggression?" I asked.

"I assumed that he was under stress of some sort," he answered. "I think he was under pressure from his father to perform athletically. At least that's what he implied, very indirectly, a few times. But his aggression seemed to get worse through his high school years. By his senior season, he was almost expelled twice for fighting. I had to constantly intervene on his behalf." He hesitated and then said: "I was not surprised to hear that Mitch had been arrested for fighting in that downtown bar."

"Sherman's March?"

"That's the one," he said. "Mitch seemed to be moving toward that kind of involvement with the law."

I asked him if he was still in touch with Mitch, and he said that Mitch called him every so often to talk about his problems.

"I'm always happy to talk to Mitch," he said. "He's a nice young man who has some problems that he has to work out. The most important of these is his aggression."

"Could he really hurt someone?" I asked.

"He might if the circumstances were right," he said.

I thanked the Kaufmans for their assistance and gave

them my card. "If you hear from Mitch, please let me know," I said. "I'm anxious to find him before he does something that he'll regret."

The Kaufmans assured me they would stay in touch and showed me to the door.

"By the way," Kaufman said as I walked out, "one person you should talk to is the Antaglia family maid. Mitch always spoke of her as the person in the household who he was closest to."

"I'll talk to her when I get a chance," I assured him.

Walking to my car, I reflected on Kaufman's concerns about Mitch. He seemed to think Mitch was capable of doing real harm to people who crossed him and that worried me. Rachel apparently didn't think so, but she didn't see Mitch as objectively as Kaufman did. I hoped to find Mitch before he had a chance to cause serious trouble.

Chapter 6

I followed the professor's directions and soon found myself in another subdivision of Ithaca. Hers was east of campus, almost in the next county. The houses were all large and set back from the street on spacious lots. Most were made of brick with slate roofs. I took a turn off the main road, followed it a few blocks, and then turned again, onto Starling Street. Night had fallen, and it was hard to see.

The professor must have done well with her publishing because her house was one of the biggest in the development. It sat on a corner lot, on Starling Place and Starling Circle, back among a stand of trees. A long driveway went from Starling Place to the house, and I took it up to a parking circle. Surprisingly, the house was dark and the porch light was off. I checked my watch: 8:33. After parking and walking to the front door, I pushed the illuminated button. When the bell rang, some scuffling inside took place inside, and a dog barked. After a moment, I rang the bell again. That nobody answered concerned me.

Fearing something was wrong, I walked back to my car and got my flashlight and .38 out of the glove compartment, put the pistol in my jacket pocket, and walked around the house, playing the beam along the ground. In back, a cement walk disappeared into a pitch black copse of trees and bushes. I pointed my flashlight onto the house to find the back door.

Suddenly, just stepping onto the walk, I heard the sound of something large thrashing through brush and before I could react, a big man was on me, running hard. It was too dark for me to get a good look at him before he knocked me to the ground and kept running. My flash flew from my hand, hit the ground, and went out. I fumbled for it on my knees. When I found it and shook it back on, the man was well down the path and my beam did not illuminate much. I just got a glimpse of him disappearing around a bend.

"Halt! Police!" I shouted, getting to my feet and starting after him. The runner did not stop but continued to Starling Circle. By the time the street came into view, a large, dark, lightless vehicle was screeching away, disappearing into the night. It was too dark to see a licence plate or identify the make of the car other than it was big and black. I turned back to the professor's house and took out my revolver.

The door was unlocked but no lights were on. I entered the house and felt for a light switch. A small dog began yapping and jumping up on me. It was some sort of black and brown terrier, which stood his ground with his back legs straight when he wasn't airborne. When I located the switch and the lights came on, I found myself in a large kitchen with the dog nipping at my legs.

"Calm down, boy," I said, bending to pet him with my gunless hand.

He jumped at me again. I noticed that his paws were red. My best gray suit was smeared with blood where he touched me. He calmed down a bit as I stroked his neck.

A pot of food had been left on a burner and was spewing forth plumes of smoke. My dinner, I thought wryly, turning off the burner and removing the pot.

"Professor Connolly," I called. "It's Nick Stirling."

No human answered, but my voice got the dog barking again. Noticing a closed pantry in the corner, I grabbed the whirling dervish of a dog and stuffed him through the door and shut it. He continued a muffled barking.

I looked at the kitchen floor, which was covered with red paw prints, then left the kitchen through a swinging door, entered another dark room, and found the switch with my flashlight. When the lights came on, I was in the dining room. There on the floor was the professor, face down next to a large table. A large, dark circle of blood spread out from her upper torso and red paw prints were all over the parquet floor and oriental rug. Two of the walls were spattered with blood.

I walked around the body carefully to avoid stepping in the spreading blood. A wave of guilt, followed by nausea, overcame me. The professor had struck me as a good sort in the short time we had spent together. She had seemed concerned about her students and willing to help Mitch. If only I had arrived here earlier, I might have prevented this murder. Choking back my nausea, I focused on the job before me, leaving my guilt for later.

Kneeling beside Connolly, I looked at her closely. On the side of her neck was a deep gash. On turning her gently to the side by her shoulder, I saw the gash went all across her neck. I felt her neck for a pulse. Nothing. She was still very warm, so she must have died recently, but I couldn't tell when. The tall man had run from behind the house no more than five minutes ago. He might have been the killer, but maybe not. He could have stumbled across the body like me, panicked, and run when he heard the front door bell.

A quick look around the kitchen, dining room and then the rest of the house revealed no weapon. Nor did my search turn up evidence of a break-in. The doors had not been forced and no windows were broken. Upstairs, no drawers were opened, and a bottle of prescription sleeping pills was still in the medicine closet, a sure sign that no addict had been here. The professor must have known her killer because she had apparently let him or her in.

During my search, I looked especially for Mitch's notes and the poem that Connolly had wanted me to see. They weren't anywhere downstairs. Upstairs I found the professor's study. That room looked like someone had rifled through the papers on her desk, but Connolly's office at Central, I remembered, was a bit of a mess so maybe the home office was as she had left it. A pile of student poems included one sheet with Mitch's name on it. The poem was titled "Dr. Death." Putting the gun down and folding the paper in thirds, I slipped it into the breast pocket of my jacket to read later. Certain that nobody was in the house, I returned my revolver to my jacket pocket.

After this hurried search, it was time to make a decision. Should I call the police, remain until they arrived, explain my presence at the murder scene, and spend the next three hours going over my story, or should I anonymously report the murder using the professor's phone and take off? The former plan appeared the better. I wanted to stay on the police's good side. Besides, I wanted to find out as much as possible about the time of death and other specifics. Instead of phoning the station house, I called my contact person, Detective Brett Snow, who was on duty.

Detective Snow answered her cell in two rings. I gave her a brief rundown on what had occurred and the address of the house. "You'll need the coroner, an ambulance, a crime scene specialist, and a person from animal control" I said.

"A pet?" she asked.

"Affirmative."

"I'll be right there, Nick, I'm only a mile or so away," she said.

Almost immediately, a siren screamed in the distance, getting louder and closer until it stopped with a final yelp in the parking circle in front of the house. Another siren came alive in the distance. I opened the front door, turned on the porch light, and watched Brett and her partner exit the car with their flashlights on.

When Brett entered, she did a double take when she registered my face and clothes.

"What happened to you?"

I didn't know what she meant until I looked at myself in the mirror hanging in the front hallway. My face was dirty from the fall with a bloody scratch on my forehead. I explained how a tall man had run me down in back and how the dog had walked through the blood and stained my suit jumping up on me.

"You should clean up that scratch to avoid infection," she recommended.

"I'll do that later," I assured her.

I led her and her partner to the body in the dining room. Brett first examined the professor without touching her. "Have you disturbed anything?" she asked. I admitted turning her slightly to observe the wound.

She looked at the table set for two with wine glasses and red candles.

"Looks like the professor was going to entertain someone tonight," she said. "You?"

I described my interview with her earlier and how we had been interrupted before she could show me one of Mitch's poems which might suggest where he'd gone.

By this time, two uniformed police officers had arrived to secure the scene, and the coroner entered the house soon after to examine the body. Brett told me to stay where I was while she looked around the house.

Brett's partner, Detective David Bronson, then took over the interrogation and played a version of bad cop to Brett's good.

"Don't you think it's odd that you're here in this house, all scraped up, with a dead body?" he asked.

"As I explained to Detective Snow," I responded, "I came here working on a missing person case. I'm a private detective hired by Abraham Seamer, the Athletic Director at Central. I'm also cooperating with the Ithaca police department. Professor Connolly said she had some evidence about the possible whereabouts of Mitchell Antaglia. That's why I'm here tonight."

"What kind of evidence?" he asked.

"A poem and some notes, Professor Connolly said."

"Did you find any of that stuff?" he demanded.

"Negative," I said.

"So you looked over the house," he said, accusingly.

I decided not to cooperate fully about my search. "No, I just looked around the kitchen and the dining room. Nowhere else."

"Mr. Stirling," he said, "did you kill Professor Connolly?"

"No," I said, and we went around in a few circles before Brett returned. The two of them asked some more questions until the coroner, a small neat man who exuded competence, came over to us.

Brett asked him if he knew how the murder took place. From the angle of the gash on the throat, he said, he could tell that a tall person, probably a male, came up behind her, grabbed her head, probably by the chin, and pulled a sharp knife across her throat, cutting the jugulars. Then the professor bled to death.

"Look what I found," he said to Brett and Bronson, holding out his gloved hand.

I looked over Brett's shoulder and saw a small enamel pin with a brightly colored figure on it. Brett, with her gloved hand, picked it up and held it in her palm. "Where did you find this, Hugh?" she asked the coroner.

"In the professor's right hand," he responded. "It looks like it is a pin that she pulled off the assailant's shirt as the two were struggling."

"Can I take a look at that?" I asked.

"Yes. Just don't touch it," Bronson warned.

I examined the pin. It had a bit of white cloth attached to it. On the pin's front was a funny-looking but familiar cartoon bird with a red head, big yellow beak, and over-sized yellow boots. For a moment I couldn't place the figure. Then it came to me.

"This little creature is a Jay Hawk," I said. "It's the mascot of Kansas University."

All four of us looked at the pin for a moment.

"Could the murderer have some connection with the University of Kansas?" Brett asked us.

"You might be right," I responded. But what? I thought to myself. The only connection that came to mind was Jineral Jackson, the basketball phenom who had transferred to KU in Lawrence, Kansas. But what could he have to do with this murder? I decided not to mention such a long shot to the police.

By the time I had completed my official statement down at the police station it was 1:35 in the morning. I said my goodbyes to Brett and thanked her for her help. She was holding the terrier, who was shivering anxiously in her lap. Animal Control was going to pick him up from the station, she said, stroking the dog's head. "He's a sweet little guy, a rat terrier."

Could she recommend a good motel, I asked, too tired to discuss the dog, and she sent me to the one next to campus.

"Good night," I said.

"Stay in touch on this case, Nick," she said. "Stick around for a few days while the coroner develops more information on the death."

"I will," I promised.

While driving to the motel, I thought about the Antaglia case. Missile Mitch was missing. Sherman, who had known Mitch all his life, claimed that Mitch's father practically abused him as a child, forcing him to play basketball at the expense of everything else. Professor Connolly, now deceased, had told me that many of Mitch's poems expressed a hatred of his father. Was this some sort of unresolved Oedipal Complex? In the morning I'd have to see Coach Seamer to bring him up to date. And to tell him an interview with Antaglia was essential if I hoped to find Mitch.

I showered, cleaned my wound, and, in bed, read Mitch's poem titled "Dr. Death" from Connolly's desk :

I've known you long, my Dr. Death
You come to me at pa's behest
With your needle sharp and straight
To shoot me with your drugs of hate

To shoot me with your drugs of hate
You come to me at pa's behest
I've known you long, my Dr. Death
With your needle sharp and straight

With your needle sharp and straight
I've known you long, my Dr. Death
To shoot me with your drugs of hate
You come to me at pa's behest

You come to me at pa's behest
To shoot me with your drugs of hate
With your needle sharp and straight
I've known you long, my Dr. Death

Who is Dr. Death, I wondered? The piece apparently was some kind of practice poem that Connolly had assigned. After reading it twice, I turned off the light and dreamed of my dead father with a knife at his throat. Professor Connolly was calling me from the other side of a blood-red lake. She was beyond my reach.

Chapter 7

My cell alarm woke me at 6:30. The mirror showed that my face was clean, but bruised on my forehead, which had a scrape that had scabbed over. After using peroxide from my medicine kit to clean the main wound again, I covered it with a large band-aid and shaved. Then I put on a clean shirt and another suit brought in from my car. A quick breakfast in the motel's dining room consisted of a bagel with black coffee. When finished, I stopped by the main desk and told Linda, the blonde behind the counter, that I would stay another night. She tapped at her computer and smiled. I noticed she had no wedding ring.

"It's all set, Mr. Stirling. Can I help you in any other way?" she asked with a hint of flirtation.

"Not now," I smiled, "maybe later," and drove to the athletic complex.

"If you're still lookin' for info on Missin' Missile Mitch," Clarence, the guard, said, "you've come to the right place. His daddy is here. Just walked in the door madder than a rattler."

"Thanks, Clarence," I said and retraced my steps from yesterday to Seamer's office to inform him that I had to see Antaglia to crack the case. I just hoped he wouldn't fire me. The case had dug its claws deep in me, and I wanted to solve it. To the right of her desk in the outer office, Candy stood with her ear to the door. She grinned at me nervously and waved me over.

"Sounds like a good fight going on," I said in response to the muffled shouts.

"Coach Antaglia got here fifteen minutes ago and started screaming about Mitch being kidnapped," she said, her eyes wide, stepping back from the door. "He's blaming Coach Seamer for it."

The door burst open, and a small, furious man dressed in golf attire flew out, with Seamer in his wake.

"It's not our responsibility to keep tabs on our athletes every minute of the day and night!" the Athletic Director shouted at Antaglia, who turned on a dime and shouted back, "At least you can make sure your players aren't kidnapped from under your nose, you moron!" He took a step or two and turned again. "Especially a player of my son's stature!"

By this time Antaglia was almost on top of me, and I put my hands out to prevent a collision. He was small enough for me to stop, and he turned to glare at me.

"Get out of my way!" he growled.

Seamer finally noticed me and saw an opportunity to use me to control the situation before it spun out of control.

"Antaglia," he said, "the man you just about ran down is Mr. Stirling, the private investigator from Atlanta that I hired yesterday to locate Mitchell. I told you about him a minute ago."

Antaglia turned toward me and thrust his face into mine. His small eyes were a milky blue, and his nose was veined from too much alcohol. His hair was white and needed a trim. Although in his seventies, he had the bearing of an athlete, quick on his feet and strong for his age and size.

"Hello," I said, grabbing his hand and shaking it to control his movement. "What's this about a kidnapping?"

"I just told Seamer all about it. Ask *him*. It's his fault it happened. He's responsible," he continued, glaring again at Seamer.

Seamer gestured for me to come closer to him, and whispered, "He's going to cause a major problem if you don't get him out of here. Take him down to the parking lot before he does something really stupid."

"So you don't mind if I talk to him?" I asked.

When he sighed and whispered "O.K.," I followed after Antaglia as he made his way toward the elevator.

Antaglia spent the ride down glaring at me and muttering about Seamer's incompetence. "The bastard wasn't much good as a football coach, and he's even worse as an AD," he said to no one in particular.

When we got out the door and onto the parking lot, I managed to make him look at me.

"Tell me about the kidnapping," I said. "I have some experience with that kind of thing and might be able to help."

Antaglia hesitated and then looked down for a moment. When he looked up, he said, "I don't know much about what's going on myself. I got a call at home this morning from someone who said he had Mitch and wanted money for his return."

"What'd you say to the kidnapper?"

"I told him I would do anything to get my son back!" he asserted.

"How much money did he ask for?"

"If you must know, he asked for $110,000. I'm on my way to my broker to raise the ransom now," Antaglia said. That's an odd amount for a ransom, I thought.

"The kidnapper said he'd call back tomorrow afternoon, about 2:15, and give me instructions about how I should get the money to him," Antaglia continued.

"Have you gone to the police?" I asked.

Antaglia stiffened. "No. The bastard said no police. If the police get involved, I'll never see my son."

I encouraged Antaglia to notify the police, explaining that they could help in kidnapping schemes. They had the manpower to do a full search, and in some circumstances, they could bring in the FBI. But Antaglia continued to insist that he would handle this himself.

"I would be happy to help," I said, hoping he'd agree. I was worried that Antaglia was so erratic that it was more than likely he would foul up the trade-off of money for his son.

My offer seemed to calm him down a little. His breathing slowed and his eyes cleared.

"I have to arrange for the funds and get back to my wife," he said. "She's been horrified by the recent events—Mitch's disappearance and now the ransom request."

He hesitated, looked down again, and said, "I'll consider your offer. I'll talk it over with my wife. If we decide to accept your help, can you come over later?"

"Yes," I said and gave him my card with my cell number. "Call me if anything happens today," I said. He gave me his home number and address, which I wrote in my notebook.

As Antaglia drove away, honking his horn imperiously at Clarence to let him through the gate, it occurred to me this case might not be what it seemed. For a ransom, the sum was small. A professional kidnapper would investigate the wealth of the victim and ask for as much money as he or she could possibly pay. From what I had gathered from Seamer, that was not the case here. Antaglia was supposedly rich and could afford a substantial sum, especially for a beloved son. And the money requested was an odd total. It seemed as if the kidnapper had decided on a hundred grand and then added the $10,000 as something extra. Why? I wondered.

Parking my car beside the athletic complex, I asked Clarence how to get to the campus bookstore.

"You must thinks I be a campus road map, Mr. Stirling," he said in his best Step'n Fetchit imitation. "Yessiree, you must sees me as a map for this here university."

I shook my head at his strange joke, followed his directions on foot, and found myself at the college bookstore. Once inside it, I asked for a copy of *Coaching Genius*, Antaglia's book on coaching basketball. A cashier directed me to the faculty publication section where the book was sitting near the beginning of the alphabet. I bought it and walked across the street to the student café to sit and read it.

The book was published by a small press that specialized in minor sports books. *Coaching Genius* must have made the press's year financially because it was in all of the Atlanta bookstores. The review I'd read in the Atlanta papers hailed its approach to training as an innovative method to make exceptional basketball players out of all talented boys.

I bought a cup of coffee and sat down in a quiet corner. As I read, it became clear that Antaglia had an odd relationship with his son. While much of the book argued for what one would expect—encourage your son to love basketball, give him opportunities to play in different venues, reward him when he does well—other advice was unusual, even monstrous.

The main problem was that any father following his advice would have to keep his son busy with basketball every spare moment the boy had. Antaglia claimed, for instance, that he made Mitch run four miles every morning. "Road work is essential to develop stamina and coordination," the father wrote. "There is no substitute for putting in the miles every single day." Antaglia claimed that Mitch loved getting up at 4:30 a.m. to do his running before school. How much did Mitch enjoy getting up that early during winter mornings? I wondered. "Once your son loves to run and does it willingly every day, then you can give him an occasional day off and have him instead ride his bike ten miles or pedal his stationary cycle for an hour," Antaglia wrote.

After the road work, Antaglia recommended that boys do an hour a day of weight lifting. They should do this to build strength and endurance. Boys should do multiple sets of lifts with at least twelve reps. As they grow older, Antaglia advises, they should lift heavier weights to put on bulk. "Do not listen to those who claim that bulking up slows a player down. The opposite is true," Antaglia argues. Throughout this training, he had Mitch drink high protein drinks and take other sport supplements to increase his muscle mass. I wondered what he meant by other supplements.

Another piece of odd advice was the inordinate amount of practice on the basketball court he required of Mitch. Antaglia said that he built a backyard court for his son for this purpose. But if a father couldn't afford to build one, he could take a membership to the Y and work with his son there. And work Mitch Antaglia did. From the time Mitch got home from school until dinner, the older Antaglia had his son on the court working on drills. He taught Mitch to dribble, to shoot, to pass, and, to lesser extent, to guard opponents. "The goal of all this work," Antaglia wrote, "is to make your son a scoring machine. For your models, look at the best NBA players. They are quick and inventive in their play, and you want your son to perform in the same way." He went on to say that he started each practice with Mitch doing wind sprints on the court before putting four hours in on the drills, especially dunking the ball when the boy got tall enough. When Antaglia himself couldn't coach Mitch due to a conflict, he had an older player drill him.

After dinner, Antaglia advised, fathers should watch three hours of video footage highlighting the greatest basketball players in the NBA. He especially mentioned dunking competitions. He recommended that fathers get as many DVDs as possible, including making their own by recording pro games that could be replayed. It is especially important to slow great plays down so that the boy can learn precisely how these shots work in slow motion. "One advantage of having your own court," he noted, "is that you can take your son out to copy the plays that you see on the DVDs no matter how late at night it is."

Adding up the hours that Antaglia made Mitch work out and practice basketball each day was an eye opener. Mitch ran for an hour in the morning, lifted weights for another hour, practiced basketball for about three hours after school, and then watched NBA DVDs for three hours at night. When did Mitch have time to do anything else?

Antaglia had a long chapter on summers. He planned Mitch's summers so that the boy focused only on basketball. He played on several youth teams so that he gained experience competing at an early age. When Mitch got older, he participated in AAC programs in Atlanta. When he got to high school, he participated in basketball camps and played on traveling teams that competed in games set up by the major shoe companies such as Addidas and Nike. "The purpose of this play is not only to give your son the highest level of competition but to expose him at a young age to the college and pro scouts who will determine his future." When, I wondered, did Mitch have time to do anything besides play basketball? Studying or socializing with friends seemed out of the question.

I couldn't help but notice the ambiguity in the title. Did Antaglia mean coaching a genius such as Mitch? Or did he refer to himself as a genius of a coach? From what I could tell from my interviews, Mitch's coaches at Central didn't think Mitch was a genius on the court, and Seamer didn't consider the father a genius of a coach.

The method may have backfired on Mitch. When he was entering his junior year in college, he was, according to Rachel Stone, burnt out on basketball and ready to take up poetry. The intensity of Antaglia's method might well have driven his son out of the game.

I put the book down on the table and went to get another coffee. When I got back, my cell buzzed.

"Stirling," a voice practically shouted in my ear. "Coach Antaglia here. Where are you? I need you immediately."

"What's going on?" I asked.

He explained that he and his wife had talked it over and decided that they wanted to hire me to help with the ransom negotiations. He asked me the size of my retainer, and I gave him a high figure. Seamer was already my client, and I didn't need a second one, especially one as erratic as Antaglia. He surprised me by agreeing to the amount and invited me to come to his house as soon as possible to discuss strategy. Before I could advise him again to get the police involved, he hung up.

Just as I replaced the phone in my jacket pocket, it rang again. "Yew owe me ten dolla, cowboy," Jules said. "The Smiths is returned to they room."

"How long ago did they arrive?" I asked.

"They jest did," Jules said. "When do I git my money?"

"I'll be out there in the late afternoon," I said, "and I'll give you a third ten if you can get the car's licence plate number."

"O.K. I'll be right back."

The phone clunked as he put it down. A small beep sounded in my phone telling me that another call was coming in.

"Are you the guy who promised me ten dollar to tell you when the Smiths got back?"

"Robin, right?" I asked.

"That's right. Well, the Smiths are back. Hey, who's fighting out there?" she said, as if fights were a fairly common occurrence in her world.

"Hold for a moment, Robin," I said and switched back to Jules.

A commotion was going on in the motel office, and an unfamiliar voice said, "What the hell you doing lookin' at my car, you dwarf!"

"Hep! Hep! Murder!" Jules yelled. Then the phone went

dead.

I connected again with Robin.

"You better call the police!" I asserted. "Your father is being beaten up in the office!"

"He can take care of hisself," Robin said calmly. "He wouldn't want me to call the police."

Some of the reasons why were clear.

"Robin," I said. "I need the licence number of the Smiths' car. I'll give you ten more dollars if you get it for me. Just walk outside and read it off."

"I ain't dressed for going outside," she said. "Why do you want that number so bad anyway?"

"This is an emergency," I said. "The Smiths might have something to do with a missing person case."

She agreed to get the number. I heard the door shut and the sound of her walking across the gravel to the car. She read off the number, and I wrote it in my notebook. Then she yelled, "You O.K., daddy?" and her cell went dead.

I called the police department and reported the fight at the Lions Den. The officer on duty did not seem concerned. "They're always fighting there," he said, "but I'll send a cruiser over to check things out if we have time."

While collecting my things to go, I found that my copy of *Coaching Genius* had been stolen when I'd gone for more coffee. Having read enough, I didn't need another copy.

Chapter 8

On my way back to the athletic complex on foot, I called my contact at the Division of Motor Vehicles. Wendy had been a telephone friend since my days on the Atlanta police force more than twenty years ago.

"I haven't heard from you for a while, Nick," she said peevishly. "I'm still looking forward to that date that you keep promising."

"I thought you were married, Wendy."

"I was but Jerry decided after twenty years of marriage he needed some new experiences," she said.

"I'm sorry to hear that," I said. "Maybe we can go out on a date soon."

"Hah!" she snorted. "That'll be the day. I'll bet you have a license number for me and want an address."

"That's right," I said and read the number to her. I heard her clicking away on her keyboard.

"I come up with a Harold Westerly," she said and gave me an address in Atlanta. The neighborhood was a familiar one consisting of modest homes that had been built after WWII. Mr. Westerly certainly did not live in the lap of luxury.

"Make sure you call me when you're ready for that date, Sugar," she laughed.

I had known Wendy for almost twenty-one years and didn't know what she looked like.

At the athletic complex, I got in my car and waved at Clarence as I drove out of the lot. I didn't stop to ask him directions, and he gave me his mock salute.

I made my way across town and found the Antaglia house, arriving a little after 1:00 p.m. It was a McMansion in an unimpressive housing development. It looked like the Antaglias had demolished the original house on the lot and put up a gray stone mansion. It had a turret on the right side that towered over the modest homes surrounding it. I wondered what the neighbors thought of the Antaglias with their architectural pretensions.

Parking in front, I walked across the spacious, manicured lawn that had gone dormant during the winter months. I rang the bell once, then twice, before a black woman in a maid uniform opened the door.

"You must be Mr. Stirling," she said.

"Yes," I responded. "And what's your name?"

"Stella," she said. "Coach and Mrs. Coach are waiting for you in the library. I'll show you in."

She led me through several long hallways to the back of the house. Then she tapped on a closed door. "Come in," Antaglia snarled with his usual charm.

Stella opened the door on the Antaglias. They were sitting together on a large leather couch in the middle of a large room. You could cut the tension between them with a knife. The walls were covered with shelves of books on sports. The focus of the room was a large wooden desk on which sat a red telephone. To the side were two antique wooden file cabinets.

When the Antaglias stood up, I was surprised that the wife was several inches taller than the husband. She was a striking woman closing in on fifty with long blonde hair going grey. She wore it braided and coiled on the back of her head. Her nose was long and straight; her eyes, a striking blue. She was dressed in lavender golfing attire. In fact, the two of them looked as if they had just returned from a round of golf. It was surprising that they had been golfing when their son was kidnapped and they were awaiting a ransom call.

Antaglia had a highball glass on the table in front of him. He got up and made another drink at an unobtrusive bar behind the couch. He was a bit unsteady, which didn't bode well if anything developed later with the kidnapper. He would need his wits about him.

"Thank you, Stella," Mrs. Antaglia said in a patrician tone that did not seem natural. "I'm Linda Antaglia, Mr. Stirling," she said, turning to me. "My husband is too busy getting drunk to introduce us." Antaglia glared at her. "May I get you something to drink?" she continued.

"Thanks, but not right now," I responded as Antaglia poured himself a tumbler full of scotch and took a long pull.

He walked over to the desk, picked up a check, and handed it to me. It was for $4000 drawn on a local bank.

"Thanks," I said.

"Now that you're working for us, I want you to sever all ties with that idiot Seamer," he said.

"I'll call this afternoon and do that," I assured him.

Antaglia waved me to a chair across from the couch, and the two of us sat down, as did Mrs. Antaglia. Once we all were settled, I asked them to tell me about the kidnapper and his demands. Linda Antaglia looked at her husband and said, "Coach here is the one that got us into this mess—he'll have to tell you what's going on. I don't understand most of it."

Antaglia glared at her again. "My fault!" he practically

shouted. "All I did was try to make the boy a man! I wanted to cut the apron strings that you tied around his privates!"

"How dare you blame me for all of this, Alberto," she said coldly, her eyes steely slits.

It was clear that this was going to become a full marital battle if I didn't control the situation.

"Folks, I know you're under a lot of strain, but if I'm going to help, you've got to calm down," I said, trying for a calm but firm tone. "I need both of you to help by giving me information to find your son. Blaming each other doesn't help matters." It was like talking to a couple of ornery children. "Why don't we begin with the person who called asking for the ransom? Who took the call?"

"I did," Antaglia said.

"Did you recognize the voice?"

He said that he didn't, but he recognized the accent as Midwestern, maybe from Nebraska. "He kind of sounded like Johnny Carson used to on the old *Tonight Show*."

"So he wasn't from Georgia, or even the South," I said.

Antaglia agreed.

"Did he seem to know you?" I asked.

"He did," Antaglia said. "He knew my name and knew I had been a coach."

"Did he seem to know Mitch?" I asked.

"He did," Antaglia said. "He claimed that he had had his eye on Mitch for many years and thought it was time that he stepped in and took over his life."

"What did he mean by that?" I asked.

"How the hell do I know?" Antaglia growled. "He's a damn kidnapper. I guess he researched Mitch. The boy's one of the greatest college power forwards in the nation. A lot of people know about him." Antaglia gave me the impression he was holding something back.

I asked him to tell me about the demands again. Antaglia repeated details about the ransom demand and the amount demanded, $110,000. He informed me that he now had that amount in cash, in the small unmarked bills that the kidnapper had demanded.

Turning again to the police, I advised the Antaglias to notify them immediately, going over in more detail how the police could help in catching the kidnapper. If this person operated across state lines, the cops could bring in the FBI.

Antaglia looked at me with his eyes blazing.

"How many times do I have to tell you, Stirling, that the kidnapper told me no police if I wanted to see Mitch alive? Do you have children?" he asked.

"No," I said.

"Then you can't understand how far a father will go to save his son," he said. His wife looked at him strangely.

"If you don't want the police involved," I said, "will you let me make the drop, wherever the kidnapper wants it to be?"

"Are you mad, Stirling?" Antaglia snapped. "The kidnappers said only I should come with the money in a plain brown paper shopping bag. If anyone else appears, the bastard said he'd kill Mitch. He said that twice."

I then decided to broach the subject that had been bothering me all day. "I understand that Mitch disappeared one time before, when he was in high school."

"Where did you hear that lie?" Antaglia said bitterly.

"From Seamer," I responded.

Linda Antaglia looked at her husband. "We'd better tell Mr. Stirling the truth, Alberto."

She hesitated, collecting her thoughts. "Yes, Mitchell ran away from home once, about seven years ago," she admitted. Antaglia sat glaring in his corner of the couch.

"What were the circumstances?" I asked.

"He got mixed up with a loose girl in high school by the name of Jenny Nelson. She convinced Mitch to go to Atlanta with her. They stayed there a couple of weeks."

I wrote the girl's name in my notebook. "I also heard they pretended Mitch had been kidnapped and asked for money,"

I said.

Linda Antaglia looked uncomfortable. Antaglia looked furious.

"The girl called us up and said that she and a gang of kidnappers had Mitch and wanted $10,000 for his release," she said. "She even put Mitch on the phone, and he cried and told us that the kidnappers were threatening to murder him if we didn't give them the money."

"Cried like a little girl," Antaglia said.

I ignored Antaglia. "How did the incident resolve itself?" I asked.

"We hired a PI to look into the situation, and he found out pretty quickly it was a scam," she said. "He went down to a flea bag motel in Atlanta, caught them, and brought them home."

"What happened then?" I asked.

Linda Antaglia looked uncomfortable. "We made certain that the two of them didn't see each other again," she said. "Alberto threatened to sue the girl for kidnapping, but the DA wouldn't press charges. He said Mitch was not kidnapped, which was a lie. He claimed my son was in on the subterfuge. That's the word he used. But he didn't know Mitch very well. He wouldn't have gone with that girl on his own. She tricked him. I'm his mother. I can tell about such things."

I hesitated before asking the next question. "Could the current kidnapping be similar to the first one, with Mitch somehow involved?"

Antaglia's face reddened, and he began sputtering.

"We asked you to help us find our son, not to imply that he's some sort of criminal!" he shouted. "If you're not going to help us, give us our money back, you SOB!"

I considered doing so for a moment but resisted the impulse. From everything found so far, Mitch seemed like a good kid who was in some sort of trouble. I didn't want to give up on finding him before something else horrible happened. It was time to change the subject.

"I suppose you heard about Professor Elaine Connolly," I said.

The two looked at each other. "We know who she was," Linda Antaglia said. Antaglia himself looked blank.

"She was Mitch's English teacher," she said to him. She was used to his confusion.

"Oh, her," he responded.

"You didn't like her?" I asked him.

"She was a meddler," he said gruffly. "Got him interested in writing poetry when he should have been paying attention to his future in the NBA."

"Don't you think he should develop more interests than that?" I asked, testing his response. It was not beyond the possible that Antaglia had murdered Connolly in one of his rages over Mitch.

"I've heard that crap for years—that Mitch needs outside interests," he shouted, "that he needs to develop his mind. Do you think Michael Jordan would have been Michael Jordan if he had developed his mind instead of his fade-away jump shot?"

His wife looked at him as if he had passed gas at a fancy dinner party. "Calm down, Alberto," she said. "Mr. Stirling doesn't want to hear your theory of education right now." She infused the "theory of education" phrase with heavy irony that apparently went over his head. "I was sorry to hear about the professor's death," she said to me. "She apparently was very kind to Mitch."

"She was," I confirmed. "She taught him in three classes and thought he had talent as a poet. He called her his spiritual mother," I concluded.

Linda Antaglia stiffened.

"I'd like to see him try to eat those poems," Antaglia said.

He looked at his watch, and I glanced at mine. It was almost 2:00 p.m., and the kidnapper had promised to call at 2:15.

Antaglia turned to me and said: "When the bastard calls,

Stirling, I want you on the other line taking notes. I want a complete record of what he says—where I'm supposed to meet him, when, and so forth. There's a second phone on the main house line in the living room. I'll show you where it is."

He finished his drink and moved toward the bar for a fresh one.

"Don't you want to be clearheaded during the phone call?" I asked. "Is it wise to keep drinking?"

He stopped on the way to the bar and swayed briefly before catching himself. "Mind your own business, Stirling. I know what I'm doing."

But he put his empty tumbler on the bar and turned to the door. He led me silently down the hall to a large, tastefully-decorated sitting room. It had Louis XVI stuffed furniture, thin-legged symmetrical tables, and scenes of the 18th-century French countryside. Mostly pictures of dogs and horses on hunting excursions hung on the walls.

"Must be your French Revolution room," I said.

"You'll have to ask my wife about that," he responded absently, pointing to the phone. "When it rings, pick up and let me do the talking. Just listen and take notes," he said as he walked out of the room.

Since 15 minutes remained before the scheduled call, I used my cell phone to contact Seamer and inform him that Antaglia had hired me. He didn't sound disappointed.

"I read about Professor Connolly's murder in this morning's paper," Seamer said. "Is it connected with the Antaglia kidnapping?"

"Might be," I said, "but I don't know how."

"When I talked to Chief Madison this morning, he said Connolly was Mitch's teacher. True?"

"Yes."

"This is getting too complicated for me," he said. "Could you do me a favor?"

"I'll try."

"Keep the Athletic Program out of the murder

investigation and publicity surrounding it," he requested. "We don't need any more bad publicity connected to our basketball program."

He was probably referring to the recruiting scandal, and I promised to do my best to control whatever media attention the program got. I also offered to return by personal check the unused money he gave me. He said that would be fine, and we parted on friendly terms.

Just as I hung up, the house phone rang. Antaglia picked it up on the first ring, and I picked up a moment later, after the conversation had begun.

"What was that sound?" a flat Midwestern voice said. "Is this line tapped by the police?" He had heard me picking up the hand set.

"No," Antaglia insisted. "I've followed your orders to the letter. No police."

"If you want to see that boy of yours alive, you better continue cooperating with me," the voice said.

"Before I do anything else," Antaglia said, "I want to talk to Mitch. I want proof that he's alive."

"I'm not going to let you talk to Mitch," the voice said. "You have to take it on faith that he's alive. The best way to ensure that he remains alive is to cooperate with me 100 per cent. If you don't, you might find your son dead in a ditch. So shut up and listen to me. I know that's hard for you to do, but this time I'm in control, not you. First off, do you have the money?"

"I had my broker sell some stocks, and I have the money you asked for in unmarked tens and twenties," Antaglia said.

"Did you put them in a shopping bag like I told you?" he asked.

"Yes."

"Good," the voice said. "Now listen carefully to what I say because if you screw this up Mitch will be dead. Drive north to Comfort. Do you know where that is?"

Antaglia said he did.

"There's a golf course there called the Sunshine Country Club. Are you familiar with it?"

Antaglia said that he had played the course many times.

"I didn't ask you if you played golf there—just if you know where it is."

"I do," Antaglia said.

"OK, meet me there at midnight, behind the clubhouse. I'll have Mitch with me. If everything looks good to me with no police or other people around, and you have the bag, we can make the exchange."

"How will I know it's you?" Antaglia asked.

The voice hesitated, as if he had not planned on this question.

"I'll whistle," he said.

Antaglia didn't seem to think this was odd, but I did. This setup was planned by an amateur.

"OK. I'll be there with the money," Antaglia said. His voice had lost it assertiveness.

"Good. I'm glad that you trust me," he said. "Trust is the most important ingredient in this transaction."

"You will have Mitchell with you, won't you?" Antaglia asked.

"Yes, I will. It'll be like old home week," the voice said, chuckling.

"What do you mean?" Antaglia asked.

"You'll find out soon enough, Coach," the voice responded sarcastically, and then hung up.

I put the hand set in the cradle and leaned back. Sweat ran down my back. What a mess this case was becoming, I thought, looking over my notes on the conversation. It was clear that the kidnapper knew Antaglia from the past. Proof of this was in his references to "this time" he was in control and to old home week. Getting up to find my way back to the study, I wondered how much information Antaglia was hiding from me.

In the study, Antaglia was getting another drink from the

bar, and Linda Antaglia was sitting on the sofa crying. She had apparently listened in on the speaker phone.

"How could you have let things go this far?" she sobbed.

"What do you mean, Mrs. Antaglia?" I asked.

She looked surprised to see me, as if she had forgotten I was in the house.

"Only that Alberto has worked Mitchell so hard that he drove him away," she said. "Into the clutches of this awful kidnapper."

Antaglia stared at his wife with rapier eyes.

"Shut up, Linda," he said. "Now's not the time to worry about how we got here. If we want to save Mitchell, we'll have to do what this kidnapping bastard wants us to do."

I again recommended that the Antaglias contact the police. They both said no at the same instant and looked at each other.

"If you won't contact the police," I pleaded, "at least let me make the exchange."

"No," Antaglia shouted. "Didn't you hear what the man said? He wants to see only me."

While not liking his decision, I agreed to help any way possible. Perhaps I could drive to Sunshine with him, I suggested. Again he refused.

"I want you to stay here, with Linda," he said.

Linda didn't seem excited about the possibility. Antaglia intended to leave for the exchange at 10:30 that night and asked me to be back before then.

"Will do," I said.

In the meantime, I had some errands to run and left, stepping out into a dreary, rainy afternoon.

Chapter 9

The first was to drive out to the Sunshine Golf Course to get the lay of the land. I took a road map out of my glove compartment and looked for Comfort, GA. It was about thirty miles to the north of Ithaca. On the map, the town had a little green flag signifying the golf course. After jotting down the highway numbers and turns in my notebook, I drove out to the highway.

Outside of Ithaca, the landscape turned rural. I passed old farm houses that were in various states of disrepair. Around them spread fields with cows and a few herds of goats. The fields were often separated with lines of trees, and along the highway small shacks had fallen into ruin. Often the only structure left standing was the old brick chimney that looked ready to crumble. The highway passed through two one-light towns until I reached Comfort and turned left at the only major intersection. My directions took me through some residential areas with modest homes. Then the golf club appeared, which consisted of a small clubhouse on top of a large hill. It had taken me more than half an hour to make the drive. It would probably take a little longer at night, much longer if it were raining heavily.

The course fell off below the club house with the most prominent feature being a large pond in front of the last green. The edges of the fairways were covered with thick stands of trees, and these trees came right up near the clubhouse. They provided the perfect cover for the exchange, or for a murder. I didn't like the look of things.

Back on the highway, I took a different route home—all roads lead to Ithaca around there—and returned to my motel room. I brought in my laptop, went online, and looked up Jineral Jackson at Kansas University. No luck, but after nosing around a bit, I found a phone number for the basketball program. It was 6:00 here, which would make it 4:00 there. The secretary I reached connected me to the office of the head basketball coach. Lying to the woman who answered, I claimed to be a representative of Nike shoes and wanted to talk to Jackson about his shoe deal because a minor glitch had developed in his contract. A problem with Jineral's future sneaker contract would get his attention.

"Uh-oh," the secretary responded when I explained the problem.

"Can you put me in touch with Jineral?" I asked.

"Well, it's against policy," she said. "But if you give me a number, I can have him call you back."

"Fine," I said, not expecting much.

I cleaned my .38, thinking I might need it that night, and had just gotten back online to look up Harold Westerly in case I had time today to phone him about the black Caddie registered in his name that Smith was driving. Before I got far, my cell rang.

"You call about my Nike contract?" a voice asked.

"Is this Jineral Jackson?"

He said it was, and I gave him a line that Nike had concerns about their future contract with him. "Are you wearing our shoes now?" I asked.

"Of course I am," he responded. "You know Kansas is a Nike school."

"Well, I talked to an old friend of yours, Missile Mitch Antaglia, who tells me you might jump over to Addidas."

"Why would Mitch tell you that?" he demanded. "I haven't talked to that boy in six months."

"Well, thank you for clearing that up for us," I said.

I explained how important it was for Nike to get college players to sign contracts early so that they would continue the association during their pro career.

"Tell me something I don't know," he responded.

"And we're always looking for new people to sign," I continued. "Do you think Mitch would be a good prospect?"

"Mitch is a good friend," he said, "but despite what people in Georgia Central think, he's nothing more than a good college player. That's as far as he goes."

"When I was talking to Mitch," I said, "he told me about a guy at Central named Dr. Death. Do you know anything about this?" There was a long pause on the other end.

"Who you say you are?" he demanded. "Are you trying to ruin my career with this Dr. Death shit? Let me tell you something: that was a long time ago, and I only did it once and then I quit. I don't need this shit. Who you say you are?"

"Nick Sterling," I admitted. "I'm a private investigator working with the Ithaca police department on the possible kidnapping of Mitch."

"Dr. Death? Kidnapping? This is getting too hard on me. You stay away from me. I'm finished with all that shit at Central."

My cell went dead. But I had learned something important. Jineral knew who Dr. Death was. I'd have to look into that. But before doing that, I had a visit to pay. It was now 7:00. I needed to check on things at the Lions Den. Mitch's key to room 32 was still in my pocket, and this time I would use it.

When I drove up to the motel, it was raining hard and dusk was falling. The building looked deserted. No cars were in front. Lights were on in the Robins Nest and in the main office. Maybe Jules and his daughter were still about.

On entering the office, I found a stranger behind the desk. "Where's Jules?" I asked him.

"In the hospital."

"What happened?" I asked, but I thought I knew.

"Some guy beat him up bad."

This information didn't surprise me given what I had heard over the phone.

"Is he O.K.?" I asked, wondering if all the night clerks in the place kept their information close.

"He'll live, I guess. Do you want a room?" he inquired, as an afterthought, as if people stopping by wanting rooms were unusual.

"No thanks," I said. "I'll go by the hospital to see my buddy Jules."

"Didn't think he had any friends," he said as I left.

I drove over to the county hospital and asked at the front desk for Jules's room. They gave it to me and sent me to the seventh floor where I located the room. Inside, Jules lay in bed with his head and face fully bandaged except for a mouth hole. Robin was with him, feeding him some sort of a liquid through a plastic straw.

"Look what the cat dragged in," Robin said, glaring at me.

"Who's here?" Jules asked. "Cain't see a thing."

"It's me, Jules, Stirling," I said, trying to sound friendly.

His bandaged form raised itself from the bed clothes. He looked like the ghost of a child.

"Where's my money, you bastard? You owe me lotsa money for gettin' beat up for you," he shouted.

"And where's my money?" Robin joined in to form a loud duo.

I reached in my back pocket, took out my wallet, and lay forty dollars on the table beside Jules's bed.

"There's your money," I said, "and thanks for helping me out."

"How much he give me?" Jules asked. "I cain't see."

"I know, Daddy," Robin said, patting his hand. "He gave you ten dollars." She tucked the other thirty into her cleavage.

I left them squabbling over the money and decided to return to the Lions Den to check out room 32.

When I left the hospital, the rain had turned into a storm, with thunder and lightening punctuating the gloom. I drove across town toward the motel. Near its vicinity, I heard a huge boom and recognized the sound of a transformer exploding due to a lightening strike. Both street and traffic lights went black. Fortunately, I was past the major intersections and made it to the Lions Den with little trouble.

The motel had no lights and looked empty. I knew Jules and Robin were at the hospital, and no cars were parked in front of the rooms. If the manager was there, he was in the dark. I parked my car near the road and took my .38 and my flashlight out of the glove compartment, placing the pistol in my right jacket pocket. Going to the back of the Honda, I took my raincoat out of my trunk, put it on, and walked the short distance to room 32 in the rain. I looked in the window but the curtains were closed. Lightening flashed, and the hair on my neck stood up. The strike must be close, I thought, when the thunder clapped an instant later.

I reached in my pocket for Mitch's key, unlocked and opened the door a crack, then pushed. The door hit something hard. When I pushed harder, the impediment moved six inches. I stepped into the room and immediately felt my foot slip on something wet. I pointed my flashlight beam into the room and saw unmade beds with suitcases on them. Looking down along my beam, I found that the door was stopped by what looked like a body with a pool of blood around its shoulders and head.

"Not again," I muttered.

My light revealed that I had stepped in the coagulating

blood. Walking back to my car, I took a towel out of my trunk and used it to clean the soles of my shoes thoroughly before walking back to the room.

I looked in the door again using my light and surveyed the extent of the blood. It was spattered across the opposite wall and ceiling, and it had pooled about three feet out into the middle of the room. Setting my back foot, I hopped over the area, fell forward, and found myself next to the bed. I reached over the body and locked the door.

Pointed down, my flashlight revealed the victim's face. Ghastly white, it had a prominent misshaped brow and sharp check bones. My hand felt the neck for a pulse. Nothing. When I looked closely at the neck, I found the same gash that the professor had. A slasher was on the prowl.

I then examined the body. The woman was clearly tall, over six feet, "model tall" as Rachel had said.

Next, I examined the room. Nothing was in the bathroom except for some tissues in the trash and some disposable razors and an empty shampoo bottle. I checked the closet and then the bureau drawers. Nothing. The occupants had packed to leave.

Looking through the suitcases on the bed turned up a mess of women's clothes thrown together in knots. Whoever packed was in a hurry. In the bottom of the suitcase, I found a few personal items: two old snapshots of a baby and a professional photograph of a young woman in her early twenties wearing an old-fashioned basketball uniform with short pants. She was in the defensive stance, long legs bent with arms flexed, her face smiling. It was a glamour shot. Whoever this was did not look much like the woman on the floor. The girl's face was beautiful. She looked like a movie star. The face on the floor looked like a boxer's. What had caused that deformation? I wondered.

I directed my beam on the back of the photo and saw a studio identification that read, "Richard Reeves, Sports Photography, Atlanta, Georgia, 1987." I wondered if Richard

Reeves remembered the beautiful young woman he photographed so many years ago.

I carefully placed the materials in my right armpit to keep them dry. After one more look around, I bent over the pool of blood to open the door and hopped out into the rain, shutting the door behind me.

It didn't take me long to decide not to wait for the Ithaca police. It would be hard to explain being found at two murders so similar two nights apart. I drove my car to the nearest gas station with a pay phone and dialed 911 and reported a murder in room 32 of the Lions Den. The operator did not seem surprised as she took down the information. That area of town did not have a good reputation. When she asked for my name, I hung up and started back to the Antaglias' house.

I wondered if Mr. Smith realized that Mrs. Smith was singing with the angels. I also wondered if he had arranged a one-way ticket for her.

Chapter 10

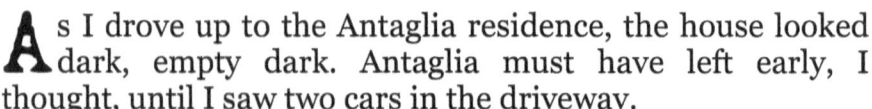

As I drove up to the Antaglia residence, the house looked dark, empty dark. Antaglia must have left early, I thought, until I saw two cars in the driveway.

When I rang the front doorbell, Stella, the maid, answered.

"It's good to see you again, Mr. Stirling," she said, taking my raincoat and hanging it on a rack next to the door. She seemed genuinely happy I was there.

"Do you generally stay here all night?" I asked.

"No, sir, but Mrs. Antaglia asked me to stay tonight. She said she'd need my help for when Mitchell comes home." She hesitated. "He's coming home, isn't he?"

"Hope so," I said as Stella led me down the long hallway. But a long night lay ahead of me. And a lot had gone badly the last two nights, especially the two murders. Were the baby pictures from room 32 Mitch's? If so, who was the murdered woman? Rachel thought she was Mitch's new girlfriend, but I thought she might be a relative, an aunt of

Mitch's maybe.

"What kind of kid was Mitch?" I asked Stella. She looked uncomfortable, as if it were out of place for her to talk.

"Was he kind to you?" I asked.

She said he was but was also a bit lost. Then she whispered to me that she couldn't talk here and to call her later. I nodded.

By this time we had arrived at the study and found the Antaglias facing each other tensely in the middle of the room. They had been arguing, and Antaglia was drunk. Mrs. Antaglia looked slightly disheveled, as if she had exerted herself.

Had the Antaglias been fighting? I wondered.

"About time you got here, Stirling," Antaglia snarled. "I want to go over with you the procedure to use during the exchange."

I told him how he should handle the meeting. He agreed to follow my advice. When he put on his coat, I noticed that he had a gun in his belt.

"Why the gun?" I asked.

"In case I have to protect myself or my son, you idiot," he answered.

I took a deep breath to control my temper. "It's not a good idea to carry a gun because you'd be tempted to use it," I explained as calmly as possible.

"I might just do that," he snapped. He was not a friendly drunk, and the tension of the situation made him even more difficult.

He picked up the bag from the corner and started to walk but stumbled and almost fell before catching himself.

"You're pretty drunk, Coach," I said. "Why not let me drive you to Comfort and wait in the car."

"Mind your own business, Stirling," he snapped. "The kidnapper told me to come alone, and I'm going to follow orders to make sure I get Mitch back!"

"Let him drive you, Alberto," his wife said, as he left the

room.

He glared back at her and departed.

When he was gone, Mrs. Antaglia looked at me.

"Mr. Stirling, will you please follow him? Try to keep him out of trouble. He's so drunk, I don't think he'll make it to Comfort in one piece."

"I'll follow in my car," I said. The heavy rains that affected visibility worried me. I hurried to the front door and watched as Antaglia put the bag in the car, got in himself, and backed out of the driveway. When he was half a block away, I put on my rain coat, got in my car, and followed him at a distance.

The rain was now coming down in sheets, and, on the highway, cars had pulled off to the side because the drivers couldn't see. The lack of visibility didn't affect Antaglia, who drove much too fast, his car fish tailing on the slick road. When he got behind a slower car, he tailgated, flashed his lights, and blew his horn until the car pulled over to let him by. It was hard to stay close, but I managed to keep his tail lights within sight.

We were making pretty good time until we hit Gilbert, the first town north of Ithaca. A huge tree, a water oak, had blown over onto the right side of the highway, and the Gilbert police were directing traffic. I caught up to Antaglia and was afraid that he might see me and do something stupid. But the police officer directing traffic let our line of cars go through, and Antaglia began his erratic driving again.

We reached Comfort at 11:05, five minutes late. As Antaglia turned off the highway toward the golf course, I realized my car was almost out of gas. Bad planning, I thought, as I pulled into a station on the corner. The pump didn't have an outside pay function, so I had to prepay inside. After throwing the cashier a ten, I filled up my car half way, and took off after Antaglia toward the course. His tail lights were lost in the gloom. In the club's parking lot, his was the only car. The kidnapper was either not there or had parked elsewhere.

After parking next to Antaglia's car, I got out my .38 and my flashlight, and stepped into the storm. It was raining hard, and the wind howled through the surrounding trees. Walking along the side of the club house, I kept my light off.

As I turned the corner, a flash of lightening lit the landscape, and two men appeared, one tall, one medium, facing each other. No third figure was visible, but I might have caught a glimpse of someone at the edge of the woods. Maybe not, I thought, as the thunder clapped.

Through the wind and rain, snatches of shouts, but nothing coherent, reached me.

"...he's not your son, you..."

"Cynthia's not..."

Another lightening flash illuminated the two figures grappling together, fighting for the shopping bag. It was time for me to intervene, and, flicking on my flash, I saw two darts of light and heard two pops—the sound of gunfire. I pulled out my .38, and ran toward the two men.

In the next lightening flash, I saw the tall man limping toward the woods with the bag. Antaglia was not visible, until I reached the spot of the transfer and found him on the ground. When I pointed my flash at his face, he grimaced and said:

"Where the hell you been, Stirling. You let the bastard get away!"

It didn't seem the best time to point out he had told me not to come.

"Did he shoot you?"

"Yes."

"Where?"

"In the chest, I think," he said, "but I got him, too."

Holding the light in my teeth, I unbuttoned his rain jacket, which had a bullet hole in the front. Underneath was a blood-soaked shirt.

"Where's Mitch?" he asked, forgetting that his son had not appeared at the exchange.

"He's not here," I responded.

"Where's he gone?" Antaglia asked. He appeared to be going into shock.

The next decision was how to get Antaglia to the hospital. We were far away from an ambulance service, so we couldn't wait here for help. I called Ithaca 911 and told the operator that Antaglia was badly wounded and needed an ambulance. "Send the ambulance up the Comfort highway," I shouted. "I'll drive back toward Ithaca and flash my lights to stop the ambulance when I see it." She said O.K., but didn't like the plan. We didn't have much choice because too many wounded people bleed to death waiting for an ambulance this far from regular service.

Placing my handkerchief on the wound, I pressed down to staunch the bleeding, and told Antaglia to hold it there. Then I dragged him to my car, got him in, and headed toward Ithaca.

As we drove, Antaglia became more delirious and began yelling at people who were not present. He complained that Roy had shot him and that Mitch was not Roy's son. He said that he never loved Cynthia, whoever she was. And he yelled at Dr. Meluso, saying he needed more injections, right away. Could that be his physician? In less than a mile, he passed out.

Half way to Ithaca, the emergency lights of the ambulance appeared. I flashed my headlights on and off, and the ambulance pulled off the highway as did I. The medics got Antaglia on the gurney and into the ambulance while I told them about the wound and the time it occurred. One of the medics entered the back to treat the patient; then the other turned the vehicle around and sped back to Ithaca.

Following along without trying to keep up, I called the necessary people on my cell, starting with Linda Antaglia. When I told her that her husband had been shot, she asked, almost hopefully, "Is he dead?"

"Not when I saw him last, Mrs. Antaglia," I said. "You

should call the hospital for details later."

"When can I see you?" she asked.

"I can meet you at the hospital in about an hour," I said, and she agreed.

The next call went to Brett Snow. When she answered with a sleepy "Detective Snow," I realized I had awoken her. My watch said it was 12:45.

"Sorry to wake you, Detective," I said, starting to hang up.

"Nick?" she said, more alert. "Is that you?"

I identified myself and caught her up on what she needed to know. "Holy cow!" she exclaimed, and invited me to her house to discuss events in more detail. She gave me directions, and I arrived in about 15 minutes.

Brett opened the door in her wool bathrobe. On her feet were two bunny slippers with rabbit ears and bushy pom poms for tails on the heels. She saw me look at them.

"I've had them since I was thirteen," she said. When I smiled, she said, laughing, "I don't let just anybody see me in them!"

We sat down at the table, and she asked me if I wanted some wine.

"I don't drink wine," I said.

"Whiskey? That's all I have on hand."

"OK," I said, and she put a bottle of Wild Turkey with a glass of ice in front of me.

When we were settled and sipping our drinks, I reviewed the events of the day, holding back only what was necessary.

I explained about Mitch's kidnapping and the Antaglias' refusal to notify the police, against my repeated advice to do so. I told her of Jules being assaulted by a mysterious Mr. Smith, who might be the kidnapper. I told her about the botched ransom exchange at the Sunshine Country Club, which was technically out of her county. And I told her about the murder at the Lions Den that I phoned in anonymously. For each item, I filled in a few details.

All the while she looked at me, sipping her wine and

running her fingers through her hair. Every once in a while she'd ask a question, and then go back to looking and listening.

When finished, I apologized for not having kept her better informed as events unfolded.

"What you're really telling me, Nick, is this little missing person case has turned into a kidnapping, a felony assault, a gun battle, and two murders in just two days, and the Ithaca police had no idea much of this was going on."

"I did report the two murders." I reminded her.

She paused a moment, laughing at me. "That you did," she said. "I don't know if this is funny or sad," she continued, "but we'll find out tomorrow when we report to Captain Madison. How about meeting him with me at 9:00 in the morning?"

"I'll be there to take my medicine," I said.

She asked me if I wanted anything to eat, and I said "No thanks, I have an appointment at the hospital."

She led me to the door and held out her hand. As I took it, a spark of static electricity snapped between us. We looked at each other and laughed.

"Looks like something's happening between us!" she exclaimed, smiling at me.

"Why don't I take you out to dinner to explore what that something is?" I suggested.

"Let me know when, Nick," she said as I walked out the door.

After driving across town, I parked my car on a dark street near the hospital and walked to the main entrance. At the desk, after identifying myself, I asked about Antaglia. The woman checked her records and said he was out of the Emergency Room and in Intensive Care. "I work for the family and want to talk to his wife," I explained, and she dialed a number and said a few words.

"You can't see him," she said, "but Mrs. Antaglia will come down."

About ten minutes later, Linda Antaglia exited the elevator, got her bearings, and walked toward me.

"Thank you for coming, Mr. Stirling," she said. We shook hands formally.

"How is your husband?" I asked.

"Not well," she said, explaining that he was in Intensive Care, on life support. He had lost a lot of blood—plus the bullet had damaged his lung.

"I'm sorry to hear that," I said. "I was worried about the exchange. I was afraid that it wouldn't go well, especially with your husband being so drunk."

"Alberto has not been at his best the last few days," she said. "Mitch's disappearance affected him deeply."

"Your husband mentioned several names when I was driving him toward town. The two he mentioned most were Roy and Cynthia, and he seemed to see Roy as some sort of competitor. Cynthia sounded like an old friend. He mentioned Dr. Meluso once in connection with some injections, perhaps because your husband was in pain and wanted relief."

Linda Antaglia glanced around to see if anyone was within hearing range. Then she looked at me.

"Dr. Meluso is a lab technician in the Ag School who does research on pigs. From what I've heard, he is breeding a wild pig for wealthy hunters."

"Why would that be useful?" I asked.

"I'm not sure. You'll have to ask Dr. Meluso," she said.

"How does your husband know Meluso?" I asked.

'I don't know when they met," she said, "but I think it was somewhere in Kansas. I know they worked together on projects concerning athletic endurance."

I asked a few more questions about Antaglia's condition and then asked the main one:

"Do you want me to stay on the case, Mrs. Antaglia?"

"Yes," she said. "I'd like you to catch the person who shot my husband and kidnapped my son. I want this beast punished for his crimes. And I want you to find Mitchell and bring him home."

"I'll do my best," I promised, and then mentioned my two clearest leads, the photographer who took the picture of the basketball player and the owner of the black Cadillac that the Smiths were driving. I was beginning to be certain that Smith, now without his female companion, was the kidnapper I was searching for.

Chapter 11

Next morning, after a quick breakfast, I drove to the police station for my meeting with Brett and Madison. I was not looking forward to it and expected a tongue lashing.

On arriving, the secretary showed me into Madison's office, where the Captain and Detective Snow were waiting. Brett caught my eye and gave me a joke frown. Madison waved me to the seat beside her and looked at me.

"Stirling," he said, "when I first saw you I thought you might be trouble. In fact, I called Lawrence Kimble, the DA of Fulton County that Seamer mentioned had referred you, and Kimble told me that you were a trustworthy investigator, one of the best that he's ever worked with." He stopped and made a steeple out of his fingers and looked through them at my face.

"But now that I see the mess you've made out of what seemed to be a simple missing person case, I wonder if I was right to work with you. Let's just go over what has happened since you arrived in Ithaca two days ago. First, a professor was murdered, and we found you on the premises. Then, a man was assaulted and sent to the hospital. Next, a woman apparently named Smith was murdered in a room in the Lions Den, again with you on the premises. Note that the two murders took place within two days. Finally, you neglected to inform me about the kidnapping of the Antaglias' son, which resulted in Antaglia being shot and nearly killed."

His eyes had darkened and his fists had clenched. "Didn't I ask you to keep my office in the loop? And didn't I give you Detective Snow as your contact person?"

Silence filled the room. I wanted to make sure the Captain had finished before mounting my defense. But Brett answered first.

"Chief," she said, in a calm, firm tone, "I just want to remind you that Mr. Stirling did keep me informed about what was going on. In fact, in the Connolly murder, he waited around for us and helped with the crime scene. If it hadn't been for Mr. Stirling, we might have missed a few key pieces of evidence."

"I follow you on that, Detective," Madison said, "but what about the other murder, the woman at the Lions Den?"

She looked over my way and frowned again. "Mr. Stirling even helped us there," she said. "Don't forget that he called in the murder and alerted the force about it. While I too wish he had stayed around," she looked sharply at me, "he did have to get over to the Antaglias to advise on the ransom money."

"Which he didn't notify us about," Madison practically shouted.

"You're correct there, Chief," Snow said, "and I've reprimanded him for that. But keep in mind that the Antaglias did not want the police involved."

"And what about the Antaglia shooting?" Madison asked.

I decided to speak up. "Technically that's not even in your jurisdiction, Captain Madison. It occurred in another county."

That fact calmed him down. He wasn't responsible for that one.

"And don't forget, Chief," Brett said, "Stirling is handling a case that we refused to take on. If it weren't for him, we probably wouldn't have any idea why these murders took place."

"But without him, maybe they wouldn't have occurred," he said. "He's like a kid who knocked over a bees' nest. The bees only swarmed because he angered them."

We all three sat looking at each other for a moment or two.

"Oh, hell!" Madison exclaimed. "The damn horse is already out of the barn so there's no use in trying to get him back in."

I thanked Madison and brought him and Brett up to speed on the case and told them Mrs. Antaglia had asked me to remain in her employment. "I promise," I continued, "to keep Detective Snow informed on my progress."

Madison accepted my promise, and Brett and I left his office.

As we walked down the hall, I thanked her quietly for helping me with Madison.

"Hell, Stirling," she said, "I was trying to save my own neck as much as yours. I wanted to make it look like I knew what was going on, even though I didn't."

"I'll keep you better informed with a phone call every afternoon or evening," I promised.

"That would be nice, Nick."

I drove south to Atlanta and stopped by my office to check my mail and land-line messages. Along with the usual advertising circulars and bills appeared a letter from Mrs. Gentry's lawyer, Harold Robinson, with a check for my work on her divorce. She was a nice woman, and my having to present her with the results of my investigation into her husband's philandering bothered me. Robinson attached a note saying that he had more investigative work for me, but playing the Peeping Tom in divorce cases was getting old. I decided to put him off until I needed work. I still had the bulk of Antaglia's $4,000, which would see me through the next two weeks at least. After this case, if all went well, I would go to Florida to play golf.

Checking my machine, I listened to a few messages until I heard one from Brett, which she had recorded after I left Ithaca. She told me how much she enjoyed talking last night and hoped we could get together again. I did too. She was sharp as a tack and attractive, too.

Sitting at my computer, I began some background research on the Antaglia case. I googled "Richard Reeves Sports Photography" and came up with a number of hits on sports photography and one on Reeves Sports Photography from a number of years ago. I jotted down the address and phone number. Dialing the number connected me to a beauty solon at another address. The manager was not familiar with a Reeves or a photography studio. Running a MapQuest on the address showed that it was fairly close to my office. I could run by and take a look. I also MapQuested Harold Westerly, the owner of the Smiths' old Cadillac, and got directions to his house. It was time to pay Mr. Westerly a visit, too.

Upon arriving at the Reeves address, I found the sign for the Richard Reeves Sports Photography Studio above a doorway, parked out front, and went in. The studio was on the second floor with the door open. A man in his late twenties was behind the counter, working at a computer. He smiled when he saw me and asked if he could help me. I identified myself as a private investigator and mentioned the missing person case that might now be a kidnapping.

"A gumshoe, eh?" he said pleasantly. "How exciting."

"Not as exciting as you might think," I laughed.

"What can I do for you?" he asked, moving to the counter.

I placed the picture of the woman basketball player on the counter. "I'm trying to identify this woman," I said. "This photograph was apparently taken by Richard Reeves." I turned it over to show the name.

The man picked the photo up and examined it carefully.

"This looks like Dick's work," he said.

"Is Dick around?"

He said that he wasn't. He had worked for Richard Reeves for about five years as an assistant. Then, when Reeves was ready to sell the business and retire, he had bought it. He had kept the original name for the goodwill.

"Can you tell me anything about the photo or the girl in it?" I asked.

"I'm afraid I can't," he said. "This picture was taken, I'd guess, in the 1980s. At least that's the time period the uniform suggests." The uniform consisted of hot pants and a low-cut top.

"Does the name Atlanta Bees mean anything to you?" I asked.

He thought for a moment. "I think Dick said something about the Bees. If I remember correctly, it was one of the women's semi-pro teams that were in existence in Atlanta about twenty or so years ago." He stopped for a moment and then said that he might be able to help me.

"Dick left all his files in the back room. Thought they might help me drum up some business. I remember seeing a file on the Bees."

He led me through the door to the storage area, turned on the lights, and then began looking through file drawers.

"Ah," he said. "Here it is, the Atlanta Bees. A bunch of photos."

"May I look through them?"

"I don't see why not," he said. "In fact, you can take whatever you want. The Bees are long gone, and I still have the negatives if anyone wants more copies."

Looking through the files, I found a large number of pictures of women basketball players. Some were in posed shots like the one in the Lions Den. Others were action shots of a game. One was a picture of Mrs. Smith, gracefully shooting a lay up over the outstretched hand of an opponent. I took that picture. Nothing else seemed connected to my case, so I returned the file to its drawer and went out.

"Thanks for your help," I said, "Mr?"

"Oh, sorry. My name is Adam Lasner. Now that I'm in business myself I need to develop better business manners, like giving people my name." He laughed at his ineptness.

I showed him the picture I needed, and he said, "Fine, take it."

"By the way, is Dick still in town?" I asked.

Adam said he was and lived now in an apartment across town. "Let me give him a call," he offered. He speed-dialed a number, and let it ring about ten times before he looked at me and shrugged. "He's not there now, but he's usually around these days." He gave me the phone number and apartment address.

"Thanks for your help, Adam," I said when leaving.

"Good luck," he said. "And if you need any pictures, I'd be happy to take them. I'm expanding from sports photography to general work." He looked a little desperate to me, and I wondered how long he'd stay in business in this recession.

It took me half an hour to arrive at Reeves's apartment. When I called his number on my cell, he answered almost immediately. I explained my business and that Adam had sent me to find out the name of a woman on the Atlanta Bees basketball team in the 1980s. Reeves seemed interested and invited me up to the third floor.

A short, thin man of seventy or so greeted me and invited me into a small apartment filled with photographs of athletes and athletic events. He was surrounded by photographs of race cars and their drivers, golfers hitting various shots at the Masters, baseball players and their team photographs, football players, and basketball players, both male and female. He offered me coffee, and we sat down in his living room. Across the room on the opposite wall, tucked away in the corner, was a picture of the woman from room 32. I took my two pictures out and put them on the coffee table. "This is the woman I've been trying to identify. The same woman on your wall," I said, pointing her out.

"You mean Cynthia Barnes," he said. "Cynthia Barnes of the Atlanta Bees."

"That's her name? Barnes not Smith?" I asked.

"Not Smith. She's Barnes, from Laurel, Kansas. Is she O.K.?" he asked. "I just saw her a few weeks ago when she came back to visit her brother-in-law in Atlanta. I used to watch the Bees play," he explained, "and she and I got close."

How close? I wondered.

"I'm afraid that I have bad news," I told him. "The woman in your picture was murdered in Ithaca last night."

He put his face in his hands, and then got up and walked into the next room. He rummaged around in some files and returned in a few minutes, with a handful of photographs that he placed on the table next to my two.

When he sat down, he had tears in his eyes.

"If Cynthia's dead, I know who killed her," he said in anger.

"Who is that?" I asked.

He spat out the name Roy Harrison. "I think he was her husband," he added.

"Who was Cynthia?" I asked, and he began a long story. Cynthia was a young basketball player from a small Kansas high school. She loved the game and had a single backboard and hoop over her barn door in Kansas where she practiced shots for hours a day. She had hoped to get a scholarship to play at a major university (her parents were far too poor to send her anywhere), but this was before women's athletics had taken off and little money was available to support a female basketball player. But Aurora College, a small Bible school in eastern Kansas, was interested and offered her a scholarship that included a tuition waiver and some work study funds that made it possible for her to play. She did well and hoped to move to a better school. All four years she was at Aurora she applied to major universities with no luck. When she left Aurora without graduating, she hoped to continue playing. She tried out for the Olympic team but didn't make it. She tried out for a spot in the NWBA—that's the old National Woman's Basketball Association—without any luck. The only team she could play for was the newly formed Atlanta Bees, a semi-pro outfit that was supposed to be a feeder team for the NWBA. She thought if she did well there she'd have a chance to make it to a professional team.

"I met Cynthia when I was hired to take the photographs of the Bees," Reeves continued. "I was to take what they called the glamour shots, the shots designed to make the girls look beautiful. These were supposed to attract male fans."

"Did the pictures work?" I asked, glancing at the ones on the table.

"Not really," he said. "From what I could tell, it mostly attracted creeps who tried to hit on the girls."

"Including Cynthia?"

"Especially Cynthia," he said. He pointed to the pictures he had collected. "Take a look at those."

The photos consisted of Cynthia in various poses. Some were more or less cheesecake, with Cynthia without her uniform top, her arm folded over her breasts. Others were pictures of her playing: shooting jump shots, blocking shots, guarding other players, and so forth. Other pictures looked like they were taken after a game, with Cynthia and her teammates, now in street clothes from the 1980s, at parties with various men. In one such picture, in the background, stood a young man with a cocked eye looking into the camera.

I held the picture up and pointed at the figure. "Who's this?" I asked.

"That's Roy Harrison, the man she married," he said. "He's the guy who killed her, I'll bet."

"What happened to Cynthia when you knew her with the Bees?" I asked.

For a while she disappeared, he explained. She left the Bees on short notice. When she came back, about eight months later, she wanted to rejoin the team, but the coach would have nothing to do with her. She had left the team right when it was making a run for its conference title. She was the team's power forward and top scorer. So the team fell apart without her and didn't amount to much that year. The next year, the league disbanded, and the players had to find new teams. Cynthia tried to stay in basketball but couldn't. She just didn't have the connections to find a new team.

"Then she just drifted away," Reeves said. "One of the last things I heard was that she married Harrison and returned to the Midwest. I also heard she was an assistant coach of her old college's women's basketball team but can't be certain of that."

"But you said you saw her a few weeks ago," I reminded him.

"I did, but only for a moment. She wanted to talk about the old days with the Bees, and I showed her some of the team pictures. She was very moved and kept one of them."

That was the photo I found in her luggage, I realized.

"Did she look O.K.?" I asked.

"I couldn't see her face very well. She wore a large hat and sunglasses. I assumed she didn't want anyone to see her because she was older. She was a beautiful girl when she played for the Bees."

Or she didn't want anyone to see her deformed face, I thought.

"I get the impression, Mr. Reeves, that you were close to Cynthia," I said.

"I think it'd be better to say I loved her," he responded.

"Portrait photographers must always fall in love with their subjects if they want to catch them at their best. But I felt more than that for Cynthia. I was confused, though, because I was married at the time and also loved my wife. But Cynthia was special. When she returned from her disappearance from the Bees, I tried to talk to her about us marrying."

"What'd she say to your proposal?" I asked.

"Oh, it wasn't a real proposal," he said, "just a trial one, and she wasn't interested. She said as a kind of joke that she had too many men already. Later I learned that she married Roy."

"Who were the other men?" I asked.

"She mentioned once a coach at Aurora College that she had an affair with," he said.

"Do you know his name?" I asked.

"No," he said.

I glanced at my watch and realized it was 4:00, time for me to leave. I promised to tell Reeves if I discovered anything about Cynthia's murder.

"Please do, Mr. Stirling."

After he closed the door, I heard a sob.

After reviewing my MapQuest directions, I headed toward Harold Westerly's house. I figured the rush hour traffic should get me there by 5:20, when Westerly might have gotten home from work. My estimate was close, and I knocked on Westerly's door at about 5:40. The door opened a crack and a woman's voice asked me what I wanted.

"I'm here to talk to Harold Westerly about his Cadillac," I said.

The door opened wider, and a small heavy woman stepped out on the stoop. She had dyed red hair, heavy makeup, and a red muumuu that billowed around her. She smelled strongly of alcohol.

"Has something happened to that car?" she asked, as if she expected it had.

"Not that I know of," I responded. "But the driver of the car might be a witness to a murder."

The woman's face was suddenly suffused with anger. "What has Roy gotten himself involved in this time?" she demanded.

"I also want to discuss the murder of a woman named Cynthia Barnes," I said.

"Cynthia's dead?" she exclaimed. "Roy's wife is dead?"

She invited me in and pointed to the couch in the living room.

"I'm waiting for my husband to come home," she said. "I'm Jeanie Westerly. In the meanwhile, I'm having a little cocktail. Would you like one?"

If you want to get information out of drinkers, you'd better at least appear to be drinking with them. Otherwise, they think you're being judgmental.

"I'd be happy to join you," I told her.

"Is Southern Comfort on the rocks O.K.?"

"Fine," I said, thinking of tomorrow's hangover if I overdid it.

When she returned from the kitchen with her drink refreshed and a new one for me, I asked if she knew Cynthia well.

"I certainly do," she responded. "She's been my sister-in-law for more than twenty years. But I haven't seen her that often. She and Roy live in Kansas and only get out this way every five years or so."

"I take it you've seen her recently," I said.

She said she had last seen Cynthia and Roy about four weeks ago. "They flew into Atlanta from Kansas City. Dick, my husband, picked them up and brought them here. They stayed for two weeks until I had to make Dick kick his dead-beat brother out. I don't mind Cynthia, but I can't stand

Roy."

"Why not?" I asked.

"Roy is a shiftless dog, and nothing but trouble," she asserted, as she finished her cocktail. When she looked at my glass, her face registered disappointment that so little headway had been made.

"I'm getting another. Can I freshen yours?" she asked, as she stumbled to her feet.

"Sure," I said, and watched her walk unsteadily toward the kitchen with the two glasses.

When she got back, she plopped herself on the sofa next to me and fell against my shoulder. "Oopsy," she said, and looked up at me with wet puppy eyes.

Just then a key turned in the front lock and the door opened to reveal a large man with blonde hair wearing a cheap suit and carrying a briefcase. It didn't take him long to survey the situation and draw some negative conclusions.

I decided to take control by jumping up and walking toward him with my hand out. He didn't take it.

"I'm Nick Stirling," I said. "I want to talk to you about your brother Roy and his wife."

Westerly ignored me. His attention was focused on his wife.

"Drunk again, I see," he said to her. She hung her head. He grabbed her arm and pulled her to the kitchen. I stood in the living room, listening in case I needed to intercede. It didn't take me long to push through the kitchen door after hearing some heavy thumps and a glass breaking.

Westerly was standing over his wife with a wooden spoon held threateningly. She cowered under him like a frightened dog.

"How many times have I told you I don't like coming home and finding you drunk?" he hissed, raising the spoon higher in preparation to strike,

I grabbed his hand before it descended, and Jeanie scurried over to the opposite corner. Westerly glared at me with mean eyes.

"And who the hell are you, drinking with my wife? What else have you done with her?" he yelled.

"Calm down, Mr. Westerly," I said. "I'm here on business and your wife was nice enough to let me wait for you inside."

"What are you here about?" he said, his voice dripping with suspicion.

"I'm here to talk about your brother Roy," I responded.

"We've been talking about Roy and Cynthia," Jeanie said from across the room. "He told me Cynthia's been murdered," she continued, trying to get his attention.

"Murdered? Cynthia? I just saw her a few weeks ago, and she was fine," he retorted.

"I found Cynthia dead at the Lions Den in Ithaca last night," I explained.

"Did Roy kill her?" Westerly asked, as if it were a good possibility.

"I don't think so," I told him, "although that is not an impossibility. Did Roy have a reason to kill his wife?" Dick Reeves had thought he could have. Did Westerly agree with him?

The tension between husband and wife had dissipated, and I suggested that we sit down in the living room to discuss the case.

When we were seated, with fresh drinks made by Jeanie, I gave the Westerlys a quick rundown on what I knew. I told them about being hired first by Coach Seamer and then by Antaglia to find Mitchell, who might have been kidnapped. I told him details about the incident, mentioning the Smiths, who I now was sure were Roy and Cynthia. I described the botched money exchange and the shooting of Antaglia. I also mentioned the murder of Professor Connolly and seeing a man that looked like Roy running away from the scene in the dark.

Westerly took this all in, his face changing shades from near white to bright red.

"How do you know that my brother Roy killed all these people?" he asked.

"I don't," I responded. "But I'm pretty sure that Roy shot Antaglia because I saw him."

"You saw him in the dark," he said. "Could you swear in a law court that he was the shooter?"

"I can't be 100% certain, but that's why I've come to talk to you," I said.

"Me?" he practically shouted. "I don't know much about what Roy is doing now!"

"Well, maybe you can just give me some background information," I responded. "Let's start with his full name."

"His name is Royston Harrison," Westerly said.

"Why the different family name?" I asked.

"We're not full but half brothers," he explained. "We had the same father but different mothers. Roy used his mother's last name."

He went on to clarify his relationship with Roy. His mother had married his father, Jesse Westerly, after he returned from a tour of duty in Viet Nam. They had met in high school, got engaged, and she had waited for him to return. When he came home, he took a job as a salesman for a farm machinery company and traveled throughout his territory, which included eastern Kansas and parts of Missouri and Nebraska. Westerly was born about two years later.

Everything had seemed fine until his mother received a call from a strange woman when Westerly was about two. This woman, whose name was Sally Harrison, claimed that she just gave birth to Jesse's baby, a boy named Royston. The woman thought that Jesse was going to marry her, but she had found Westerly's mother's name and address in Jesse's briefcase. She found Westerly's mother's phone number through information and called her. It turned out that Sally and her baby lived just fifty miles down the highway from the Westerly home.

Westerly's mother confronted Jesse with the woman's claims. While Westerly was too young to remember any details, apparently his parents had a huge fight and his mother almost left her husband. Jesse claimed that he wanted the marriage to continue. Westerly's mother demanded that he never see Sally and her son again.

"He might have agreed to this demand," Westerly continued, "because my mother stayed with him. Whether or not he ever saw Roy and his mother, I don't know. But I do know that I didn't even know Roy existed until my senior year in high school."

"Why did you see him then?" I asked.

"My father died," he said. "And my mother learned that Jesse had been giving his other 'family' money all those years. Not much, but enough to supplement Sally's income as a cashier. When the money stopped, Sally came to see my mother to beg for support. I remember the first visit very well. My mother and Sally sat on the porch and talked things over. As strange as it may sound, the two women got to be friendly, and my mother did help her out as much as she could."

"So you didn't know Roy until he was about sixteen," I said. "What was he like then?"

"He was wild, a really troubled kid," Westerly said. "My mother always said that he was wild because he didn't have a father to raise him right. That might be true. He always seemed to be in trouble."

"What kind?" I asked.

"He was thrown in jail for stealing cars and getting drunk and fighting. We were very different kids. I was raised in the Church of God of the Living Saints. Roy had no religion that I know of. He was an athlete in high school, a basketball player. He hung out with the jocks, who were really wild at his school."

"When did Roy meet Cynthia?" I asked.

"I'm not sure," he said, looking at Jeanie. "Do you know?"

Jeanie said in an unsteady voice that Cynthia told her Roy and she knew each other in high school but that she didn't like his wild streak. "They did share an interest in basketball—Cynthia played on the high school girls' team, you know, but I think Roy kind of followed her around for a while. She said she couldn't shake him."

"So they didn't get married after high school?" I asked.

"Not till after college, or at least Cynthia's college," Westerly said. "She got a basketball scholarship to play at some small Bible school in Kansas. Don't know the name."

"Aurora College?" I asked.

Westerly thought for a moment. "That could be right."

Suddenly the case began to come together. Could Antaglia have known Cynthia twenty years ago in Kansas? Mrs. Antaglia had told me her husband was in Kansas at some point.

"What about Roy?" I asked. "Was he at Aurora?"

"No," Westerly said. "He was in jail for breaking and entering." He seemed a bit embarrassed to be related to a person like Roy.

"Your wife told me that you now see Roy fairly regularly," I said.

Westerly glared at Jeanie, who pulled her neck in like a turtle.

"We don't see him that often," he said. "But when he comes, he usually wants money for some new plan to get him back on his feet. He always wants to make a fresh start."

"And you always help him," Jeanie said angrily. She was drunk enough now to attack her husband, and I got a clearer sense of the emotional issues in their marriage: her drinking and his giving money to his brother.

"What did he want this time?" I asked, already knowing about the car.

"He didn't ask for money," Westerly said. "He just wanted a place to stay..."

"Until I kicked him and Cynthia out," Jeanie interrupted,

slurring her words.

"He just wanted a place to stay and the use of my old Cadillac," he said, glaring at his wife again.

"You lent the car to him?" I asked.

"Yes, he did," Jeanie said. "He also let him stay in my father's old office building."

"What's that about?" I asked him.

Westerly took a deep breath; he looked like a man carrying heavy burdens. "I work for Jeanie's father in his insurance business. We moved offices recently and haven't been able to sell the old building. And I didn't just let him stay there," he said sharply to his wife. "We needed a night watchman to keep an eye on the place."

I asked for the building's address, and he gave it to me. I wrote it in my notebook.

"Let's get back to the car," I said. "Why did you loan it to him?"

"He said he had a big deal to conclude here in Georgia."

"What kind of deal?" I asked.

"Someone owed him a great deal of money," he said, "someone who had hurt him and Cynthia in the past. And he said he would make it worth my while. He'd give me $10,000 for all that I had done for him over the years."

"I'll believe that when I see it," Jeanie said.

That explained the odd $10,000 of ransom money, I thought.

I asked Westerly for the phone numbers and addresses of Roy's mother and Cynthia's parents. Westerly went over to a desk for his address book and looked in it. He gave me the address of Roy's mother in Stovington, Kansas, saying that she did not have a telephone.

"She's lived her life close to hunger," he said. "If my mother hadn't given her some money along the way, she would have been in the proverbial poor house." He continued: "I don't have any information on Cynthia's family. I've never even met them. They didn't approve of their daughter's relationship with Roy, and there was a break between Cynthia and her parents." He hesitated for a moment as a truth sank in. "They'll never be reconciled now that Cynthia's gone," he said.

"Do you know where Cynthia grew up?" I asked, and he said in Laurel, Kansas, because she often talked about her girlhood there.

Our little party was breaking up, and I rushed to finish my questions. Jeanie was slipping down in the sofa, her eyes closing, her breathing getting heavy. Westerly looked at her disdainfully.

"Could I see the office building where Cynthia and Roy had been staying?" I asked, and Westerly agreed to take me over. "I'd like to see what they've done to the place," he said.

After following him across town in my Accord, I parked next to him in a small lot attached to a two-story cinder-block building and got out. A large sign on the building said Renco and Westerly Insurance, with Renco in bigger letters. It was clear that Mr. Renco saw his son-in-law as the lesser partner.

Westerly unlocked the front door, and we entered the stale-smelling building. Westerly flipped on the light to reveal a few old pieces of office furniture that had remained after the move, including old file cabinets with their drawers hanging open.

"Let's go to the second floor," he said, pointing to a set of stairs in the back room.

The second floor had dilapidated living quarters that included two bedrooms, a full bath, and a small kitchen. The space felt deserted.

In the first bedroom was a single camp cot. Against the wall was an athletic bag with Central's logo on the side with clothes spilling out. Most of the clothes looked like athletic gear—shorts, sweat shirts, a letter jacket, and cotton socks. My guess was that this was Mitch's room and he had planned to come back to collect his clothes.

In the other room, Westerly was nosing about. This room had two single beds that had been pushed against opposite walls. On one bed were several reddened towels that someone had used to staunch the flow of blood. Looks like Antaglia was right when he claimed to have shot the kidnapper during the botched exchange, I thought. In the only closet, women's clothes were hanging. Two large floppy hats of the kind Cynthia wore had been thrown on the floor in the corner. In the bathroom off the bedroom were some makeup and other personal things belonging to Cynthia. The clear plastic walls of the small shower were covered with splattered blood. Roy had obviously taken a shower to clean his wounds, which were significantly bloody.

Returning to the bedroom, I looked through the chest of drawers. It was full of women's clothes, including panties, nightgowns, and various tops, skirts, and slacks. It appeared that Cynthia was planning to return. But Roy wasn't. None of his possessions remained.

"Looks like Roy has moved out, Westerly" I said. "He must have collected his belongings and left recently."

"The bastard could have at least told me he was leaving," he responded. "Now I'll have to hire someone to clean this place up."

His lack of brotherly feelings surprised me.

The setup of the apartment was interesting because it looked like a family's domicile: mother and father in one room, with the beds pulled far apart to suggest some degree of estrangement, and the child in the second. No evidence existed that Mitch was kept there against his will. It looked to me that he could come and go as he pleased.

I gave the rooms another search, looking under beds and in the medicine cabinet, and found nothing of interest.

"I've seen enough," I told Westerly. "I'm taking off. Thanks for your help."

"I'll see you out," he said, and led me down the stairs and out the door.

Chapter 12

For the first time in three days, I went to my apartment and called Brett to explain my recent discoveries. She didn't pick up her cell, so I left a long message summarizing my day and informing her I was heading to Kansas tomorrow morning. It had become clear that the case had originated there, and that was where it might be solved. I asked her to run a background check on Dr. Herman Meluso, who apparently worked in some capacity at Central and was connected, I suspected, to the case. I also asked her to check into the death by drowning of Mitch's little sister, Christa, about eight years ago.

I then called Linda Antaglia to inform her of my findings and plans. When she picked up on the third ring, I asked how her husband was doing.

"Not so well," she said. "He's still on life support, but the doctors say he is stabilizing. So I hope he will be better soon."

"I hope that's the case," I said, "and please give him my

best when you see him."

"Thank you for your concern. Have you found Mitchell?" she asked.

"No, but I am certain that Mitchell is unharmed," I said. "I'll find him soon and return him to you." My attempts to keep her interested in the case worked. She told me to continue searching for Mitch and to keep her informed about my progress. After offering her my condolences for her husband again, I hung up.

I assembled the phone numbers needed in the morning to make appointments for tomorrow and the next day. Online, I found Aurora College and the number of the school's president, G. Ransom Sparrow. He might shed some light on what happened at the school twenty years ago. The other numbers were on my cell speed dial.

Then my thoughts turned to the case itself. It was looking less and less likely that Mitch had been kidnapped. Instead, it appeared that he went willingly with Roy and Cynthia to Westerly's office building, where he apparently stayed with them for several weeks. No telling where he was now, but it didn't seem reasonable that he had been harmed by Roy and Cynthia, who appeared to have some sort of a relationship with him.

That left the two murders in Ithaca. The evidence of the throat slashing from behind in both cases suggested that the same person murdered both women. No convincing suspects with motivations for killing Professor Connolly and Cynthia Barnes existed as yet. The most likely suspect was Roy, who I might have seen running away from Connolly's house. But what motive did he have to kill the professor? I had found some indications that Roy and Cynthia were not on the most affectionate of terms. But why would he want to murder her? The other possible suspect was Mitch. Professor Connolly reported that he was so furious at her for rejecting his poems that he frightened her. It seemed less likely that he murdered Cynthia Barnes, a woman he appeared to know well, but such a murder was not an impossibility.

Turning again to my computer, I made a reservation online for the first flight out of Atlanta for Kansas City, Missouri, at 5:45 a.m., printed out the itinerary, and arranged a rental car at the airport. Then I called up Central's web page and put in the name Meluso. The information that came up identified him as Herman Meluso in the Agricultural School. When I went online to the Ag School, I found a bit more about him. He was a laboratory technician who worked on hogs and swine. Not much more information was available.

Next I googled Herman Meluso and got several minor hits that identified him as working in Central's Ag school. One story discussed his innovative work on the artificial insemination of swine and hogs. He apparently was also working on the genetics of the domestic pig. The last piece on him, written about a decade ago, was the most interesting. In a brief exposé of East German scholars who came to the US around the time of the fall of the USSR, Herman Meluso was identified as Herman Schultz, an East German MD, who, the author claimed, came to the US in the mid-1980s and disappeared in the American university system. I printed out this item and put it in my briefcase. On returning from Kansas, I would look into Meluso/Schultz, and see if Brett had used her impressive investigative talents to unearth anything else about him.

I showered, went to bed, and slept the sleep of the exhausted.

In the morning, I caught my flight and landed in Missouri at 7:35. My rental was awaiting me, and I drove toward Lawrence, Kansas, stopping for breakfast at an Alan's Burgers on the road. After eating, I made some phone calls, starting with Coach Seamer. Candy answered.

"Mr. Stirling!" she exclaimed. "I wondered what had happened to you."

"I've been busy, Candy."

"Have you heard about Coach Antaglia's being on life support?" she asked.

"Yes," I said.

"We're all shocked," she exclaimed. "He seemed so loud and healthy just the other day."

"Certainly loud," I agreed.

"Have you found Mitchell yet?" she asked.

I explained my Kansas trip to work on the case and asked her to do me a favor.

"Anything," she responded.

"I need a better sense of Antaglia's career," I explained, "especially where he coached before he arrived at Central. I especially want to know if he has any ties to Kansas. Do you have that kind of information handy?"

"We keep old files in the basement," she responded, "so I can go down there and see what we have on him."

I thanked her and asked to speak with Seamer. She put me through.

"How can I help you, Stirling?" he said abruptly.

I explained in general my progress so far, and then got to my main point: my need to talk to Jineral Jackson at KU. I had spoken with him briefly on the phone, I explained, but didn't get much information because Jineral was afraid I might be a reporter digging up dirt on him. "Do you know anybody at KU who might be able to help me meet with Jineral, Coach?" I asked.

He told me he did. The Athletic Director there was an old friend, and Seamer said he'd be happy to give his friend a call to set up an appointment that morning if possible. After thanking him, I asked him to call me on my cell when he knew something and hung up.

I then called Aurora College and made a 1:00 appointment with President Sparrow through his secretary, explaining that I was a private detective looking for information on Cynthia Barnes, a former student. I also mentioned that Cynthia had been murdered. "That's a shame," she said.

I was finishing my second cup of coffee and looking over my Kansas map when my cell rang. It was Seamer, who told me that his friend at KU had set up an appointment for me with Jineral at the Brew-4-U coffee shop on Massachusetts Avenue in downtown Lawrence at 10:00 a.m. I thanked him again and headed there.

My morning and early afternoon were accounted for. During the rest of the day I would try to make contact with Cynthia's and Roy's parents for background information on those two. I wondered if Cynthia's mother knew yet that her daughter was dead.

By the time I drove into Lawrence, it was 9:45. It was a typical college town, similar to Ithaca. The university was huddled on a hill called Mt. Oread and below it lay the downtown area along Massachusetts Avenue that contained bistros, coffee shops, beer joints, and clothing stores. I located Brew-4-U with little trouble, parked, and went in. It contained a large counter behind which a young woman made coffee and sold sandwiches, pastries, and salads. A row of booths lined the opposite wall, with small tables and mismatched wooden chairs in the middle. I sat at the most inconspicuous booth in the back and waited.

At 10:00 a tall, graceful young man walked in. I waved to him, and he came over. I introduced myself as the private detective working on the Mitchell Antaglia missing person case that he had spoken to on the phone.

"Look, man," he said, "I don't know why you want to speak to me again, but Coach told me I had to do this so I'm here."

"Thanks for coming," I said and asked if he wanted some coffee and food. He said he could use a ham sandwich, and I ordered at the counter, keeping my eye on Jineral in case he bolted.

When we got settled in the booth, I gave him a sanitized version about Mitch's disappearance and asked Jineral if he had heard from him.

"Heard from him yesterday," Jineral said.

That surprised me. "What'd he say?" I asked.

"He said he was tied up in some murders back in Ithaca and wanted to talk to me about them. I told him to stay away. I like the Missile pretty well, but I got to look out for myself. I don't want to be tied up in no—any—trouble."

"How'd he respond?" I asked.

"He wasn't happy but said he understood."

I asked if Mitch was in Kansas now, and he said he didn't know for sure.

"What I really need to know from you, Jineral, is what you can tell me about Mitch's relationship with his father."

"All I can say is that he hated the dude," he responded.

"Why so much anger?" I asked.

Jineral finished his last bite of his sandwich, sat back thoughtfully, and said, "I wasn't sure what the problems were between Mitch and his old man, but I do know that Mitch resented him for something big. After practice sometimes me and him would go out together to talk over basketball and our futures. Me and Mitch were on the same page about the game—we wanted to run the fast break, score on the run, play the pro game. We loved Coach Fletcher because that's how he wanted us to play."

"And you didn't love Coach Brown?" I asked.

"It's not that I didn't like Coach Brown," he replied. "He was a good man and a brother who finally got a break. But I think he was too worried about not screwing up to let his players play they—their—own game."

"Did Mitch feel the same way?" I asked.

"Yes, but Mitch couldn't transfer," he said. "His old man wouldn't let him so he stayed and hated every minute of it."

"How good is Mitch?" I asked.

"Mitch is the Missile, know what I mean?" he said. "If truth be told, he ain't as good as me, but who is?" Jineral was beginning to let himself go. "Mitch was fast, and a good college player, but he didn't play good D like me, the Stonewall."

"Where did you learn to play basketball?" I asked.

"I played my ball in New York City. I played on the playgrounds, know what I mean? And I played in the shoe leagues, on traveling teams, and that's where I first met Mitch. He was a skinny white kid, thirteen years old, same age as me. He didn't seem good at all then, but he got bigger and faster quick. By the time he was a senior in high school he was a star because of his quickness and power. Few players improve like that."

"What do you attribute this improvement to?" I asked.

Jineral looked uncomfortable. "I think his father drove him pretty hard." He hesitated a moment. "Maybe that's why he didn't like his father very much. Drove him too hard."

"What about this Dr. Death person that we discussed before?"

He looked at me intently. "I don't want to talk about no Dr. Death," he said, and forced his big frame into the corner of the booth, sulking.

"I found a poem Mitch wrote about him," I said.

"Mitch did get caught up in writing his poems," Jineral responded.

A silence fell across the table. I could tell that it wasn't going to be easy to get Jineral to talk about Dr. Death.

"Look, Jineral," I said. "You seem to know something about this guy but you're afraid to tell me. You mentioned on the phone that you thought I was trying to ruin your career. I assure you I have no interest in doing that. Just tell me what Dr. Death did to Mitch. Did he inject Mitch with drugs of some sort?"

Jineral looked at me, sizing me up. He apparently thought he could trust me, because he began a long story about Dr. Death's involvement with the basketball program. He said that Dr. Death, who was Meluso, worked in the Ag School on pigs but came to the athletic program regularly with a black bag full of vials of drugs. Coach Fletcher wanted the players to take them. None of the players knew much about the drugs except that they were some sort of combination of steroids and Human Growth Hormone. Some of the players took them regularly, but Jineral took an injection only once but didn't like the way it made him feel. "Kinda dizzy" was the way he put it.

"Besides," he concluded, "I don't need crap like that to make me good."

"Did Mitchell take the injections?" I asked.

"Yeah, he did," Jineral said. "He seemed to think that taking these drugs was a normal thing to do. In fact, he seemed to know Meluso well. They kind of joked around together."

"So Meluso knew Mitch already?" I asked.

"I think they knew each other for a while," Jineral said. He then lit up with another insight. "Hey, do you think Mitch got so much stronger and quicker when he was a kid because he took those drugs?"

"That's a good possibility," I said.

By the time the two of us left, I was impressed with Jineral. He had a good head on his shoulders and had his future worked out for his own benefit. He had survived a near tragedy at Central, but successfully navigated the transfer to a much better basketball program. Mitch had not been able to do that. I shook hands with Jineral outside the Brew-4-U, got back on the highway, and drove west toward Aurora.

While driving, I called Brett, who picked up immediately.

"Nick," she said. "Where are you?"

"Lawrence, Kansas," I said. "I just spoke with Jineral 'Stonewall' Jackson at KU, and he gave me some interesting info on Meluso."

"I found some, too. What's yours?" she asked.

"According to Jineral, Meluso, at Coach Fletcher's request, provided the basketball players with some sort of performance enhancing drugs," I said. "He also said that Mitch appeared to know Meluso well. There seems to be some history between the two. What'd you find out?"

"We looked into Meluso and discovered the guy is in the country illegally. He doesn't have a green card, and he's not a citizen."

"When he got the job, how'd he get through Central's hiring channels?" I asked.

Brett explained that Meluso arrived at Central twenty years ago, before there was much concern about illegal immigrants. He seems to be valuable to the Ag program, too. "I interviewed Dean Sibble over there," she continued, "and he sang Meluso's praises for his work on what he called 'porcine genetics.' Plus they don't have to pay him much," she added. "He's a lowly lab technician."

"Did you find anything on the drowning?" I asked.

"Not yet," she said. "But I have an appointment this afternoon with John Millar, the detective who investigated the incident at the time. He's now retired but told me over the phone that he had some interesting information on the case."

"Keep me informed, Brett," I said. "I'll be back in Ithaca in two days."

"Should we pick Meluso up now on the illegal immigration charge?" she asked.

"Better not," I said. "We'll be able to find out more about Mitch if the good doctor thinks he's safe."

Before I hung up, Brett said: "I'm still interested in that dinner invitation, Nick. Just let me know which night."

"Will do," I responded.

I then called Seamer and got Candy again. "Please thank your boss for setting up the appointment with Jineral," I said and asked if she had found anything about Antaglia's past coaching positions.

"I did, and I was just about to call you," she said.

"Did he work in Kansas before Central?" I asked.

"When I checked his last resume, he listed no positions in Kansas," she said.

"That's too bad," I responded, thinking I'd have to reconsider the Kansas connection.

"But when I looked at his earliest resumes," she continued, "I found a different story. Antaglia had coached for one year at a small Kansas college called Aurora."

"Candy!" I exclaimed. "I owe you a steak dinner when I get back to Ithaca!"

Aurora College sat off the highway and looked like it had seen better times. The sign at the front gate read "Aurora Bible College: Where God Makes the Future Possible." Most of the buildings needed a coat of paint, so I guess God didn't put maintenance high on his agenda. Driving onto campus, I didn't see a single student. Suddenly, a bell tolled, and thin ribbons of young scholars filed out of the buildings. After parking my car in the visitor lot, I asked one of the students where the president's office was. He was a thin boy with close-cropped hair wearing a white dress shirt. He didn't look far from the farm, but he wasn't the one lost. He pointed out a large building to the right and said, "God bless you, friend."

By the time I got to Sparrow's office, it was a minute after 1:00. I introduced myself to his secretary, an attractive brunette wearing a long gingham dress and a bouffant hairdo. She said that President Sparrow was expecting me and pointed to his office door

People's names don't always fit them, but Sparrow was a perfect name for the quick little man with a big nose sitting at his desk. He stood up and walked with a hopping motion around his desk to shake my hand. His office looked like a nest. The President had surrounded himself with books, which seemed about to fall in on him. His desk was covered with papers and the remains of his lunch, which he had just finished. When he offered me coffee, which I accepted, he walked over to the coffee pot in the corner, poured two cups, and handed me one as he returned to his desk.

When we were settled, he looked at me with bright eyes and said he had not been entirely surprised when he heard of my interest in Cynthia Barnes.

"Why was that?" I asked.

"Her son stopped by yesterday," he said. "When he told me that she had been murdered in Ithaca, Georgia, I was, of course, horrified, because I remembered Cynthia as a young athletic college girl. The boy hadn't known his mother well, he said, and wanted to see if he could look through our library archives for information on her."

"Who is the son?" I asked.

"A nice young man named Mitchell Barnes," he said, checking a note pad in front of him.

That's interesting, I thought. Mitch is using Cynthia's last name.

"He explained that he had been adopted as a baby," Sparrow continued, "and just found out that Cynthia was his mother. I felt so sorry for the young man—to find your mother and lose her to a murderer almost immediately is too hard. God works in mysterious ways," he concluded sententiously.

"I'm working with the Ithaca police on the same murder case," I said. It was a lie, but a small one since I knew that the murder was connected to the disappearance of Mitch, and solving the murder might well lead me to young Antaglia.

"You mentioned to my secretary you were working with the Ithaca police, and I took the liberty to check into that claim and made a few calls. I spoke to a Detective Snow, who vouched for you enthusiastically. So I'm perfectly willing to help solve this terrible murder. I knew Cynthia. I taught her while she was here. She wasn't a great student, but she was famous on campus as a basketball player. We all expected great things from here in that arena, but for reasons I don't understand she did not succeed."

Sparrow went on to say that he gave Cynthia's son permission to search in the library archives with a librarian. "I didn't want the young man burrowing around in our papers without guidance," he noted. The two of them unearthed some information on Cynthia's days at Aurora and brought the material to Sparrow's office. He pointed to a pile of papers on the corner of his desk.

"Can I look through this material?" I asked.

"Certainly," he said. "Don't think you'll find much. Most of it consists of athletic photographs and stories about her in the student paper."

Sparrow called in his secretary and told her to set me up in a nearby conference room with the archival material. Before leaving Sparrow, I asked if he remembered a Coach Antaglia from about the time that Cynthia was a student at Aurora. Sparrow thought for a moment.

"No, the name doesn't ring a bell. But I'll have my secretary check to see if she can find the name in our records. I'll also call over to the Athletic Program."

In the room, I began reading about Cynthia's college life twenty some years earlier. Included among the materials were four yearbooks in which Cynthia appeared. She was always pictured among her class and in various photographs related to women's basketball. In her junior and senior years, she was a member of the homecoming court. I looked carefully through the last book, which was her senior year, and found another picture of interest. Herman Schultz was pictured as an assistant professor of chemistry. He had a chiseled, handsome face with a sharp nose and dark hair. Was this Meluso? I wondered. I looked for Antaglia's picture with the women's basketball team but found nothing.

Most of the material Sparrow gave me consisted of puff pieces on Cynthia as a female basketball star. A lot of the loose pictures showed her taking shots. One showed her as a member of the homecoming court. Her date did not look like Roy. About to give up, I found a game picture of Cynthia making a bounce pass to a teammate. Aurora's bench was in the background, and on the end of it sat a younger Coach Antaglia, yelling at Cynthia.

I took the material back to Sparrow, with the picture of Antaglia on the top, and showed it to him. He looked at it for a moment and said he did remember that person.

"That's Albert Craft," he said. "He was an assistant coach for the women's basketball team."

"Can you tell me anything about him?" I asked.

"I barely remember him," he said, "but I do have a sense that we had some problems with him."

"What kind of problems?"

"There was some sort of scandal associated with Craft," he said. "Whatever it was was handled quietly by the Athletic Program itself. The rest of us didn't know much about it."

"Is there anyone else on campus who might remember more about this?" I asked.

He thought for a moment. Then he picked up the phone and pushed a button on his speed dial. After a short conversation, in which he mentioned Craft and Cynthia, he hung up.

"I just spoke with Cherry Penny, who is our women's basketball coach. If anyone can remember what happened to Craft, it would be Coach Penny. She was a player under Craft and a teammate of Cynthia's."

He gave me directions to the arena building where the athletic offices were. He said that Penny was expecting me and sent me on my way.

"May I take the picture of the coach with me?"

"Yes, if you promise to return it to the library," Sparrow said.

Chapter 13

Following Sparrow's directions across campus, I noticed that the students had scurried back into the classroom building for their mid-afternoon classes. Differences between Central and Aurora were pronounced. The Central quads were filled with students every minute of the day, while Aurora's was empty.

Rounding the corner of the library, which was the largest building on the quad, I saw the arena before me. It looked like a Buckminster Fuller geodesic dome. I entered at the main door and found the office of the Athletic Program. Inside a smallish room sat the program's secretary, and I asked for Coach Cherry Penny, explaining I had a 3:00 appointment. The woman lifted her phone, pushed a button, and announced that Penny's 3:00 was here. She sent me to the second floor, where I walked half way around the arena to Penny's office.

The door was open, and I stuck my head in to find a tall, slim fortyish woman standing in the middle of the office, gesturing for me to enter.

"Mr. Stirling?" she asked.

"Yes," I said.

She asked me to sit down and offered coffee. As she walked over to the shelf to get the pot, I observed her. Her blond hair was close cropped, and her navy suit was complemented with a white dress shirt and small black tie. She moved with a quick grace. When she handed me the coffee, I noticed that she wore no makeup.

She looked at me quizzically with striking blue eyes and asked what she could do for me.

"I'm here to talk to about Cynthia Barnes," I said, assuming that she knew about the murder.

"Oh," she said brightly, "how is Cynthia? I haven't seen her in forever."

I was surprised to see that she thought Cynthia was still alive.

"I guess you haven't heard that Cynthia was murdered in Ithaca, Georgia, two nights ago," I said.

She looked at first as if she didn't follow me. Then her face crumpled with grief. She emitted a strange, low moan, and put her hands over her face. I sat quietly as she absorbed what was obviously an emotional blow.

She stood up and walked unsteadily toward her desk. Halfway there she almost fell, and I jumped up to grab her arm. She let herself fall against me, putting her chin on my shoulder. We stood together for several minutes as she wept. I could feel the tears on my neck.

"Can I get you something?" I asked after she grew calmer.

"I'd like to sit down," she said, and I helped her back to the chair at the table and took my seat across from her.

"You were obviously close to Cynthia," I said, watching her closely.

"You are right, Mr. Stirling," she said. "We were closer than sisters."

"Would it be better for me to come back another time?"

"No. I'm O.K.," she said, drying her eyes with a tissue from one of her pockets. "In fact, it would help me to learn what happened to Cynthia."

I explained as much as I knew about Cynthia's death, beginning with the kidnapping of Mitch and Cynthia's apparent involvement in that.

"Cynthia would never do anything illegal like kidnapping a kid," she assured me.

I continued, telling her about how Cynthia was seen with Mitch in Ithaca, and how Rachel, Mitch's girlfriend, was under the impression that Cynthia was Mitch's new girl. I then told her about my finding Cynthia's body in the Lions Den in room 32, which she shared with Roy, who was apparently her husband.

When I mentioned Roy, Cherry's eyes flashed in anger. "I knew that guy years ago when he was following Cynthia around. We'd call it stalking now. Everybody warned her that he was trouble, in and out of jail and always scheming to make money in some scam. But Cynthia had known Roy in high school and felt sorry for him."

"Did you know they had married?" I asked.

"I did," she said. "I was invited to the wedding but couldn't face seeing Cynthia throw herself away on such a man."

Would Penny have been willing to accept Cynthia's marrying any man? I wondered.

"I'm trying to find Mitch, who might be Cynthia's son," I said.

Penny's eyes narrowed. "As far as I know," she said, "Cynthia never had a son."

I told her I was trying to piece together Cynthia's life and wondered if she could tell me about her time at Aurora.

Cynthia, she said, loved basketball. She grew up on a dirt farm in central Kansas, an only child. Her father, who always wanted a son, encouraged her to watch sports, and he nailed a basket to the front of his barn. Cynthia spent all of her free time shooting baskets, and her father, delighted when she showed talent and interest, coached her on the basics. He had played the game in high school and taught Cynthia to love it as he did.

"Was Cynthia good?" I asked.

"She was for her time," Penny said. "But women's sports were just taking off then, and a lot of girls did not receive the level of coaching needed to make them really good."

She explained that Cynthia played high school basketball, and attracted some local, even regional, attention. Her coach at the time encouraged her to expect a scholarship to a major university, but for some reason that didn't pan out. Cynthia ended up on scholarship at Aurora along with Penny herself.

"We became teammates and best friends," Penny said. "I was a point guard, and Cynthia was a power forward. She had a great jump shot for a woman player at the time."

"So what happened to her?" I asked.

She explained that Cynthia remained obsessed with the game and wanted to play at the professional level. A professional women's league was just starting, and she hoped to be recruited by one of the teams. "But to tell the truth," she said, "Cynthia was a good college player but she was not great."

Sounds like what I heard about Mitch, I thought.

She went on to tell me how hard Cynthia trained to better herself and develop her skills. But then she got caught up with Coach Craft, and things went wrong fast.

"Is this Craft?" I asked, holding up the picture with the young Antaglia in the background.

"Yes," she said.

"What happened between them?" I asked.

"It's a long story," she said.

Craft arrived at Aurora at the end of Penny and Cynthia's junior year. It was something of a mystery why he was hired because he had never coached women before.

"Craft took a shine to Cynthia right away," Penny said,

"and they began to spend time together."

"Were they lovers?" I asked.

"They had sex," she said pointedly. "But it was a tumultuous relationship because Craft had relationships with several women on the team and was engaged to a woman back east. Cynthia and I talked about Craft many times, and I told her he was not to be trusted, but she was in love and couldn't see his many shortcomings."

"Was Craft a good coach?" I asked. "I mean, did he help Cynthia and the others become better players?"

"In my opinion, he didn't help Cynthia at all," she said. "In fact, he hurt her badly."

"How so?" I asked.

"Craft," she said, "encouraged his players to take what are now called performance enhancing drugs. He claimed that these drugs, various kinds of hormones and steroids, would take her to the next level."

"Where did he get the drugs back then?" I asked.

"Oh, he had his source on campus," she said. "There was a German chemistry professor who came the same year that Craft did . . ."

"A Professor Schultz?" I asked, interrupting her.

"I think so," she continued. "He was East German. Craft claimed that Schultz worked on the East German national Olympic team as a physician. His job was to develop drug regimens for the East German athletes to make them competitive against the US teams. Craft said he was brilliant."

"Did most of the women take the drugs?" I asked.

"Many did, but Cynthia took more than anyone on the team. She saw them as her main chance to make it to the pros," Penny said.

"How did the drugs affect her?" I asked.

"Well, she got hairy in surprising places," she said, "and she got muscular. Now it's common for young women to work out and bulk up, but back then it was unusual, even among athletes. Some of the other girls made fun of Cynthia for becoming more masculine looking, but that didn't seem to bother her."

"What about her face?" I asked. "Did it change at all?"

"I think it did," she responded. "After a while, her head seemed to get bigger, with a more prominent brow and chin. I don't mean that these changes happened at Aurora. But when I occasionally saw her later she looked different. I thought it was because of the drugs."

"I understand that Antag...I mean Craft left Aurora at the end of his first year," I said. "What happened?"

"Several things," Penny said. "One of the other girls on the team reported Craft for sleeping with the team members, including Cynthia. That didn't go over well at a small denominational institution. But it also came out about the doping. Drug testing was beginning to become an issue internationally, and when that same girl told about Craft's encouraging drug use for the team, the powers-that-be thought it wise to get rid of him. Then, surprisingly, Craft got a job at Georgia Central. This surprised us all," Penny said, "since Craft seemed to be carrying around a lot of bad baggage."

"Didn't he also get married about that time?" I asked.

"I think he did, to a woman in Georgia," Penny said. "All the girls understood that she was wealthy. I think her name was Linda, or something like that."

I told her that Craft's real name was Antaglia and showed her the old picture of him on the bench again.

"You're sure that's the man you knew as Craft?" I asked, pointing to Antaglia.

"That's the bastard!" she exclaimed.

I told her that Antaglia was now in the county hospital in Ithaca recuperating from a gun shot wound associated with the kidnapping of his son, Mitch.

"I'm not surprised to learn that Craft was not who he appeared to be," she said bitterly. "I never trusted that guy."

The past remained very much alive in her.

We spoke some more about Cynthia's tragic life, and Penny wept several times as she reflected on her friend. It became clear to me that the two women were very close, and I respected the deep feelings that Penny still had for Cynthia. When we said goodbye, Penny and I hugged, and she said, "Find the bastard who murdered Cynthia for me, Nick. And let me know who it is."

I promised her, and myself, that I would.

By the time I left Aurora it was 6:00 p.m. I stopped at a small restaurant for a quick sandwich before starting out across the Kansas plains for the nearby farming towns where Cynthia and Roy grew up. After I ate, I put in a call to Linda Antaglia to report my progress. She didn't pick up, and I left a brief message on her answering machine about what I had accomplished.

When I started for Laurel, Cynthia's hometown, my shadow was long across the ground. I drove to the highway and pointed my car west. The highway was straight as a ribbon stretching before me across the plains. It seemed to go on forever through fields of winter wheat and hay. According to my map, Laurel was only 50 miles away from Aurora College, so I drove into town just as the light began to fade.

Laurel was a typical small farming town. It was organized along a single street, named Main, with several cross streets intersecting it. Main Street had on it a cluster of business buildings, including a small savings and loan, a feed and grain store, and a hardware store. I drove up and down a few of the side streets and found about a third of the houses with"For Sale"signs. A few had their windows boarded up. It looked like some of Laurel's residents had packed up and left.

Needing directions to the Barnes's house, I stopped at one of the two gas stations on Main. A man crawled out from under a car in one of the bays, wiping his hands on a dirty rag. Tall, dressed in blue coveralls with his name, "Stretch," stitched above the pocket, he was the dirtiest human being I had ever come across. "Do you know the Barnes family?" I asked.

As he filled my tank, he scratched his head, and said the name "Barnes" several times.

"How about Cynthia Barnes?" I asked. His face lit up.

"Oh, them Barneses," he said. "They live out on Hungry Cow Road, about three miles out of town."

He gave me directions, took my money for the gas, and, as I was leaving, crawled back under his vehicle.

It took me half an hour to find the Barnes's farm, which had a mailbox on the road with "Barnes" carefully hand painted on it. I turned up the driveway, which was neatly attended with fresh gravel and cleared ditches on each side.

Rounding the final bend, I found the house. It was small and old, but its clapboards were freshly painted white and its roof newly shingled. In front, on both sides of the front porch, were flower beds that had been carefully mulched for the winter. To the left of the house toward the back was a barn. I could just make out Cynthia's rusty basketball hoop attached above the door. That's where Cynthia first honed her basketball skills, I reflected.

I parked and walked toward the door. A large dog suddenly bounded at me, barking protectively. I put forward the back of my hand, and the animal wiggled toward me, with her head down and ears back. Not much of a guard dog, I thought.

"She won't hurt you," a voice said as the front door opened and the porch light came on. "She's a good old girl, aren't you, Molly?"

Before me stood a tall man, in his mid-sixties. He was dressed in blue jeans and a flannel shirt. His hair was iron grey and closely cropped.

Molly began to dance about me, happy to have a guest.

"How may I help you, mister?" the man said.

"I'm here to talk about your daughter, Cynthia," I said,

wondering if he knew that she was dead.

"I haven't seen Cynthia for near ten years," the man said. "As far as I know, she's been dead that long."

"Don't say such a horrible thing, Hank!" a woman's voice said as a slim form appeared behind the man.

"I'm Hank Barnes, and this is my wife, Thelma," the man said. "Who're you?"

I told the Barneses my name and occupation and explained my search for a missing person, Mitch Antaglia, who was in some way related to Cynthia.

Mrs. Barnes stepped into the light. She was almost as tall as her husband. That explained Cynthia's height, I thought. Her hair was grey and neatly done in a bun behind her head. She was dressed in a simple calico house dress with a navy blue cardigan sweater over it.

"Won't you come in, Mr. Stirling?" she said. "We're having our evening tea. Would you like a cup?"

"That would be nice," I said as they showed me into their front parlor. It was decorated simply, with clean colors and old-fashioned furniture. Mr. Barnes pointed to an easy chair for me, and they sat close together on a sofa. Mrs. Barnes poured me a cup of tea and asked me how I took mine. "Just plain," I said, and she handed it across the table to me.

"I get the impression, Mr. Stirling, that you don't have good news about Cynthia," the mother said.

No matter how many times I've had to do this, I've never found a good way to tell a mother that her child has died. Mrs. Barnes looked at me intently.

"Cynthia's dead, isn't she?" she asked.

"Yes," I said, trying to cover my surprise.

"How?" Mr. Barnes asked as he took his wife's hand.

"She was murdered in Ithaca, Georgia, two days ago," I said.

A silence descended over the room, and the Barneses looked at each other. The wife began to cry quietly as the husband put his arm around her shoulder. I gave them time to process the horrible news.

After a few minutes, Mrs. Barnes dried her eyes with a tissue and looked at me.

"Thank you for bringing us this sad news, Mr. Stirling," she said. "It can't have been easy for you. But surely you didn't come all the way from Georgia just for that. You could have just telephoned."

I explained my finding Cynthia's body while working on a missing person case. The case involved a college athlete, a basketball player, named Mitchell Antaglia. This young man might be Cynthia's son, I continued.

The Barneses audibly gasped in unison at the mention of a son. I immediately felt a stab of guilt, not knowing for certain that Mitch was Cynthia's son.

"I'm not 100 percent sure of this," I continued. "But I'm certain that Mitchell himself thinks this is the case. He now goes by Mitchell Barnes."

"Odd that he'd use Cynthia's name. Who is this boy's father?" Mr. Barnes asked.

"Again, I'm not certain," I said, "but some evidence points to Roy Harrison. He at least appears to be Cynthia's husband."

"Oh God, no! Not him!" Mrs. Barnes gasped, looking at her husband with wild eyes.

Hank Barnes calmed his wife and turned to me. "You have to understand that Roy Harrison is the one who ruined Cynthia," he said. "She was a wonderful young woman until she got involved with him."

"What was the problem with him?" I asked.

Hank explained that Royston Harrison was one of the boys in this county who was always in trouble. He didn't have a father, and he ran wild. He stole cars, got in fights, and eventually was sent to prison for breaking and entering.

"How'd he get involved with Cynthia?" I asked.

"Cynthia was obsessed with basketball," he explained. "She played in as many girls' leagues around the area as she could. I spent my weekends driving her and her teammates around to every gym and playground in the three-county region," he concluded. He seemed to remember those days fondly.

"You have to understand," Mrs. Barnes said, smiling at him, "Hank always wanted a boy and Cynthia was him."

Hank mumbled that that wasn't true, but he was glad that Cynthia loved playing basketball. Unfortunately, though, all this travel put Cynthia in touch with the ball players in the area, including Roy Harrison, who appeared to be one of the boys with some talent in the sport. At first, Cynthia ignored him, but he persisted in pursuing her until she began dating him occasionally in high school. "But she dropped him when he began getting in serious trouble," Hank Barnes said. He went on to explain that Cynthia seemed to do well until she didn't get a basketball scholarship to a major school. The only place that wanted her was a little Bible college down the road named Aurora, and things didn't go well for her there.

"What went wrong?" I asked.

"She seemed to kind of go crazy," Mrs. Barnes said. "She began having relationships with women." I could tell by the way she used this term that she meant sexual relationships. "And her senior year she began sleeping with her coach, a man named Craft."

"How do you know that?" I asked.

"For several reasons," she said. The main one, she continued, was because Craft's fiancée from "back east" called her and demanded that she make her daughter stop sleeping with her future husband.

"What was this woman's name?" I asked.

"It was some sort of a German name, I think. But I know her given name was Analinda or something like that."

Another piece of the puzzle fell into place: Linda Antaglia knew that her husband, before they got married, had had an affair with Cynthia.

After speaking with the Barneses for another half hour, I

asked why Cynthia did not remain in touch with them. Hank Barnes said he thought that she was ashamed of herself.

"Why?" I asked.

"She knew we didn't approve of Harrison," he said. "But more importantly, she was ashamed that she had never made it in basketball. I think she thought I wouldn't respect her for failing." This assertion didn't ring true. These people were too kind to mistreat their daughter in this way.

Soon after this I left, telling them I would keep in touch. I also gave them the number of the Ithaca police department to make arrangements to have Cynthia's remains returned to Kansas. Giving them my card, I asked them to call if Mitch should contact them.

While driving away, I thought of the sad couple sitting together on the sofa wondering where they had gone wrong with their daughter.

Chapter 14

I looked for a motel on the way to Roy's hometown, Stovington, which was fifty miles west of Laurel, and drove twenty miles before finding one. While driving, I reflected on how a teenaged Roy must have felt traveling back and forth from his town to Cynthia's. Sounds like their relationship in high school was complicated, with Cynthia being unsure of her feelings, given his wild streak.

I checked into the motel, and, while lying in bed, I thought some more about the relationship. Cynthia seemed to be the less interested of the two. Both her mother and Coach Penny had said that she couldn't get rid of Roy but wanted to. And she did go to Aurora without him, where she might have fallen in love with Penny, and from what I had learned so far, did not reconnect with Roy until they went to Atlanta together. This was when she played for the Atlanta Bees, her last basketball team.

The next morning, I checked out and had a quick breakfast on the road. When I drove into Stovington, it was

8:30 a.m.

Stovington looked like a rundown version of Laurel. It had the familiar single main street, but the stores were on their last legs and several were abandoned with the windows boarded. The doctor's office had closed, and I wondered if the doctor had left for better pickings or if he or she had retired and no one wanted to assume the practice. Neither option was good for Stovington.

I needed to find someone to ask about the Harrisons, and stopped at the only business that seemed to be open at this hour, a diner called Sherry's Eatery. On entering, I found a woman with "Sherry" stitched on her blouse with a single customer. This morning, at least, things didn't look good financially for the only restaurant on Stovington's main drag.

"How may I help you?" Sherry asked, giving me the once-over. She did not wear a ring, and I caught her glancing at my unadorned ring finger. Her most notable features were her bright red hair, dyed, and her heavy makeup.

I sat down at the counter, ordered coffee, and asked for some information.

"Whatcha need, hon?" she asked, putting the full mug down in front of me.

"I'm looking for the Harrison family who lived outside of Stovington," I said. "Do you know them?"

"Is one of them named Roy?" she asked.

"Yes. Royston Harrison."

"Well, Roy's famous around these parts," she said. "He was a wild one back in the day."

"That sounds like the family I'm looking for," I said. She took a paper napkin from the holder and drew a crude map on it ending in "Roys House" with a childish picture of a house with curly-cue smoke coming out the chimney. "That's if the place hasn't fallen down," she said. "Last time I seen it, it looked ready to. Kinda like this whole town, I guess."

I thanked her for her help and got up to leave.

"If you see Roy say hi," she said. "I used to date him in

junior high."

Sherry's map led me through the Kansas countryside. After driving half an hour, I found a mail box that had the name Harrison scrawled on it. The driveway that went off the highway was overgrown with vegetation and a dead tree had fallen partially across it. Two hand-lettered signs stood near the main road. One said "No Trispissing" and the other, for good measure, said "Keep Out That Meens You."

I turned into the driveway and drove carefully up it, avoiding the biggest ruts. On catching sight of the house, I stopped. There in front of it was a black Cadillac. Driving closer, I saw it had Georgia plates and wondered if Westerly knew that his car had been driven half way across the country. After parking my rental short of the house, I walked up to the Caddie and, looking in the window, spied a tangle of clothes and two suitcases in the back seat. The front seat was more interesting. It was covered with blood, with a bloody towel on the passenger-side floor. Someone had driven Roy across five states to his mother's house.

The domicile stood before me, a two-story clapboard farm house. At one time it had been painted blue, but the clapboards were now bare wood bleached white. The roof sagged and needed a new set of shingles, and a brick chimney protruded through the roof at a crazy angle. It looked ready to fall.

While walking up the front steps, I felt one of them give under my weight and just managed to hop up on the front porch without falling. Someone inside heard me. A pair of eyes stared at me through one of the dirty glass panes in the front door.

When I walked toward the door and knocked, the eyes disappeared. A few moments later, the front door opened to reveal a tall woman in a worn grey house dress.

"Ms. Harrison?" I asked.

The woman looked at me suspiciously, her mouth tightly scowling. "Don't you read?" she said. "My signs say keep away from here."

"I'm sorry to intrude, Ma'am," I replied, "but I'm looking for your son, Roy. I have reason to believe that he's in your house."

"Yew a cop?" she asked.

"Not exactly," I said. "I'm a private detective working on a missing person case."

"Who's missing?" she asked.

I gave her a watered down version of the story of Mitch Antaglia's disappearance without mentioning her son's involvement in the kidnapping or the ransom demands.

"Why're you coming here? I don't know no Mitch Antaglia. Sounds like a wop name to me," she said distastefully.

I asked to come in, and she reluctantly consented. We sat down in the front parlor, which contained a few pieces of old furniture. She sat with her back to the stairs that led to the second story. On the walls hung a few family pictures, including a photograph of Roy as a boy, wearing a baggy baseball uniform and holding a bat. He had a lazy right eye.

"Roy was quite an athlete," I said, motioning to the picture.

"He was an athlete," she agreed.

"I understand he played basketball, too," I said.

"He's tall like me," she said. "He could dunk the ball."

"I also understand that he married a basketball player," I said.

"Yew mean that Cynthia Barnes?" she asked.

I nodded.

"He never married that little bitch," she said, her voice dripping with disgust. "He had more sense than to marry a whore like her."

"A whore? Why a whore?" I asked.

"Because she shacked up with anything in pants," she said.

"Who do you have in mind?" I asked.

"Why that coach of hers at the Bible college down the road for one," she said.

"Aurora?"

"That's the one. She shacked up with her coach there. His name was Gaff or something like that," she said.

"I thought she married Roy and had a baby with him," I said, trying to get her to talk more freely.

"She would have been lucky to marry my boy," she said. "But she didn't want him. She thought she was too good for him." She glared at me for suggesting that Roy had married Cynthia. "As for a baby, Roy ain't got no children," she asserted.

As we spoke, a loud moan came from the second floor of the house. Ms. Harrison turned around. When she looked back, she had a horrified look on her face.

"Sounds like someone's hurt up there," I said, pushing my way past her chair and taking the stairs to the second story. Another moan come from a door that opened to a bedroom. On walking in, I found Roy lying in bed, moaning and shivering. I put my hand on his forehead. It wasn't warm but hot. When I pulled down the bed clothes, the telltale smell of putrefying flesh hit me. Roy was sick, very sick, from Antaglia's bullet wound that had needed attention days ago.

"This man's sick and needs a doctor," I said to the old woman, who had followed me into the room.

"He's all right," she said. "I've been praying on him to get better."

"He needs a doctor, not prayers," I said and asked her the number of the nearest hospital. She walked out and came back a few minutes later with a number on a card.

"Ain't got no phone," she informed me.

"Don't worry," I said and punched in the number on my cell, identified myself, and ordered an ambulance to the

Harrison place. When the emergency operator asked where that was, I gave her the address and my cell number.

Sitting down on the bed, I looked at Roy. He appeared to be much older than his forty-some years. His eyes were bloodshot and his skin was yellow. Glancing around, I saw we were in his boyhood room. Cowboys populated the wallpaper and various toys and sporting goods stood on the shelves over his desk. His baseball glove was there along with a deflated basketball. What had his life been like, growing up fatherless on this isolated farm? I wondered.

At that moment, a door slammed downstairs, and I jumped up to look out the window. Below, a tall young man leapt down the porch stairs and headed toward the Cadillac parked in front. He opened the door, but didn't look up. That's got to be Mitch, I thought, as I tried to open the window to yell out to him.

I heard a sound behind me and turned in time to see the old woman bring Roy's childhood baseball bat down on the side of my head. I fell to the floor and the world stopped.

I found myself looking into a bright pen light held by a man in white. It took me a moment to realize he was a medic.

"He's coming to," the medic said to another man standing over him.

Looking up, I saw a tall, heavyset man in a brown suit staring at me. He held a police shield down in front of me that said Detective Laurence Henderson of the county police.

"Can you please tell me what's going on here?" he asked. "We've got a man with a wounded leg who is half dead, you unconscious, and an old lady who claims you broke into her house to rape her."

I tried to get up but couldn't until the medic helped me to my feet. The room swam around me, and I sat down on the now empty bed that smelled of putrid blood. I asked for a drink of water, which the medic brought me from the bathroom in a dirty cup.

"So what's going on here?" Henderson asked.

I explained as clearly as possible my relationship with the Ithaca police on a kidnapping case that involved Roy Harrison, the man who had been in the bed. He had been shot in Ithaca, Georgia, during a botched money transfer associated with the kidnapping. Mrs. Harrison was the owner of the house. It was she who had clubbed me with a baseball bat. Someone else in the house, possibly a young man named Mitchell Antaglia, who may or may not be Roy's son, had just driven away before I was knocked out. The car was a black Cadillac with Georgia plates, probably headed east.

"May I see your licence?" Henderson asked.

I fumbled for my wallet and gave him the licence.

"Nick Stirling," he said.

"You're the person who called the ambulance," the medic said.

I nodded.

The medic told Henderson that he had to get me to the hospital to check for a concussion. Roy was already in the ambulance, which awaited me on the driveway. I mildly protested going to the hospital, but soon agreed, realizing the wooziness might indicate the need for treatment.

The medic helped me down the stairs to the door where Henderson had stopped to talk with Mrs. Harrison.

"Why would a man come into your home to rape you and then call an ambulance to save your son?" I heard him ask. I learned later that he talked Mrs. Harrison out of filing charges against me.

In the ambulance, another medic was working on Roy. When the medic saw his partner and me, he moved out of the way and helped me into the vehicle and onto a seat to the right of Roy's gurney. He crawled back in to tend to Roy and the door closed just as the siren blared and the ambulance rattled down the driveway. Out the back window, I saw Henderson following in a patrol car and one of his men driving my rental.

As we sped along, I tried to talk to Roy, but the medic told me to stop. He had given Roy a sedative to put him to sleep.

At the hospital, the emergency room doctor gave me a quick checkup and recommended that I lie down for a few hours. The hospital then released me when I paid a bill for $593.23, which I put on my MasterCard. As I was leaving, Detective Henderson found me and gave me the keys to my rental parked outside.

"Glad I caught up with you, Stirling," he said. "We did a background check on Roy Harrison and found an outstanding warrant for his arrest for attempted murder in Ithaca, Georgia. Is that warrant connected to the kidnapping case?"

"That's correct," I said and explained in more detail the situation in Ithaca.

"Harrison might also be responsible for the murder of a faculty member at Georgia Central University," I concluded.

"Roy gets around," he said. "He has a rap sheet a yard long here, mostly from when he was a teenager. But his only major felony was breaking and entering in the 1980s. He went to prison for that one."

"Do you know anything about what he broke into?" I asked.

"No," he responded, "but I can look it up for you tomorrow in the office."

I gave him my card and then asked if he remembered Cynthia Barnes. He said he did. "She was hot stuff around here in the '80s. The first of the big girl athletes. Played basketball and was a real beauty back in the day."

I told him she was dead, and he looked sick.

"That's a damn shame," he said. "We all thought that Cynthia would make something of herself in basketball. She had everything: talent, looks, ambition. It just didn't work out for her."

"Do you have any idea what happened to Cynthia?" I asked.

"I don't but I know who might. Lou Worshing," he said.

"Who's he?"

"He was the best local sports reporter in the three-state area," Henderson said. "He's long retired now, but I bet he would tell you everything you need to know about Cynthia." He explained that Worshing had worked for the Kansas City *Star* for forty years as a sports columnist who specialized in the local sports scene. He was the only sports reporter at the time who followed closely the regional high school and college players. Even now, said Henderson, he writes "Whatever Happened to ..." columns for the local papers on forgotten prep and college athletes. Henderson said he just saw Worshing interviewed on a TV sports show a few days earlier, and he was still sharp. Henderson recommended that I contact the *Star* when I got to Kansas City to find his phone number and address.

"Good idea," I said.

I reminded Henderson that the Ithaca police would like to have Roy extradited to Georgia, and Henderson said he would see if that could be arranged. Thanking him, I gave him my card, shook hands, and left for Kansas City.

On the highway, I stopped at a fast food restaurant and had a hamburger and fries. After eating, I got the number from information in Kansas City for the *Star* and called the main number. I was passed about through the bureaucracy until I found a secretary willing to help. She had no problem giving me Worshing's number.

"He loves to talk to people," she said affectionately.

I called the number she gave me, and Worshing picked up immediately. "I'm a private detective working with the Ithaca,

Georgia, police on the Cynthia Barnes murder," I explained.

"Cynthia's dead?"

"She died two days ago in Ithaca under mysterious conditions" I said.

He agreed to talk to me.

"Cynthia was one of our first female basketball stars around here," he said. "She was a little early to have a pro career since the WNBA began and then folded in the mid-1980s. But in my opinion she got a raw deal at Aurora. Sounds like she got a raw deal in the rest of her life, too."

"What kind of a raw deal?" I asked.

"I'd rather not talk about it over the phone," he said and gave me his address and directions to his house.

"I'll be there in a few hours," I said.

"I'll be looking for you this evening about 6:00."

Worshing's house was close to an exit from the highway, and I parked in front. It was a small ranch with a closed-in carport that made an extra room. When I knocked, a small neat man with long gray hair opened the door. He wore gray slacks with an Oxford blue dress shirt and bedroom slippers. He shuffled me off to the living room to sit down.

When we were settled, he asked me details about Cynthia's death, and I told him what I knew.

"Cynthia was destined for a hard life," Worshing said.

"Why is that?" I asked.

"She wanted things too much," he said, obscurely.

"Can you be more specific?" I asked.

He sat for a moment before he began his story.

"Cynthia fell in love with basketball as a child," he said. "She spent her free time shooting baskets at her home. Her father had wanted a son, she told me once, and had treated her like a boy. They hunted together and watched sports on TV, especially the Olympics because women competed there.

She particularly liked women's basketball. She came along at the right time because high schools and colleges were beginning to field women's teams. There were even the beginnings of a women's professional league. So Cynthia glimpsed the possibility of a sporting life."

"I met her parents," I said, "and they seemed like nice people."

"The salt of the earth," he responded. "They raised her to be a gentle person, and she was. Perhaps too much so for her own good."

"What do you mean?" I asked.

"Cynthia was taught that the world was filled with people she could trust," he responded. "She wasn't at all prepared for the shark-infested waters of college and professional basketball. She was one of the best prep women players around, but she was not recruited by a major program. That surprised and disappointed her. I interviewed her at the time, and she cried like a baby."

"But she did go to Aurora," I pointed out. "Wasn't that at least a decent opportunity for her?"

"It should have been," Worshing said. "Aurora was a place with some potential. The president at the time had decided he would put the college on the map by making it an athletic powerhouse, especially in women's sports. The school fielded softball and field hockey teams. It also started a women's gymnastics team that received some attention. And basketball, of course. Cynthia, in fact, was supposed to be one of the main attractions of the women's sports program. And she certainly did her part until she ran into trouble during her senior year."

"What happened then?" I asked.

"I don't want to be the source of your information," he said. "But I can give you access to what I know about Cynthia."

"How?" I asked.

"Follow me," he said, as he got up and walked through his

kitchen to the carport, where his office was set up. The right wall was lined with an array of battered metal file cabinets of various colors ranging from tan to army green.

He invited me to sit on a couch along the front side of the room and opened a drawer marked "B" in the first cabinet. He fanned through the folders for a moment and then pulled out a thick one. He sat down at his desk and opened the folder in front of him.

"I keep files on all the major prep and college players," he said. "Each one contains my notes on them plus any published material and interviews I had with them. This file is on Cynthia Barnes."

I walked over to take a better look. Worshing, sitting, looked up at me.

"You are welcome to examine this material as long as you don't attribute anything to me," he said.

"Why not?" I asked.

"In my business you have to be discreet, particularly when you are dealing with young people," he said. "If I told you everything in this file, I wouldn't have a snowball's chance in hell of getting another interview with a high school kid. His or her parents wouldn't let me."

"That makes sense."

"You can stay here as long as you like, Mr. Stirling, and look through Cynthia's file," he said. "Over there is a small duplicating machine. Please use it sparingly. Shut the door completely to lock it when you leave. But if you ever claim that I gave you any material from that file I will deny it. And my word is worth something in these parts."

Thanking him as he left the room, I sat down at his desk and began reading the file, taking brief notes in my notebook. I lost track of time reading until, looking at my watch, found it was 10:35 p.m. Upon leafing through the last of the papers, I found a note scribbled by Worshing that said, "See Becker file."

I retrieved that file from the cabinet and examined it. It

contained notes and an article on Wilhelm Becker, a German industrialist who in the mid-'80s was visiting the US to find a location for a plant to produce veterinary medicines in the US. Worshing interviewed him because Becker had been an Olympic decathlon star in Germany during the '50s. According to notes in the file, Becker had narrowed the potential location of his plant to two university towns: Lawrence, Kansas, and Ithaca, Georgia. Included in the file was a December 1987 newspaper article, with several pictures of Becker being wined and dined by the President of KU and various local politicians trying to influence his decision. One picture included Becker, his daughter Linda, and several other people. Linda was dressed in a diaphanous gown and was on the arm of Alberto Antaglia. So Antaglia had met his wife in Kansas, I noted. Standing next to Becker was Cynthia Barnes, looking out of place. The article discussed Becker's Olympic career and his current business interests in the production of veterinary medicines. The article went on to identify Aurora College's coach Albert Craft as Linda Becker's fiancée. So while Antaglia was engaged to Linda, he was having an affair with Cynthia, who appeared in the picture to be Becker's date for the evening. A modern arrangement, I thought.

I duplicated a few pieces from the two files, and returned both to the cabinet. After writing a note of thanks to Worshing, I left it along with my card on his desk. I then walked out of the house, closing the door tightly behind me, and drove to a motel I had passed on my way to Worshing's.

I brought in my laptop, set it up, and googled Wilhelm Becker. I learned that he was a member of a prominent German family of industrialists that specialized in producing chemicals and medicines. One area of specialization was veterinary medicine, which was produced under the Markardial name. Markardial was an international corporation, and its US plant had been until recently located near Ithaca, Georgia. Last year it had succumbed to financial pressures and closed its U.S. operations. So twenty years ago Georgia had beaten out Kansas for the plant, I thought.

In bed, I reflected on my discoveries in Kansas. I had learned that the Antaglias had met there in the mid-1980s. I had learned that Roy had been driven home in his half brother's Cadillac by Mitch, who I just got a glimpse of as he roared off in the vehicle. Roy's mother had tried to hide her wounded son in her house without medical attention. She was probably honoring Roy's request to avoid going to a doctor with a bullet wound because the doctor would be required by law to report it to local police. She also denied that Roy and Cynthia, whom she plainly despised, had ever married. And, finally, I learned from Worshing's file that Cynthia was psychologically destroyed at Aurora College.

This last piece of information came in the form of a set of notes for an article that the journalist never wrote. Based on interviews with various members of Aurora's athletic program and the administration during 1987, the notes made clear that Cynthia had been expelled the previous year from the college for old-fashioned moral turpitude. Her sins, the notes suggested, included taking performance-enhancing drugs and having a year-long affair with Coach Craft, who was fired that same year. Cynthia was forced out of Aurora with her reputation in tatters. The notes implied that she had been manipulated by powerful figures who wanted to protect the reputation of Aurora College at all cost.

No wonder none of the six WNBA teams would touch her after this scandal, I reflected.

I fell into a troubled sleep dreaming of Cynthia being stripped of her future.

Chapter 15

Early the next morning, I drove to the airport, turned in my rental, and caught the first flight into Atlanta. By the time I picked up my Honda and drove to my office, it was after 10:00. My messages consisted of the usual array of people wanting my services to help with divorces and to find lost loves. I made a list of five names and numbers to call later. My mail included a check from Mrs. Allen's divorce attorney for services rendered, which I put in my wallet to deposit in my bank account. There was also an overnight express letter from Linda Antaglia, which read,

Dear Mr. Stirling,

This letter is to inform you that my husband and I no longer want to continue your services. Please cease and desist all activities connected with the kidnapping of our son, Mitchell Antaglia. If you continue working on the case, we will have to take appropriate legal action. Thank you for all the work you have done. Now it is time for you to stop.

Sincerely,
Linda Antaglia.

The letter was dated yesterday, when Linda Antaglia received my last report on her message machine outlining my progress in Kansas. It looked like I was hitting too close to home for the Antaglias. Something was bothering them.

My cell buzzed.

"Henderson here," a familiar gruff voice responded to my hello.

"Detective Henderson," I said. "What's up?"

"I wanted to update you on Harrison," he stated.

"Shoot."

In the precise language of most police officers, Henderson outlined what he had found out about Roy Harrison. "First of all," he said, "the boy's one sick puppy. The doctor treating him said the bullet had nicked a major vein in his leg, which bled for a couple of days. So Harrison lost a lot of blood. This blood loss lowered his resistance. When infection set in, it spread quickly through his body and has affected his organs, especially his heart. He may have to have his leg amputated if the infection is not controlled."

"So no extradition in the immediate future," I responded.

"Right," he confirmed.

"Can I talk to him by phone?" I asked.

"Not now, but maybe later today," he said. "I'll keep an eye on the situation for you. I'm pretty sure he's hired a lawyer, who will try to limit what he says from this point on. I've called the Ithaca police department and informed them of the situation."

"Who'd you talk to?" I asked.

"A Detective Snow," he said. "She sounded very concerned about not hearing from you, Stirling. I suggest you get in touch with her pronto."

"I'll see her later today," I assured him.

"I also unearthed some details of the breaking-and-entering conviction of our boy Roy in the '80s."

"What'd you turn up?"

"Roy was accused of breaking into the apartment of a guy named Herman Schultz," he said. "Does that mean anything to you?"

"It might," I said. "I'm almost positive that Schultz is the real name of a pig scientist at Georgia Central named Meluso."

"That's a powerful coincidence," Henderson said.

"You bet. Schultz seems to be mixed up in this crazy case," I said. "Did you get a sense of what happened in the b-and-e?"

"I phoned the lawyer who represented Harrison twenty years ago," the detective said, "and he said it was a rush to judgment. Of course, defense attorneys always say that. But in this case the claim had some merit."

"How so?" I asked.

"Harrison apparently knew Schultz well and was in and out of his apartment regularly. The attorney thought Schultz was trying to cover something up by having our boy arrested."

"Interesting," I said.

"Does it help your case, Stirling?" he asked.

"I think so, but I'm not sure how," I said. "I'm going to try to see Meluso this afternoon to get a sense of the guy." The case had me by the neck and wouldn't let me go, I told Henderson, but I couldn't see how to resolve it. It had started out as a fairly straightforward missing person case but had turned into at least two murders seemingly connected to the original incident. And these murders appeared to be connected to events that happened in Kansas two decades ago. Thanking him for his help, I asked him to call when Roy could talk.

"Glad to help, amigo," he said, "and call Detective Snow. She seemed worried, especially when I told her you'd been clubbed with a baseball bat."

"Thanks for telling her," I said, shaking my head. I didn't want Brett worrying about me.

I jumped in the Honda and headed to Ithaca. The traffic near the town was heavy, which suggested some athletic event was drawing a crowd. I called Brett and invited her to lunch at Sherman's March. She seemed noncommittal but agreed to meet me.

Before heading downtown to the bar and grill, I went to the athletic center. As I drove in, Clarence pulled me over.

"Where you been, my man?" he asked.

"Clarence, I've been in Kansas," I answered.

"Corn country," he responded. "Did you find the Missile there?" he asked.

"I'm pretty sure I saw him from a window getting into a black Caddie," I said.

"One of the members of the basketball team claims that he saw the Missile here last night," Clarence said. "Said he looked done in."

"Well, he would be if he drove back from Kansas in one night," I responded. "Who saw him?"

"Ricky Wright," Clarence said, and I promised to find him.

Clarence waved me through, and I went up to Seamer's office and found Candy at her post.

"Mr. Stirling!" she said with a smile. "Back from Kansas, are we?"

"Yes," I said, "and I owe you a dinner."

"Any time," she said.

"Is Seamer in?" I asked, and she said he wasn't. I wondered if that was true. He might be happy to have the Antaglia mess off his back.

"Any word on Coach Antaglia?" I asked.

"Coach Seamer told me this morning, before he left, that Antaglia was getting out of the hospital this afternoon."

"Good," I said, and left.

I caught the campus bus to the Schmeling-Wilder Center, went in, and found Coach Shuster running practice as if he had been there since I left him four days ago. He was less than happy to see me. I was a person non gratis in the athletic program.

"Have you seen Mitch Antaglia?" I asked, and he said no. "Could I talk to Ricky Wright?" I continued, and Shuster pointed out a lanky African-American player practicing defense who looked familiar from my last visit.

When I called him over, he looked in Shuster's direction. He apparently got the nod, and came over.

"Have you seen Mitch?" I asked.

"Yeah, I seen the Missile," he said, not volunteering much.

"Here in Ithaca?" I asked.

"Where else would I have seen him?" he asked.

I ignored his sarcasm and asked, "When was this?"

He thought for a moment. "Late last night," he said.

"What'd he say?" I asked.

"Not much," he said.

"I think you can do better than that, Ricky," I responded, looking at him hard

"He said he just drove back from Kansas where he went with a dude he thought might be his father," Ricky said.

"Thought might be?" I asked.

"Yeah, but he said it turned out this guy wasn't his real father," he said.

"How'd he know that?"

"The guy told him he wasn't," Ricky explained.

"Where is Mitch now?" I asked, and he said he didn't know. I thanked him for his help, gave him my card in case he remembered something, and caught a bus downtown.

I arrived at Sherman's March about ten minutes late to find Detective Brett Snow sitting at a table looking a bit

peeved but as attractive as ever. She had her blonde hair up in a bun, and her lipstick was the color of coral. I was drawn to her brightness like the proverbial moth.

"Hello, Brett," I said.

Her eyes caught mine. They flashed with a hint of anger.

"Nice of you to show up, Nick," she said. "I have only twenty minutes left on my lunch break."

"Sorry, I got caught up in an interview," I explained and asked if I could make it up to her by taking her to the dinner I had promised her.

"Well, that would help," she said, smiling in spite of herself.

After we quickly ordered lunch, she asked me how the trip to Kansas had turned out. I gave her a quick rundown on Roy and Cynthia and Antaglia and Schultz.

"The four of them have some sort of a connection that goes back twenty years," I explained, "and the Antaglias met and were engaged there in about 1987."

I also reviewed information about Wilhelm Becker, Linda Antaglia's father, and the Markardial plant that he had established in Ithaca.

"That facility used to be a few miles down the highway toward Atlanta," she said. "It was closed last year when the recession hit. Its closing was a financial blow to Ithaca."

She asked me about my head wound, and I told her about Mrs. Harrison and Roy's childhood bat. "Nothing much came of it," I explained. "Mrs. Harrison's pretty frail."

"Those are the kinds of things that can be harmful in the long run," she said, touching my knot across the table, and I agreed to keep my eye on it.

"What'd you find out about Meluso/Schultz?" I asked. She explained that she and a few officers had kept an eye on him and that she was working with the Immigration and Customs Enforcement to have Meluso eventually deported to Germany, where he was still a citizen.

"Is Meluso acting strangely?" I asked, and she said he

didn't appear to be. "He's been going to work about 6:00 in the morning and going home about 7:00 at night," she said. "Regular as clockwork." I told her I was going to visit the good doctor.

Our sandwiches arrived, and we began eating.

"I talked to John Millar yesterday about Christa Antaglia's drowning," Brett informed me, before taking a second bite of her sandwich and chewing it.

"Great!" I exclaimed. "Learn anything interesting?"

She swallowed, and said, "As a matter of fact, I did. Millar was convinced that the drowning was not accidental."

"Why did he think that?" I asked, putting down my cup of coffee and looking at her.

"His main concern was that the lock usually on the pool gate was gone, lost, and Linda Antaglia was the only person who could have removed it."

"How did Millar conclude that?"

"He interviewed all of the people in the house—Mitch; Stella, the maid; and Coach Antaglia," Brett explained, "and they all claimed that the lock was on the gate when they left the house. Mitch left for school out the back door and said he saw the lock on the gate as did Antaglia himself, who went into the back yard that morning to check on the basketball court he had just had built. He claims he checked the lock by pulling it."

"What about Stella?"

Brett sipped her sweet tea and said, "Millar remembers that Stella took the day off to deal with a family problem. One of her older relatives had passed away. But she was certain the lock was on the gate the evening she left. She checked the lock several times a day to make sure Christa couldn't fall in the pool."

"So what was Millar's conclusion?"

"After interviewing the three I mentioned, Millar interrogated Linda Antaglia and concluded, after catching her in some inconsistencies, that she had unlocked the gate and allowed her daughter to wander into the pool and drown. Then she didn't call an ambulance until four hours later. She claimed that she thought Christa was in the house but didn't know where."

I whistled softly. "That's a long time not to know where your toddler is," I said. "Why would she want to kill Christa?" I asked.

"Millar was a bit vague on that," Brett said, "but he was convinced that Mrs. Antaglia saw her daughter as an imposition. He said it became clear to him that she wanted to get rid of Christa by setting up what appeared to be an accident."

"Did the DA indict Linda Antaglia for the murder?" I asked.

"Millar said that the evidence was circumstantial but convincing," Brett said, "but the DA eventually came to believe that he couldn't win the case. Linda Antaglia was connected to the Markardial Corporation outside of town, was wealthy in her own right, and could afford the best legal guns in the area. One of her lawyers in particular was highly aggressive, and the DA didn't want to go up against him after losing cases to him three times earlier."

"Just what we need," I said, "a frightened DA."

"Millar," Brett concluded, "is convinced to this day that Linda Antaglia murdered her daughter. She said some things that made him believe she hated being a mother. What apparently brought things to a head was Stella taking the day off and leaving Christa with her mother. Mrs. Antaglia had to miss a social engagement to stay home with her child."

"There are always baby sitters," I pointed out.

"That apparently didn't occur to Mrs. Antaglia," Brett responded.

I noticed that Brett was getting her things together to leave.

"One more question, Brett," I said. "Was Millar a good

investigator? Is he trustworthy?"

"He was one of the very best," she responded, and "I found him convincing when I talked to him about the case."

"Thanks for looking into this, Brett, and I'll see you tonight," I said as she got up and left. I stayed and checked the back office to see if Mark Sherman was there. He wasn't, so I wrote a brief note on one of my cards that I had dropped by to say hello and was still looking for Mitch. After taking the bus back to the athletic complex, I got my car and headed across town to the county hospital to see Antaglia. My thoughts about Mrs. Antaglia began to shift. If Brett's report was correct, it appeared that Antaglia's wife had had some sort of a hatred of her daughter.

On reaching the front desk of the hospital and asking to see Antaglia, I was surprised that the receptionist looked at a list on her computer.

"Are you Mr. Stirling or Mitch Antaglia?" she asked.

"The former."

"Mr. Antaglia is in room 452 and wants to see you," she said.

The elevator took me to the fourth floor, and I followed the numbers and arrows to 452. When I knocked, Antaglia, in a raspy voice, said, "Come in."

"Hello, Coach," I said on entering the room. He looked small in his hospital bed with the covers pulled up around his neck.

It took him a moment to recognize me.

"Stirling," he whispered. "Where the hell've you been?"

"Just got back from Kansas," I said.

"Kansas," he murmured. "What a god-awful place that is. Did you find my Mitch?"

"I saw him from a distance," I said. "He ran away from me."

"I'm not surprised. He probably thinks you're a police officer after him. Do you know where he is now?"

"I'm not 100% certain," I said, "but I've had one report

that he is back in Ithaca."

"I hope you're right," he said. "If Mitch is here I can help him." His voice faded into exhaustion.

"I found some interesting things from the past in Kansas," I said.

Antaglia raised his hand. "I'm dead tired," he said. "Please allow me to rest before we discuss your trip." He reached up and pushed the button to summon a nurse.

"Your wife has taken me off the case," I told him. That got his attention. He looked at me with a glint of fear in his eyes.

"She did what?" he croaked.

"Here's the letter she sent," I said, giving it to him. He glanced at it and then balled it up in his hand.

"Damn that snake," he hissed. He seemed deep in thought for a moment.

"You're not fired, Stirling," he said, his head drooping. "I want you on the case. Watch her for me," he mumbled as he drifted off.

Why did he need me to protect him from his wife? I wondered. From the beginning, I had sensed tension between the two of them. But why would he fear her? Did Christa's strange death have something to do with his fears?

A nurse poked her head in the door, looked at Antaglia, and told me to leave.

"Coach needs his rest," she said.

Chapter 16

My cell buzzed outside the hospital, and Henderson said, "Hello, amigo," when I answered.

"Roy wants to talk to you," he said. "He wants you to call him 2:00 your time. As I mentioned before, he's still in the hospital and now has a lawyer, who will undoubtedly control what our boy says."

He gave me the number, and I thanked him for all his help. "I'd like to work with you again, my friend," he said as he hung up.

My watch said it was 1:45. I parked downtown, walked to Café All Day, and bought a cup of coffee. After sitting at one of the small, round tables in the corner, I dialed Roy's number. The phone rang twice before a strange voice said on the other end, "Roy Harrison's room."

"Nick Stirling here," I said. "I have an appointment to speak with Mr. Harrison."

"Thanks for calling, Mr. Stirling," the voice said. "I'm James Whitaker, Roy's attorney. I am handling his legal affairs now, including the extradition hearing that will take place tomorrow." He paused, then said, "And I might as well tell you, I have advised Roy not to talk to you, but he insists on doing so."

"I understand the delicacy of the legal situation," I told Whitaker. "My only interest is to find out the whereabouts of Mitchell Antaglia."

"I think you'll find that a lot of issues that seem unconnected are actually closely related," he warned me. "I'll be on a second line," he informed me, and then Roy came on.

"Mr. Stirling," he said, "I want to begin by thanking you for calling the ambulance for me. My doctor tells me that you saved my life."

"I was happy to help," I said. "As soon as I saw you at your mother's I knew you needed medical attention."

He went on to tell me how sorry he was that his mother hit me with the bat. "She was convinced that you were trying to harm me," he explained. "She didn't think I needed medical attention. She's a born-again type who believes that we should let things unfold according to the dictates of God's will."

I explained my familiarity of the type and gave him a brief description of my experiences with snake handlers in the North Georgia mountains a few years ago.

"Since you did me a good deed, I want to return the favor," he said. "I'll tell you whatever I know about Mitchell. My lawyer, though, doesn't want me to talk about anything connected to charges placed against me in Georgia or any other crimes I might have committed."

"I understand," I assured him. "I'll only ask for background information related to Mitch."

"Good," he responded.

"First, what is your relationship with Mitch?"

"That's a good question," Roy said. Mitch, he explained, was Cynthia's baby that she had after she left the Atlanta Bees, her last basketball team. He wasn't certain who the father was. It was not impossible that Mitch was his son, but it was unlikely.

"Could you go into more detail?" I asked.

"I'd better start at the beginning," he said. He had been in love with Cynthia since the first year of high school. He had met her when they were teenagers in Kansas. They both played basketball and participated in the various youth leagues in the area. Cynthia was one of the star players among the girls. She was tall and slim, a great athlete "for a girl at the time," as he put it, and beautiful on top of everything. It wasn't long before Roy started making passes at her and following her around. "I would have been called a stalker now," he admitted. "But back then I was just persistent."

He went on to explain his family situation. He had grown up with a crazy mother and no father. I didn't mention that his half brother had told me the whole story. Early on, he confessed, he began hanging out with a bad crowd and got into teenage trouble for joy riding and breaking into school buildings and writing on the walls. "Most of it was just stupid stuff," he said. "I got a bad rep, as we said at the time."

I heard the lawyer clear his throat.

"Cynthia was a sweet girl, and she liked me," he continued, "but her parents didn't want her to have anything to do with me. They saw me as trouble."

"Did she go out with you?" I asked.

"Some," he said. "She had a bit of a rebellious streak herself, and we dated off and on. I was the first man to sleep with her," he said, with a touch of pride in his voice.

I could imagine how Mr. and Mrs. Barnes must have felt about a hellion like Roy dating their daughter.

"Did you follow her to Aurora College?" I asked.

He said that he didn't follow her but lived in the general vicinity. He graduated from high school the same year Cynthia did. Like her, he hoped to win an athletic scholarship for basketball at a college but nothing came through, in part, he confessed, because by then he had a criminal record. "Most schools at that time didn't want to fool with troublemakers like me," he admitted, "unless they were superstars."

"Let's not go any further along this line of questioning," I heard Whitaker say.

"Anyway," Roy continued, "I took a job near Aurora and kept in touch with Cynthia. Every once in a while, she would go out with me, but for the most part she ignored me."

"I assume that hurt?" I asked.

"It did," he said, "especially when I saw her dating other people." He used the word "people" in a distinctive way.

"You mean Penny, don't you?"

"You know about Penny?" he asked.

"I talked to her yesterday," I said. "I got the impression that she and Cynthia were very close."

"They were lovers," Roy said, "and it broke my heart. I could compete against another man," he continued, "but not against a woman. So I just let her know I was still there, and she occasionally spent the night at my apartment."

"I understand that she took various kinds of drugs that she thought would make her a better athlete," I said.

Whitaker cleared his throat. "I didn't know much about that," Roy said in a strange voice. "I just know that she would do anything to improve her abilities on the court."

"Let's stop this line of questioning," Whitaker said.

I decided to return to Mitch. "So is Mitch your son or not?" I asked.

"He could be," Roy responded, "but I don't think he is."

"How could he be?" I asked.

When Cynthia graduated, Roy explained, she was at loose ends. She had been observed by various scouts for the new professional women's basketball league, the WNBA, but nothing came of these observations. "She was devastated," he said. "The only thing that turned up was a position on the Bees, a semi-pro team that emphasized looks as much as talent," he explained. "She hated the idea of joining this kind of team but saw it as the only way to stay in basketball. The WNBA had gone under after one year, so she didn't have many opportunities to play."

"She asked me to go with her to Atlanta," Roy explained. "She was afraid to go alone, and I was available and willing. She was my one true love, and I would have gone anywhere with her."

"I don't know much about that time in her life," I said. "What happened to Penny?"

"Cynthia lost interest in Penny, who stayed in Aurora and took a job as assistant coach of the women's team."

"Was she still in love with Cynthia?" I asked.

"You bet," he said. "She called all the time. If I answered the phone and someone hung up, I assumed it was Penny. Once she yelled at me for taking Cynthia away from her and ruining both their lives."

"Why were you so willing to go to Atlanta with Cynthia?" I asked.

"One advantage to going to Atlanta," Roy said, "was that my brother and his wife live there. We stayed with them when we first got to town as we were getting settled. My sister-in-law is a bit of a lush but my brother is a stand-up guy who helped me out a lot."

"Were you and Cynthia married?" I asked, remembering that both Jeanie Westerly and Reeves had said they were.

"Depends on what you mean by that term," he said. "We lived together and people thought we were married. In fact, we even planned a wedding at one point and invited some old friends, including Penny. When Cynthia died, we were certainly in a common-law union. But did we ever marry officially? No," he said. His voice was filled with regret.

"So what happened in Atlanta?" I asked.

He explained that the Bees didn't exist for long before falling apart. The team attracted few fans interested in basketball and a lot interested in the girls. "There was a photographer, one guy in particular, who had a thing for Cynthia and always took her picture," he said. That must be Reeves, the sports photographer, I thought. "I didn't mind the action pictures on the court," he continued, "but I couldn't stand the cheesecake shots of Cynthia with her jersey off."

"I saw some of them," I said.

"Where?" he asked.

"I met Reeves and reviewed some of his old photos."

"That guy never liked me," Roy said. "I think he was jealous."

Roy said that it became clear to him that there was no future for them in Atlanta, and he tried to get Cynthia to return to the Midwest, where they both had family and other connections. "Then something strange happened," he said.

"What was that?"

"Her old assistant coach her senior year at Aurora showed up," he said.

"Craft, you mean?" I asked.

"That's what he was called at Aurora," he said, "but his name is Antaglia now. He lives in Ithaca."

I decided not to tell Roy everything I knew about Antaglia nor that he had hired me. Roy would stop the interview if he knew.

He said that Antaglia started visiting them, telling Cynthia that Georgia Central was looking for an assistant coach for the women's basketball team and that he could help her get the position. "She was taken in by Antaglia," he said, bitterly. "Cynthia had had an affair with him in Kansas, and she began to go to Ithaca to see Antaglia and his wife."

"What did the three of them do?" I asked.

"I don't know exactly," he said, "but the next thing I know Cynthia was pregnant."

"By whom?" I asked.

"At the time I thought it was my child," he said. "Cynthia was sleeping with me then, but she claimed to be on birth control. But maybe she went off it without my knowing it or maybe the pill failed us and Mitch was the result."

"Did you ever ask her if Mitch was your child?" I asked.

"Yes," Roy said, "but she was vague." He hesitated and then said he would tell me about his suspicions. "I think that Cynthia served as a surrogate mother for Antaglia. I assumed at the time that the wife was infertile, and they used Cynthia to carry their child."

"Why did you think that?" I asked.

"Several reasons," he said. "Cynthia was always up in Ithaca. I assumed that she had restarted her affair with Antaglia. And I was certain that she was no longer on birth control because I found her unused pills about that time in her chest of drawers."

"Anything else confirm your suspicions?" I asked.

"Yes," he said. "Cynthia started going to an expensive baby doctor. We didn't have health insurance so I knew someone was paying her bills. One day I found a check in Cynthia's purse from Antaglia made out to the doctor." Roy hesitated a moment. "The final proof was that after Cynthia had the baby, she received a large sum of money, at least $20,000, from someone."

"What do you think that was for?" I asked.

"I'm quite sure it was payment for the baby," Roy said. "She brought Mitch home for a few days, and she really loved the little guy. She took care of him real good and read some books on how to do it right. But something was upsetting her. Then one day, when I was home, a lawyer came and took Cynthia in the bedroom and talked to her."

"Do you know who the lawyer was?"

"I'm certain he represented the Antaglias. They wanted Mitch and sent the lawyer to get him. He took Mitch away after talking to Cynthia for an hour."

"How did she respond?" I asked.

"She was miserable," he answered. "She cried for days. It wasn't until the money came that she began to feel better.

That gave us enough to move back to Kansas and get a new start. But she always told me that she would get baby Mitch back some day."

"How'd you feel about her giving Mitch up?" I asked.

"I was pretty mixed up at the time," he said. "While I loved Cynthia, I was not ready to be a father. Plus I was fairly certain that Mitch was not my son. I led a wild life back then and committed…"

Whitaker interrupted Roy, telling him not to continue that answer.

"What else do you want to know?" the lawyer asked me.

"If Mitch isn't your son, whose is he?" I asked Roy.

Roy hesitated. "As I said, I think he might be Antaglia's," he said, "but I'm not certain. He might be the child of an anonymous sperm donor for all I know."

After a pause, I asked Roy if he was the man outside of Professor McConnell's house who ran me down.

"Can I answer that?" I heard Roy ask Whitaker. They whispered back and forth until Roy's voice came on the phone. "All I can say is that I was never at the professor's house," he said.

"Do you know who the man was?" I asked.

"No," Roy said.

"Any guesses?"

"I can't say," he responded, his voice beginning to fail.

I was ready to start a new line of questioning when Whitaker came on the phone. "Mr. Stirling," he said, "this interview is over. Roy can't talk anymore."

"Thanks for your help, Roy," I said and told him I'd keep in touch. He wished me luck and thanked me again for calling the ambulance. I also thanked Whitaker for setting up the interview.

After flicking shut my cell, I finished the last of my cold coffee. Roy had not told me much that was new, but what he did say was intriguing. I learned that Cynthia and he had had a long relationship but weren't officially married. I also learned that Cynthia might have served as Mitch's surrogate mother, probably for the Antaglias. As Reeves had remembered, Cynthia had disappeared from the Bees for half a year, the break, I now understood, being due to her pregnancy. Mitch's biological father was still a mystery, and that central confusion in his life appeared to be disturbing him.

My watch indicated it was close to 3:30. My dinner appointment with Brett was at 8:00, which I couldn't miss and hope to keep her on my side. Before then, I had to interview Meluso, who apparently was deeply involved in Mitch's case. He had known Antaglia in Kansas, and had followed him to Georgia Central. He was probably Mitch's Dr. Death. I called the number Brett had given me and got a secretary, who made an appointment for 4:45 that afternoon for me to see Meluso.

I decided to get a room and returned to the motel near campus Brett had recommended a few days earlier. While I was carrying my overnight bag and laptop into the room, my cell buzzed. I recognized Rachel Stone's voice before she identified herself. She said that she had seen Mitch that afternoon and wanted to tell me some disturbing things he said. I agreed to see her immediately. For the first time Mitch seemed to be within my grasp.

"Please hurry," she sobbed. "I think Mitch is losing it."

We agreed to meet in the lounge of her dorm, and I found her there ten minutes later. She looked worn out, as if she had driven to Kansas and back herself. She was dressed informally in a gray hoodie and blue athletic shorts. Her long dark hair was piled behind her head, and she had been crying.

"Thanks for coming, Mr. Stirling. I didn't know who else to call. I had never seen Mitch so weirdly upset."

"Calm down and tell me everything that happened, starting from the beginning," I said.

"I'll try," she responded, and then burst into tears and

threw herself into my arms. I held her, hoping any passing girls wouldn't think I was making a pretty young woman cry.

She finally calmed down and took a tissue from her pocket and dabbed her eyes and blew her nose.

"I'm sorry," she said. "Mitch always tells me I'm too emotional."

"I think you're behaving normally in a stressful situation," I told her.

She looked at me gratefully.

"So tell me what happened," I repeated.

She told me the following story. Mitch had contacted her the previous night and said he was making progress on finding his father. "His *real* father," she said emphatically. She asked him if it was Roy, and he said no, not him. She asked him if it was Mr. Antaglia, and he said he wasn't sure it was him either. When she asked him who it was, he said he wouldn't say until he was certain. He then asked if he could see her tomorrow, and she said he could in the late afternoon after her morning classes.

When he arrived, he looked wild. He hadn't bathed in days. He was dressed in his workout clothes and carried a bag with the Central Lion on it. He had collected it and his clothes from Westerly's building in Atlanta, I realized.

"He told me a bunch of interesting things, Mr. Stirling," she said.

"Like what?" I asked.

"Well, he told me that the tall woman with the big hat was not his new girlfriend but his mother, Cynthia Barnes," she said. "I asked him why he didn't tell me before, and he said he wasn't sure at the time but now he was. That made me feel better."

"What else did he say?"

"This is what really frightened me," she said. "He reached into his Lions bag and pulled out a huge gun and said he was going to use it to get at the truth about his past."

The gun undoubtedly belonged to Roy Harrison. Mitch

had brought it back from Kansas.

"Do you think he meant to use it?" I asked.

"I did, Mr. Stirling," she responded. "The look of anger in his eyes scared me to death. I begged him to give me the gun or give it to the police, but he wouldn't do it and put it back in his bag and said I'd learn what he was going to do with it in the morning papers."

She burst into tears again, but this time I held her at a distance.

"Calm down, Rachel, and listen to me," I said. "Mitch has been under incredible stress for days, and he has driven to and from Kansas in forty-eight hours. Before that he learned that two of the most important women in his life had died, Professor Connolly and Cynthia Barnes. He's exhausted and not thinking straight."

She looked at me with her big brown eyes.

"It is imperative that you take your information to the police and tell them everything you told me," I insisted.

"But won't they arrest Mitch?" she asked.

"They might, but that would be better than him killing someone or getting killed himself," I explained. She nodded reluctantly.

"I have one more question, Mr. Stirling," she said.

"What's that?"

"What should I do with all this money?" she asked, pointing to a brown shopping bag on the floor between her feet I hadn't noticed. "Mitch gave it to me to keep for him."

I recognized the bag that Antaglia had put the $110,000 in to give Roy at the golf course four days earlier. "I'll take care of this," I told her after looking at the money inside. We walked out to my car, and I locked the bag in the evidence box in my trunk as she watched. "I'll count this later," I said, "and return it to Antaglia where it belongs."

On leaving, I promised Rachel to protect Mitch to the best of my ability and watched her walk back to her dorm. I then drove out of town to the agricultural centers to the north of Ithaca, hoping that Meluso would help me locate Mitch before the boy killed someone.

Chapter 17

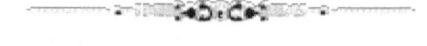

The land to the north of Ithaca was filled with centers for the study of various agricultural animals. There was a study center for chickens, sheep, cattle, and hogs. Each of these areas consisted of several small buildings that housed offices and laboratories. Connected to them were pens to contain the animals and larger fenced properties for the animals to roam in. When my wife attended Central, we took a tour of these facilities, so I knew in general how they were set up.

Driving through the rolling pastures, I kept my eye open for the hog facilities and found them the farthest out, after the sheep. The sign on the road said Hog Research Center, and the road led to a cluster of buildings to the right. Even from the main road, the smell of pig excrement was overpowering, and I felt sorry for the researchers and staff who worked there every day.

Arriving at the primary building, I parked in one of the visitor spaces, and, once in the building, easily found the main office. Four secretaries were clustered together, chatting about personal matters. I stood for a moment before interrupting them by clearing my throat. They all looked up, unhappy to see someone demanding that they work.

"May I help you?" the oldest woman asked.

"I have an appointment with Professor Meluso," I informed her.

"Professor?" she said. "He ain't no professor. He's a laboratory technician."

"He acts like he's a professor," another woman said in a high, affected voice. The others in the group chortled in unison.

The clown among the group stood up and goose-stepped around the office with her finger across the top of her lip. "Vere is Herr Meluso?" she repeated several times as the others continued laughing. Meluso was unpopular with the staff, I concluded.

An older grey-haired man in a tweed jacket and regimental tie entered the office. The secretaries scurried to their desks and tried to look busy.

"Hello, ladies," he said. "I hope you have enjoyed your afternoon so far."

"We have, Dr. Waters," they said almost in unison.

"Well, now I think we can get back to work on the report that I asked you to put together for tomorrow," he said, with a twinkle in his eye. All the women were smiling at each other and trying not to laugh.

Waters turned to me and asked what I wanted. "I'm here to see Mr. Meluso," I said.

"About what, may I ask?"

"I'm working on a missing person case that Meluso might have some knowledge about," I responded.

"Who are you working for?" he asked.

"I was hired by the Antaglias and am working with the Ithaca police to find their son. Detective Brett Snow is my contact person on the force," I explained.

"Oh, yes," he said. "I saw Detective Snow in the paper a few months ago. She participated in our local Dancing with the Stars charity event. She looked stunning in the picture wearing her tango outfit." I wouldn't mind seeing her in that myself, I thought.

The women in the office seemed a bit restless. Waters was clearly a favorite of theirs, and they didn't enjoy hearing him speak of other women.

"Well, I don't see any problem with your speaking with Meluso for a few minutes," he said. "In fact, I'll take you down to his facility."

He led me to the last building and knocked on the door. A voice with a strong German accent barked "Enter."

When Meluso saw Waters, he stood at rigid attention behind his desk. He looked like the picture in the Aurora yearbook, but the dark hair had turned grey. His face was still slender, with a sharp hooked nose upon which perched a pair of gold-rimmed glasses. He wore a white lab coat that was besmirched with filth from working with the hogs. He had attached to its lapel a small Central Lion pin.

"Meluso," Waters said, "you have a visitor that I think you are expecting."

"Mr. Stirling?" Meluso asked, glancing at me.

"That's right," I said.

Before leaving, Waters told Meluso to change his filthy lab coat. Meluso's eyes flashed with angry humiliation.

"Yes, sir," he said.

When Waters left, Meluso did not change his lab coat. Instead, he asked me what I wanted with him. His accent was strong and his language direct. He sat down at his desk and invited me to sit in a chair across from him.

"'I'm here to discuss Mitchell Antaglia, who has been missing for almost a month," I explained. "Do you have any idea of his whereabouts?"

"As you might have surmised," he said, taking a sip of water from a glass on his desk,"I know young Mitchell and have for some years. He is the child of the Antaglias. I have known Alberto and Aga—I mean Linda—for more than twenty years. We arrived here at Central the same year."

After you and Antaglia had been fired from Aurora, I thought.

"I understand that Antaglia and you had worked together at the same college in Kansas, Aurora," I said.

He looked at me blankly. "You are mistaken, Mr. Stirling," he said. "I met the Antaglias at Georgia Central. I have never set foot in Kansas."

He was lying, I knew, but didn't want to make him suspicious by calling him on it. "I must have received some misinformation," I said.

Waiting for my next question, Meluso looked at me with hard eyes.

"Do you have any idea where Mitchell is?" I asked again. "I have been working on the case for close to a week and have followed Mitch to Kansas and back to Ithaca. I'm trying to locate him and return him to his parents."

"Why in the world would Mitchell go to Kansas?" he asked, sipping his water.

I explained that he drove there with Roy Harrison, who was born in the state and was probably his father. I watched to see if Meluso reacted in any way to my claim of Roy's paternity. His eyes flashed in anger for an instant.

"I am not familiar with Mr. Harrison, but I do not think he is the father of young Mitch. I am certain that Alberto is."

Meluso glanced at his watch and then looked at me. "I am busy this time of the day with my swine," he said. "Would you like to join me as I make my rounds? We can continue talking."

Meluso was a common type I'd dealt with before. They were egotists when it came to their work and enjoyed telling anyone willing to listen about it. Since I might get some more information out of Meluso as he worked on his pigs, I accepted his offer to join him. He stood up, and I followed him.

"How many hogs do you have here?" I asked.

Meluso looked at me sharply. "Please do not call them pigs or hogs," he said. "They are either swine or boars, especially the ones I work with."

I apologized for my mistake, remembering that the sign on the road had used the word *hog* for the research center. That word must bother Meluso as he drove into the facility every morning and left it every night.

He led me to the next building to several sets of pens outside. One was filled with domestic pigs with pink skin, white hair, and loud snorts. "Are these the kind of pigs, I mean swine, that you work on?" I asked.

"I oversee their care," he said, "but I work with other kinds of swine. They are in the furthest pen to the right.

As we walked toward the pen, Meluso's attitude changed, and he started making soft snorting sounds. A batch of odd looking animals began to heave together. He took me over to the right side of the pen.

"These are my babies," he said, pointing at the mass.

As my eyes adjusted to the light, I saw a group of dark brown hairy beasts that didn't look like any domestic pig I had ever seen. Instead of being rotund, they were slender, almost sleek. They had raised backs and large heads that ended in a long, thin snout. Extending from their mouths were ivory tusks, pointed and sharp. They looked dangerous, and I noticed that for all his googooing over the animals, Meluso didn't touch them.

"These look like razorbacks," I said, referring to the mascot of the University of Arkansas.

"They are indeed related to the razorback," he agreed, "but I am attempting to develop a more aggressive swine."

"Why more aggressive?" I asked.

He took a deep breath as if he were tired of so much ignorance in the world about swine. Domestic swine, he explained, if let out into the wild, will quickly change into wild animals. They will look a bit like the swine he had just showed me. Though they go wild, they do not become fully aggressive.

"Why is it important for the swine to become more aggressive?" I asked again.

"My work is supported by the AHSA, the American Hunters and Sharpshooters Association, which is a spin-off from the NRA, an organization that I suspect you appreciate," he asserted.

While I often have appreciated my .38 in my line of work, there have been many other times that I wished the bad guys did not have their semiautomatic and automatic weaponry.

"So you're developing wild swine that are more aggressive for hunters," I noted.

"Exactly," he responded, looking at me like I was the bright student in the class.

"How are you doing that?" I asked.

Meluso mentioned that a few years ago he found a story about a group of aggressive wild boars in Wales that were attacking people and animals. The authorities were going to exterminate them, but he made arrangements to bring one of the most aggressive males to his program to mate with his female boars. It was quite difficult to get him through customs given the issues of disease transmittal. But Meluso had worked it out. The result was what he called his sounder, or group of wild boars, that he was showing me.

"Where's the boar from Wales?" I asked.

He pointed to a large animal in a distant pen. "That's him," he said. "The males don't stay in the sounders except during breeding season. I'll select the most aggressive females from his litters and breed him with them in hopes of enhancing aggression."

"Isn't it dangerous to make them more aggressive?" I asked.

He explained it wasn't so bad since many hunters will hunt his super swine from helicopters.

"Helicopters?" I asked. "Why would they want a more aggressive animal to hunt from the air?"

"Sarah Palin is a good spokesperson on this issue," he said. "She often speaks for the members of the AHSA."

I asked if he did anything else with these swine.

"I have been working on a drug regimen for swine that makes them, well, better athletes," he explained. He went on to say that he used various steroids and hormones to make the swine bigger, stronger, faster. His sounder was so aggressive he had to be careful that they didn't attack each other, he explained.

Almost on cue, two of his animals began squealing and grunting, nipping at each other's throats.

"Calm down, girls," he said firmly, picking up a wooden staff and thrusting it between the swine to force them apart. He looked at me sadly. "Some mornings I find one of my young females dead from being attacked by an older sister," he explained. "It is always very sad."

I told him that his drug treatment sounded expensive, and he agreed. "I am working to get the cost down to about $200 a swine," he said, "and I have made great progress."

"Even that sounds like a lot of money," I said.

"These swine are not for the average person," he assured me. "They are for the wealthy, who might want to populate their estates with super swine that they can enjoy hunting. But let me show you something else that I am working on."

He took me by the arm and led me to a separate pen to the left. This one was even darker. In the shadows I heard something snort and then, as my eyes adjusted to the dark, saw a massive creature heaving in the corner.

"Hello, Siegfried," he said, oddly cooing the name.

Siegfried snorted angrily. He did not want to be disturbed.

When he got to his feet, I saw that Siegfried must have weighed close to a half ton, maybe more. Like the super swine, he was long and lean, but his shoulders were even more massive and his tusks longer and sharper. He was covered with coarse dark hair, his head was elongated, and his eyes flashed anger.

"What did you do to breed Siegfried?" I asked, instinctively pulling back.

Meluso explained that he had taken a different approach with Siegfried. Instead of using drugs to make him stronger than other swine, he used artificial insemination to create a new kind of animal.

I looked at the animal and was filled with disgust. It looked prehistoric.

He explained in great detail how he bred the animal as a hybrid of a domestic swine and a wild boar. He had artificially inseminated the egg and placed it in the womb of the mother. "I have worked on this process for years," he said, "but all of my previous infant swine have died within months of being born. Only Siegfried, my Shining Lance, has survived to maturity."

Siegfried grunted in the shadows. He seemed unhappy that any other creature was alive.

"Perhaps you have heard of what the popular press called Hogzilla, which was a cross between a wild swine and a domestic pig," he said. "The creature was killed by a hunter in south Georgia a few years ago. Hogzilla weighed about 800 pounds, the same as my Siegfried. But Siegfried was not the result of random breeding as Hogzilla was. I have carefully planned his breeding. There has never been a creature like him, and I intend to clone him. The hunters will adore his progeny."

"I agree with you on that," I said. Siegfried had moved to the edge of his pen, snorting angrily at me. As he opened and closed his mouth, I could hear his tusks slashing together. "That is how he sharpens them," Meluso said with pride.

"Let me show you something," he continued. He went to a pen attached to the one Siegfried was in and opened a gate. A small domestic pig walked into Siegfried's pen, looking for food. At first Siegfried didn't seem to notice the intruder. Then his small eyes glared at the other animal. He moved his great girth like a flash and was on the smaller pig in an instant. The poor thing squealed as Siegfried dug his tusks into the animal's neck and belly. Blood spurted from the wounds, and the pig shuddered and fell to the ground. Siegfried began eating the dying creature, starting with the face. I turned away, repulsed by Siegfried and his creator.

Meluso seemed to recognize that he had gone too far and apologized if he had offended me. "I only show Siegfried to special visitors who understand the nature of scientific experimentation," he explained.

I thanked him for his information and for showing me his work. Then we made our goodbyes, and I left Meluso admiring Siegfried, who was snorting and squealing in glee over his feast.

As I drove back to Ithaca, I reflected on Meluso's character and work. His two projects were designed to challenge wealthy hunters by providing them super swine. The first project used performance-enhancing drugs to create a regular-sized but aggressive wild swine. The second used artificial insemination and cloning to create a bunch of monstrous Siegfrieds.

Meluso's background in East Germany, which was now known to have developed a state-sponsored system of providing athletes with performance-enhancing drugs, gave me pause. I remembered watching the Olympics during the '70s and '80s when the East Germans were suddenly producing world-class athletes that competed successfully against the U.S. The most famous example was Waldemar Cierpinski, the unknown East German athlete who switched from the steeple chase to the marathon in 1974 and won the event in the 1976 Olympics, beating the favorite, American Frank Shorter. Meluso, then named Herman Schultz, must have been involved in those projects. It is probable, I thought, that when he immigrated to the United States in the 1980s, he brought with him the then arcane knowledge of using drugs to enhance athletic performance. He used them at Aurora College and then here at Central. Was Meluso Mitch's Dr. Death? It was one thing to suspect but another to prove.

Returning to the motel room at 6:00 p.m., I showered, shaved, and put on a clean shirt for dinner. I then called the hospital to talk to Antaglia but found that he had been discharged earlier in the afternoon. "Who checked him out?" I asked, and the nurse at the front desk said that his wife had. I expressed my surprise that his wife had been allowed to take him given that she was not on his approved visitor list, but the nurse assured me that Linda Antaglia had every right to take her husband.

When I called the Antaglia home, Stella, the maid, answered and asked me how things were going in the search for Mitch. In the middle of giving her a very brief summary of my trip to Kansas, I heard Linda Antaglia summoning her, and she said she had to go in a minute. The Antaglias, she added quickly, were unable to come to the phone then. "They just got back from the hospital and are getting things set up for Coach," she said. I told her I'd like to talk to Mr. Antaglia as soon as possible and gave her my cell number for the coach. It was important to tell him that Mitch was back in town and seemed to be making plans that concerned them.

"Would it be possible to meet with you briefly to talk about Mitch?" I asked Stella.

She hesitated. "I'm not sure Mrs. Antaglia would like me talking behind her back," she said.

"If I hope to find Mitch," I said, "it's important that I talk to everyone who knows him well. From what everybody says, you are close to Mitch."

She said that she was like a mother to him and agreed to see me, but not at the Antaglias'. She gave me directions to her house in East Ithaca. She said she would drive home immediately. "I'll tell Mrs. Antaglia that I need to get something for tonight."

As I drove to East Ithaca, the neighborhoods began to change to smaller houses that were not kept up well. On turning down Stella's street, I saw groups of young African-American men shuffling about. It looked like they were buying and selling drugs. At the end of the street stood Stella's house. It was small but neat, painted white with a new brown roof. It stood out from the other houses on her street, which were in various states of disrepair.

Parking in front, I noticed that the closest group of men stared at me. Two broke away and walked in my direction. The door opened and Stella stepped onto the porch.

"Frog," she said to one of them, "this man is my guest. Get back to what you was doing before I call your mama to come get you."

I looked at the two males closely and saw that they were not men but boys about sixteen. They looked back at me, hesitated, and then turned and shuffled slowly back down the street to their group.

"I'm sorry, Mr. Stirling," she said when we had entered her house. "I should have warned you. This used to be a wonderful neighborhood, but it has gone down recently."

"No problem, Stella," I said, suddenly uncomfortable not knowing her last name. "By the way, what is your family name?"

"Gibson," she said, proudly. She pointed to a group of photographs on her wall of people clad in old-fashioned suits and dresses. "These are my ancestors," she said. "My family has lived in this house for four generations. I was born in the back room."

The living room was neat, clean, and carefully decorated.

The walls were painted a deep rust that matched the sofa. That and the other furniture looked old, but it was all refurbished. Most of the pieces looked like they had been in the family for generations.

Stella offered me coffee, which I accepted, and we were soon sitting together at the coffee table.

"What do you want to know about poor Mitchell?" she asked, looking at me sadly.

"I've spoken to several people," I said, "and I've gotten an inconsistent story about him. Some see him as dangerously aggressive, prone to fighting, and others see him as a young man with a sensitive, poetic nature. You've known Mitch his entire life. Can you tell me about him?"

Stella looked down as I talked. When she looked up, she had tears in her eyes.

"It's hard to explain what has happened to Mitch," she said. "I've known him since he was a baby, and he was the sweetest little boy you can imagine."

"Do you mean that he has changed since then?" I asked.

"He's changed since he learned he was adopted," she said.

This information supported what Roy had said about Mitch's birth, I noted.

"That can shake up any kid, especially if he finds out later in adolescence," I said. "Couldn't the Antaglias have children?"

"I think they tried for some time after they were married," Stella said. "I started working for them about that time, when they first came to Ithaca. Mrs. Antaglia was awful low, and I often found her crying in her room. She sometimes confided in me that she wanted a child. Then they got Mitch."

"What kind of an adoption was it, a private one?" I asked.

"I don't know how they adopted him," she responded. "The baby was just there one day, and I was supposed to take care of it."

"How did the Antaglias respond to Mitch?" I asked.

"The Coach was a typical man," she said. "He wasn't

involved with Mitch until he got old enough to play sports. Then he got real involved—maybe too involved."

"I've read his book on coaching," I said, "and know what you mean about being too involved. What about Mrs. Antaglia?"

"I've often thought about the way she treated her baby," Stella said. She explained that Mrs. Antaglia was desperate to get a baby, but when Mitch arrived, she didn't pay much attention to him. "Mostly made me take care of him and went out to see her friends," she said.

"Would you say she disliked Mitch?"

"It wasn't that," she explained. "It was more that she treated him like a little stranger rather than her son."

"Does she not like children?" I asked.

Stella shook her head. "No, because she loved her little girl, Christa" she said.

Not according to Detective Millar, I thought. He concluded that Mrs. Antaglia murdered her daughter.

"Could you tell me about Christa?" I asked.

Stella explained that four or five years after the Antaglias adopted Mitch, Mrs. Antaglia found herself pregnant. "Isn't that just the way things go?" she said.

"They often do," I agreed.

"Well, when little Christa was brought home from the hospital," Stella said, shaking her head, "Mrs. Antaglia couldn't do enough for that child. She played with her for hours, gave her the bottle, took her to the park for walks— she did everything for that girl baby that she didn't do for Mitch."

"How old was Mitch when Christa was born?" I asked.

"He was almost six, and he noticed that he was treated different," Stella said. "I could tell because he would come crying to me when his mama snapped at him or pushed him away from his sister."

"Did Mitch resent his sister?" I asked.

Stella shook her head adamantly. "No, he did not," she

asserted. "You'd think he would have, but he loved that little girl. When she died, you should have seen him cry. He was nine, and it was like the world had ended for him."

"How old was Christa when she died?" I asked.

"'Bout three or so," Stella said.

"What'd she die of?" I asked, knowing that she had drowned. But I wanted to hear Stella's version of the story.

"She drowned in the Antaglia's swimming pool," she said.

"Can you tell me how that happened?"

"Not really," Stella said. "I was off that day, and I heard later the little girl wandered into the pool and drowned. She couldn't swim."

"Was the pool not fenced?"

"It was," Stella said, "but for some reason the gate was unlocked that day, and Christa somehow got it open and fell in the pool."

"Was Mrs. Antaglia the only person home?"

"She was," Stella asserted, "but don't think she was at fault. The police checked into the whole thing and decided that Mrs. Antaglia was not responsible, not in any way. The DA considered indicting her but couldn't because she was innocent of that little child's death."

Stella seemed to be completely convinced of Mrs. Antaglia's innocence.

I decided to refocus on Mitch. "Why do you think Mrs. Antaglia treated her two children so differently, Stella?"

"I've thought on that many a time," she said. "It might have been that Mitch was not her blood and Christa was, but I always thought that something else was influencing her. It was like Mitch was tainted or something."

"Tainted?" I asked. That seemed like a strong word.

"It was as if the adoption never took," she said. "It was like Mitch wasn't really her child and never could be."

I had known many mothers who had adopted children and loved them as if they had given birth to them. It was not clear why Linda Antaglia couldn't fully accept Mitch.

Stella and I spoke for a few more minutes. She felt that she herself became Mitch's mother. Mitch came to her, not his mother, when he hurt himself or when he wanted to tell someone about his day. "And Lord I loved that boy." Gradually, she said, her relationship with Mitch changed. He fell under his father's control and spent most of his time practicing and playing basketball. "We were still close," Stella said, "but we weren't as close as we were when Mitch was young."

I thanked Stella for her time and insights into Mitch. At the door, I stopped and asked if she knew where Mitch was. "No," she said. "I just hope that boy gets aholt of himself and doesn't do anything stupid."

"What might he do?" I asked.

"I think Mitch has a lot of anger in him now," she said. "I hope he doesn't explode and hurt someone."

"Hope I find him before any explosion occurs," I responded.

I checked my watch and saw it was time to pick up Brett for dinner. Stella and I walked out together. She locked the door on her ancestors and headed to her other life in the Antaglia home.

Chapter 18

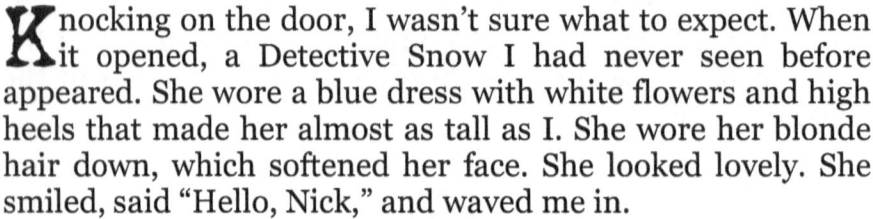

Knocking on the door, I wasn't sure what to expect. When it opened, a Detective Snow I had never seen before appeared. She wore a blue dress with white flowers and high heels that made her almost as tall as I. She wore her blonde hair down, which softened her face. She looked lovely. She smiled, said "Hello, Nick," and waved me in.

"I thought we could have a drink here before we left," she said.

"Good idea," I agreed, as I took her in my arms and kissed her.

"Easy, sailor," she said with a bright laugh. She had apparently forgiven me for being late for lunch.

She set out two glasses and poured herself some Chardonnay and me a Wild Turkey on the rocks. When she sat down, she said "Cheers," and we touched glasses.

"Now, tell me what you've discovered about Mitch Antaglia," she said.

I told her that Mitch was back in town, proof being that

two people had seen him, a teammate and his girlfriend.

"Rachel Stone?" Brett asked.

"Yes, the poetry student," I responded. "I've talked to her twice, and she seems like a wonderful girl who is pretty confused by Mitch's behavior."

"That's not an unusual feeling for a woman," she said to me pointedly. I grinned awkwardly and continued.

"Mitch now seems to be obsessed with finding his biological father," I explained. "He also is angry, probably at the Antaglias."

"Why is he specifically angry at them?" she asked.

"Mitch felt mistreated by the two of them for some reason I don't fully understand," I said. Two events in his life seemed to stand out, I continued. First, his birth to Cynthia Barnes and subsequent adoption by the Antaglias were shrouded in mystery, and Mitch now was determined to understand them. Second, Antaglia appeared to have driven Mitch hard to be a basketball star. The young man now wrote poetry and much of his work expressed anger at his adoptive father. "I don't know how far Mitch's anger will take him," I said, "but Rachel told me earlier today that Mitch had a gun and might use it on the Antaglias."

"I heard about that," she said. "Rachel reported the incident you mention to the department. There is now a search on for Mitch."

I told her about my experiences with Meluso and his super swine.

"That's gross," she said when I told her about Siegfried eating the domestic pig. "That guy should be deported to Germany where he belongs."

"Where does the deportation stand?"

"The ICE people have been put on hold until the Ithaca police give them the word to begin the deportation hearing," she explained.

"That's a good plan," I agreed. "It's best at this point not to get Meluso worked up so that we can get some cooperation from him about Mitch."

Brett looked at me closely. "You don't think Meluso is still using any of his drugs on humans, do you Nick?"

"Don't know. But I'm pretty sure he has done so in the past," I responded, telling her about Meluso teaching Chemistry in Aurora when Cynthia Barnes received her drug treatments. I also told her Meluso was probably Mitch's Dr. Death, the man who drugged up the basketball team under Coach Fletcher. "I'm not certain at this point all Meluso has done with steroids and hormones in this country," I said. "We'll have to develop a strategy for getting information out of Herr Meluso."

We spoke for another half hour about the case. Glancing at my watch, I told Brett it was time to go. I helped her with her coat and led her to the Honda. We arrived at the Fennel Seed, a downtown bistro, for our reservations with seconds to spare.

The maître d' sat us in a cozy corner, and our server, who introduced himself as Bob, had just taken our drink order when my cell buzzed.

I started to turn it off, but Brett said that I'd better answer it, especially given what Rachel had told me about Mitch and the gun. On opening the phone I heard Stella Gibson's distinctive voice on the other end.

"Is this Mr. Nick?" she asked. She was breathing hard and clearly upset.

"Yes it is, Stella," I said, giving Brett a concerned look. "What's up?"

Stella told me that Mitch had shown up at the Antaglia house with a gun. He had taken his parents hostage and made his mother call Meluso.

"Why Meluso?" I asked.

"I overheard Mitch say that he wanted all three of them together so that he could straighten something out," she said.

"Did you call the police?"

"Oh no, sir," she said. "He told me not to. He said he'd kill his parents as soon as he heard a siren or saw a police vehicle. And I believed him, Mr. Nick," she continued. "Mitch didn't look like his old self at all. No sir. He looked like he was half dead, white as a sheet with devil eyes."

"Do you know where he was taking the Antaglias?"

"He said the Swine Research Center," she said.

"You mean the Hog Research Center," I corrected.

"Where they work on pigs," she continued. "Meluso was going to meet them there."

I thanked Stella for calling and told her to stay where she was. "I'll call back later if I need anything from you," I told her.

"Yes sir, Mr. Nick," she said, sounding glad to have someone else calling the shots.

Closing my cell, I looked over at Brett. She looked back with the eyes of a police officer who was ready to take charge.

"Looks like our date is going to be interrupted," I said, tossing enough money on the table for the drinks and a tip. "I'll take you home."

"No you won't, Nick," she said. "I overheard enough to have a general idea about what's going on. You might need some backup. And if you have to arrest Mitch, I'll be there to perform the act."

"What about your shoes, your dress?"

She didn't answer but got up and led me out of the Fennel Seed to my car parked a block away.

As we drove out to the hog center, I filled Brett in on the details of Stella's conversation with me she might not have caught. I then described the way the buildings at the center were laid out. We made a preliminary plan of how we would approach Mitch and the group he had collected. We decided not to call the Ithaca police because we were afraid Mitch might hear sirens and shoot his victims. We intended to walk past the buildings from the first to the last until we found where Mitch was holding his hostages. Then we would plan our next move, depending on what we found.

As we drove into the Hog Center, I saw the familiar black Cadillac, parked in a visitor space. It now had a Kansas plate, which explained why the Ithaca police could not locate it. Next to it stood a blue Volkswagen bug that must have belonged to Meluso.

"I'll park behind the Caddie," I said told Brett, "to block Mitch in."

I then took my .38 from the glove compartment and showed it to her. She nodded in agreement that I should take it, and reached into her handbag and pulled out her pistol. I returned her nod. She left her heavy coat in the car, and we walked as quietly as possible through the complex, looking for Mitch. After passing about half of the buildings, we heard some voices in the last one, a building ahead. Brett, holding her heels in her hand because of the soft, uneven ground, and I walked up to the far edge of Meluso's building and the pen connected to it. Light flooded from the back of the building onto the concrete flooring in front of the super swines' pen. I thought I heard Siegfried grunting angrily, but it might have been some of the other swine or just the wind rustling through the trees. The two of us moved up behind the building and looked around the corner. We saw a tall young man, pointing his gun at the group. I could tell it was Mitch from the picture Rachel had given me.

One member of the group was Antaglia, looking shaky. He sat in the far corner on what looked like a box. His face was a sickly white, and his head drooped on his chest. I couldn't tell if he was sick from Roy's gun shot wound or if Mitch had recently manhandled him. Wearing a white dress, Linda Antaglia stood ten yards away from her husband with her arms crossed. They looked like strangers who happened to be waiting for the same bus. Meluso stood between them against Siegfried's pen as if at attention, with his arms hanging at his sides, his eyes fixed attentively on Mitch's face. The group had obviously just arrived, and Mitch was speaking to them as if he were a teacher making himself painfully clear to a group of slow learners.

As I watched Mitch, it became clear I had seen him twice before. His build looked very much like that of the man I'd seen running from Connolly's house in the dark, and he was definitely the person fleeing from Mrs. Harrison's farmhouse in Kansas. The Missile had a lot to answer for.

Brett was shivering, so I took off my suit jacket and put it over her shoulders. She looked up at me appreciatively. "Its cold," she whispered and returned her eyes to the meeting. A moment later she whispered, "Do you think we should call backup?"

"Not now," I replied. "According to Stella, Mitchell might shoot if he hears sirens."

"O.K.," she said doubtfully.

"And it's probably a good idea for us to remain here rather than interrupt the show," I added. I didn't mention my desire to discover as much about Mitch as possible before taking him. He'd probably clam up then.

It looked like he was ready to begin the first act of his drama.

"Let's begin with my mother," Mitch said, pointing his gun at Linda Antaglia.

"*I* am your mother, Mitchie," she said firmly. She appeared to suspect that Mitch was referring to a woman other than her.

"You? My mother?" Mitch sneered. "I'm talking about my real mother, Cynthia Barnes."

Linda Antaglia looked like she had been hit in the stomach with a bowling ball.

"I have been more your mother than that . . . woman," she said. "Who took care of you every day? Who oversaw your upbringing to make you a man?"

"You didn't take care of me, Adalinda," he said accusingly. Mrs. Antaglia jumped in surprise upon hearing that name. "Do you think I don't know your real name?" he asked. "Adalinda means noble serpent in German. I looked it up online. I don't know much about your being noble, but you certainly are a snake." He practically spit the last words out. "And you never took care of me," he continued. "Stella was the one I went to for help. If I hurt myself, she'd put a band-aid on the wound. If a child bullied me in school, she's talk to me about it. If I felt lonely, she'd be my friend."

"Mitchell, I too did all of those things for you," she insisted.

He glared at her across the pavement. "You were kind to me?" he asked. "All I remember is you rejecting me and telling me to be a little man, Adalinda."

"Well, I didn't want to spoil you like American mothers spoil their sons, making them weak. I wanted you to be strong. And look at you," she said, pointing at him. "You are big and strong, built like a tank."

"Like a Panzer, Adalinda?" he asked. "Like a good German machine with no feelings?"

"No, I don't mean you have no feelings," she said, stumbling among her thoughts. "I have read some of your poetry," she said. "You express feelings there."

Mitchell laughed. "And you want to claim that my poetry is because of you?" he said.

"Well, to some extent," she said. "I gave you, no matter how indirectly, the spirit of German Idealism."

"And no love," he responded angrily. "I only knew my real mother for a few weeks but got more from her in that short time than from you all my life. She told me about how she was forced to sell me to you. You couldn't have a child of your own so you bought me. You bought me for $20,000, cash on the barrel, and then never let her— my real mother— see me when I was a child."

"Mitchie," Adalinda said, "you can't put that on my shoulders. That's the way Cynthia wanted it. She and that husband of hers, Roy Harrison, took that money back to Kansas. She never told me she wanted to see you," she said, beginning to sob.

"And what about my other mother?" he said, glaring at her.

"I take it you don't mean me!" she snarled.

"No, I don't mean you," he snapped. "I mean Professor Connolly, my spiritual mother. She was the one who took me under her wing and taught me to be a poet. She made me come alive for the first time. She made me realize how much I hated you and him." Mitch pointed with the gun to the slumping figure of Antaglia, who was unresponsive. "And why are both of my real mothers dead?" he demanded to know.

Adalinda Antaglia pulled back in apparent fear, and said, looking at the ground, "I will talk no more about your absurd accusations."

"And what about you, my dear father?" Mitch demanded, taking a few steps toward Antaglia's hunched figure. He pointed the gun at him, and Antaglia stirred, raising his head and looking down the barrel.

Detective Snow pulled at my sleeve and whispered, "I'm getting worried, Nick. Shouldn't we try to stop this before Mitch does something stupid?"

"Wait," I said. I had the feeling that Mitch was acting out his anger rather than letting it determine his actions. He was like a playwright, and this was his production.

"What do you want with me, Mitch?" Antaglia demanded. "Haven't you done enough harm?"

"Harm?" he asked. "How have I harmed you?"

"Look at me," he said in a raspy voice. "I was wounded by Roy Harrison in a false kidnapping scheme that you helped cook up."

"What if I did, old man," Mitch said. "We decided not to ask for much money, just enough to let you know we got the better of you."

"But I ended up being shot," he complained. "I was almost killed."

"Only because you shot Roy first," Mitch said. "Instead of

just giving him the money, you shot him in the leg. He had to shoot you to protect himself."

As I reflected on that stormy night when I witnessed the transaction, that explanation of events seemed accurate. It looked to me at the time that Antaglia shot first to prevent Roy from taking the money.

"Why would you want to take advantage of me that way?" Antaglia asked. "What have I ever done to you but help make you the best basketball player you could be? You could play in the pros, in the NBA, be a white Michael Jordan."

Mitch laughed derisively again. "Haven't you figured anything out yet?" he asked. "Haven't you seen the writing on the wall? I'll never be in the pros. I'm not good enough. I couldn't even transfer to another school," he said.

"No," Antaglia said wearily. "That's not true. I made you a great player. You proved that I am a great coach. Nobody here ever recognized my greatness, but I have shown it through you, my own son."

"And how did you do that, you old fraud?" Mitch demanded.

The term *old fraud* seemed to shock Antaglia. He hesitated before answering: "I made you what you are through my method. I practiced with you every day and made you work on your stamina by running every morning. And then we watched the great players of the NBA every night to teach you their moves. I saw how great you were, Mitch, when you played in the shoe leagues and in high school."

"If I'm so great," Mitch said, "why do I sit on the bench every game?"

Antaglia said it was the new coach, who ran a sissy game of ball control and zone defense. "That's not the game they play in the pros, running the fast break and shooting on the run. You're prepared for that and will be the new great white player in the NBA, the new white Kobe Bryant."

Mitchell stood shaking his head scornfully. "You did all

this not for me," he said, "but for yourself. You wanted to prove that you were a great coach, and you used me to prove that."

Antaglia shook his head vehemently. "It is true that I was mistreated here at Central Georgia," he said. "I was going to be the head men's basketball coach. But I had enemies in the Athletic Program, starting with Seamer. He was against me from the beginning and wouldn't live up to the promises that were made to me."

Adalinda suddenly began laughing. "Listen to the man," she said scornfully. "Listen to the lies he tells."

"Don't, Linda," he pleaded. "Don't humiliate me."

"How do you think, Mitch, that your father the coach got his job at Central?" she asked. "Before he came here, he was the assistant women's basketball coach at a small Bible college in Kansas."

"Aurora," Mitch said.

"Yes, Aurora," she sneered. "And he was being kicked out of there for," she stopped for an instant, "for screwing Cynthia Barnes. Why would Central hire a loser like him?" she asked, pointing her finger at his head.

"Don't," Antaglia begged, "please don't."

"I'll tell you why, Mitch," she continued. "My family donated some money, a lot of money, to the new athletic complex that was then being planned. I gave the money for the athletic hall of fame. Have you ever walked through the hall of fame, Mitch?"

"Yes," he responded, "but I haven't looked at it closely."

"Well, if you do," she said, "you will see a list of contributors, including Linda Becker. I gave over half a million dollars, which was real money back then. And do you know what I requested for that money?" she asked sarcastically. Nobody responded. "I asked that my fiancee be hired as an assistant coach. And he was."

Antaglia had slumped back on his box. He seemed to be sobbing.

"I had thought, of course, that my wonderful husband would be successful and work his way up, become a head coach," she said. "But did he? No, he did not advance beyond the lowest coaching jobs."

"So that's why he was so determined to make me a great player," Mitchell mused, looking at his adoptive mother. "He was a failure and used me as his guinea pig to test his method, the one he wrote about in *Coaching Genius*." He stood glaring at Antaglia, who seemed to have passed out again on his box.

Mitch then turned his gun on Meluso, who stood against the fence of Siegfried's pen. He was smiling oddly at Mitch, as if he were proud of him.

"And what about you, Dr. Death?" Mitch asked.

Brett whispered to me, "So Meluso is the good doctor." I nodded.

"Don't call me that, Mitch. I am not a killer. I am a creator of new life," he claimed.

"Creator?" Mitch snorted dismissively. "You are a destroyer not a creator. Ever since I was a teenager, you came to my house and injected me with drugs that you claimed made me a better athlete."

"The drugs did not harm you, Mitch," Meluso said. "They helped you. Look at your physique. Do you think you would be as big and strong as you are without my enhancements?"

"I might not have become as strong, but I would have turned into a better person. I was sixteen before I knew what roid rage was. But as soon as I heard about it, I knew I had it. I realized that all those fights the first years in high school were due to the drugs you gave me."

"That kind of rage is much exaggerated," Meluso claimed. But his voice had lost its authority, and he began to look beaten down. "Enemies of drug enhancement claim that that kind of anger exists, but all the scientific studies I have read question its existence."

Mitch looked at him scornfully. "I don't need a scientific

study to convince me that I feel less anger now that I don't take your drugs," he said, as he waved the gun in Meluso's face. The irony of his situation apparently escaped him. "And what about my mother?" Mitch asked.

"Adalinda?" Meluso responded.

"No, my real mother, Cynthia Barnes," Mitch said.

"What about her?" Meluso asked haughtily.

Mitch said that she had told him before her death that Meluso had injected her regularly during the '80s with various kinds of performance enhancing drugs, many of which were experimental. "She said you gave her a range of steroids that came from the East German Olympics program," he said.

Meluso looked like he was losing control of his emotions.

"How dare she complain about all that I did to help her!" he shouted. "She wanted to become the best basketball player she could be and would do anything to achieve this goal. Part of what she wanted was the best steroid and hormone regimen available at the time, and I gave her that!"

Mitch looked at him with hatred in his eyes. "And what about her face?" he asked. "What about the way her face looked after your treatments?"

Meluso thought for a moment before saying, "It is true that Cynthia had some facial bone deformity that affected her looks. I told her she should not take too much Human Growth Hormone, but she insisted that the injections were helping her develop physically and always wanted more."

"Didn't you see what was happening to her? And why didn't you insist that she stop the pills and injections?" Mitch snapped.

"Keep in mind, Mitch, that I gave Cynthia those drugs before we understood much about hormone treatments. Perhaps Cynthia went too far in her requests ..."

"And you had nothing to do with this, you bastard?" Mitch snapped. "You ruined a young woman's life by causing facial deformities that she felt made her look like a monster."

Meluso shook his head vehemently to deny this last accusation. "Today many doctors give patients these same treatments to make them look younger. You'll find ads for them in the Atlanta papers. I was just a pioneer of these treatments," he claimed.

I could tell that Mitch was falling into exhaustion from the stress of this series of conversations and his recent long road trip. But he had one more act to direct.

"The last thing I need to know is, who is my father?" he asked the group before him.

Antaglia suddenly came alive again and said, "I am your father, Mitch. How can you doubt that?"

"I don't think any father would treat his son as you treated me. I was nothing more than a coaching experiment for you. But what makes you so sure you're my father?" Mitch asked. "Did you have an affair with Cynthia?"

Adalinda stiffened noticeably when she heard the word *affair*.

Antaglia looked at Adalinda before he spoke. "Yes, I had an affair with Cynthia in Kansas. It lasted for almost a year, and I had it not because I loved her but because I thought she would help me produce an exceptional basketball player. But she never got pregnant. It was later, when she was in Atlanta, that I had the idea of in vitro fertilization using her egg and my sperm. The fetus would be implanted in Cynthia's womb, she would give birth, and I would pay her a sum of money for the baby. She signed a standard surrogate contract. She was happy with it until she had the baby. Then she wanted to keep it—you, Mitch—until I paid her the money. Then she was happy to give it—you—up."

"Who performed the artificial insemination?" Mitch asked.

Antaglia looked uncomfortable. "Meluso," he murmured.

"You had a pig researcher perform the procedure!" Mitch shouted, making Antaglia jump.

Meluso stiffened and said, "Do not forget that I am a

medical doctor. In East Germany I was trained on people, not on swine."

"So Antaglia is my father," Mitch said.

Adalinda and Meluso looked at each other for a moment.

"No," Meluso said.

"What?" Mitch and Antaglia responded in unison.

Meluso looked again at Adalinda, who nodded slightly for him to go ahead.

He reminded Antaglia of the Saturday he performed the in vitro fertilization of Cynthia. Antaglia said that he remembered the day well.

"When I put that sperm sample you gave me under the microscope," Meluso said, "I found that you were sterile. Most of your sperm were dead. Those that were alive were deformed. Most had two tails. There was no way to use your sperm in the process."

Antaglia looked at him blankly, with his mouth hanging open.

"That explains, Alberto, why we could never have children," Adalinda interrupted. "It was not my fault, as you always claimed, but yours."

"So I took a sample of my own seed," Meluso said, "and used that to impregnate Cynthia. As you know, the pregnancy was successful and Mitchell was the result." Meluso looked at Mitch with that odd sense of pride I had noticed earlier.

"Wait!" Antaglia said, looking back and forth between Meluso and Adalinda. "How can I be sterile when I was the father of Christa, who was born four years later?"

Adalinda looked again at Meluso, and he nodded slightly to encourage her to talk.

"You fool, Alberto. You weren't Christa's father. Herman was."

"But we had relations about that time," Antaglia pointed out. "You let me sleep with you then."

"That's true," Adalinda said. "As soon as I found myself

pregnant, I slept with you a few times. I'm sure you remember that Christa was premature but didn't you wonder why she was the normal size?"

"So you and Herman were having an affair then?" Antaglia asked.

"We were and still are, Alberto," Meluso announced. "And we are very much in love."

Chapter 19

On learning that he was a cuckold, Antaglia suddenly came to life. He sprang off his box and threw himself at Meluso, who stood in front of Siegfried's pit. Antaglia hit him in the stomach with his shoulder, and Meluso tumbled over the fence and into the giant swine's pit. Mitch watched the action with eyes wide, shouted, "Stop!" and pointed his pistol at Antaglia, who had slumped to the ground in exhaustion. Adalinda had run to the pen, screaming hysterically to everyone to save Meluso. I could hear Siegfried grunting and squealing in excitement. Meluso screamed in either pain or fear.

"It's time to stop this!" I said to Brett, taking my .38 from my jacket pocket. "I'll take care of Mitch and then go after Meluso!" She nodded, holding up her pistol.

I rushed around the corner of the building and, five yards from Mitch, shouted, "Drop the weapon, Mitch!"

He turned from the scene in front of him and saw me when it was too late. I threw my full 200 pounds at his knees in a perfect body block and took him down. Landing on his knees, I heard a sharp pop. Mitch screamed in agony.

Brett was right behind me and picked up Mitch's gun from the ground.

"I've got him, Nick," she said calmly. She stood about five yards from Mitch with her gun pointing at his chest. I heard her tell him to roll over and put his hands behind his neck.

"My knee! my knee!" Mitch moaned.

I was already on my way to Siegfried's pit. Once there, I pushed Adalinda Antaglia out of the way. She was leaning into the pit trying to reach Meluso, who was now partially under Siegfried. I had a clear shot at the animal's head and raised my .38, aiming between Siegfried's vicious little eyes. When I fired, a stream of blood spurted from his head and splattered across the front of Adalinda Antaglia's white dress.

I jumped into the pit and watched the wounded swine struggle to move his girth to the back of his pen, his legs thrashing. When he was completely off Meluso, I shot the animal again, then again, aiming where I assumed the heart was. The giant hog squealed a few times and then began to breathe heavily until he went silent.

Meanwhile, I pulled Meluso to his feet and pushed him up against the wall.

"Can you stand?" I asked.

Meluso mumbled he could but immediately slid down to a sitting position. I examined him as best I could and saw that Siegfried had sliced him badly with his tusks across his shoulders, near his neck. He was lucky to be alive.

"How are you doing, Brett?" I called out.

"Everything's under control up here, Nick," she responded.

"Good job," I said, pulling myself over the fence and out of the pit. Glancing back, I saw Meluso sitting there, looking sadly at the remains of years of research, Siegfried.

Brett had called the Ithaca police on her cell soon after I went over the edge of the pit, and the sirens approached in the distance. She had also rounded up the Antaglias. Adalinda, Alberto, and Mitch were all seated in a line against the building. Brett stood in front of them with her gun at the ready. She grinned at me as I approached and stepped toward me.

"Antaglia has been talking," Brett said quietly.

"About what?"

"He told me his wife confided in him yesterday that she and Meluso had murdered the professor and Cynthia Barnes," she said.

"Do you believe him?" I asked.

"I'm not sure," Brett responded, "but his wife told him to shut up without contradicting him."

"I'm not sure that kind of vengeful statement made in anger will stand up in court, but we have to take it seriously," I said. "Adalinda is a wealthy woman with the means to flee the country."

"You think we should arrest the two of them?"

"Yes," I said.

Brett read Mrs. Antaglia her rights and instructed her to remain seated.

"I want my lawyer," she demanded.

"You'll be able to call one at the station house," Brett responded.

Then she turned to me. "Looks like we did a good night's work, Stirling. But I still expect my dinner."

"You bet," I responded.

Within a few minutes, four police vehicles drove over the grass, parked beside the building, and turned off their sirens. Detective Bronson, Brett's sometime partner, got out of the first vehicle with another detective, and Brett brought them up to speed on the situation. Bronson took over from Brett the oversight of the Antaglias, and I directed three uniformed officers to follow Brett and me to the pit. I quickly explained what had happened, and one of the officers said, "Suey! How 'bout that hog!" when he trained his flashlight on Siegfried lying dead in the far corner.

That officer turned to the other and asked how much bacon he thought Siegfried might provide.

"Siegfried weighs about 800 pounds," I said, and the other officer shook his head in amazement.

Two of us dropped down into the pit and handed the now semiconscious Meluso up to two other officers as Brett supervised. The five of us managed to work him over the fence and lay him on the ground. By that time, two ambulances had arrived, and the medical personnel hurried over to Meluso and began working on his wounds.

"Doesn't look too serious," one of them said to me, "but he's lost some blood and the cuts might become infected by the pig saliva."

"Swine," I corrected him. He looked at me oddly.

Meluso came to and opened his eyes. "Where is Siegfried?" he asked.

I explained Siegfried had attacked him, and I'd had to shoot the beast.

"Siegfried wouldn't attack *me*," he said, and repeated that assertion several times as they lashed him onto the gurney and placed him in the ambulance after Brett had read him his rights. He was to be taken to the hospital and later, when he was well enough, to the county jail. The second ambulance, containing Mitch, followed the first. Bronson called the station house and asked that officers meet the ambulances to oversee Meluso and Mitch.

Antaglia had come back to life and watched his wife crying about her lover's departure.

"Linda," he started to say.

"Don't call me Linda," she growled at him in a now stronger German accent. "My name is Adalinda, and I am finished with you."

"But I still love you, Adalinda," he cried.

Adalinda did not answer. She walked away stiffly and got into one of the patrol cars.

"Drive me home," she commanded.

I walked up to the officer at the wheel and told him she was not going home tonight.

"Take her to the county jail and book her for the murders of Cynthia Barnes and Professor Elaine Connolly," I said.

"People like me don't go to jail," she hissed at me.

"They do when they're accused of murder," I responded.

I returned to Antaglia, helped him up, and walked him to another squad car. "Take him home and see that he gets in," I told the two officers. When the vehicle left, I called Stella and told her to take care of Antaglia. "He'll need some assistance," I said. "Today, he lost his son, his wife, his daughter, and his self-respect." I explained briefly what I meant by that statement and told her I'd be over later that night to check on Antaglia.

I left Brett and the remaining detectives and officers to finish processing the scene and went to look around Meluso's lab. It was spotless. While inspecting the various closets and cupboards in it, I found nothing of interest. Outside, I opened a storage closet full of equipment for caring for swine. In the far corner, something caught my attention. In a white canvas bag with red spots on it, I discovered two large knives, a knife sharpener, and a hacksaw. The larger knife was honed razor sharp and covered with dried blood. It had not been cleaned after the last time it was used.

I took out the bag with the untouched implements still in it and showed them to the two uniformed officers still on the scene. One of them looked closely at the implements and said:

"My Uncle Martin uses tools like that to slaughter hogs.

That there small knife is for cutting around bone. It's called a boning knife. That big 'un with the blood on it is a butcher knife. Uncle uses it to slit the hogs' throats. The hacksaw cuts through bone."

I looked at Brett and said the butcher knife should be taken to the nearest crime lab. "I'd like to have that blood tested for DNA," I said. "I have a feeling that it might be human. It should also be compared with the blood of Cynthia Barnes and Professor Connolly. We might very well have a match. And check the knife for fingerprints," I added.

She nodded, and told one of the officers to place the bag in his evidence case in the trunk of his vehicle and take it back to the station house.

'It'll take about a week to get the results back," she said to me, "so we should get started on this now."

I looked around Meluso's lab again and found the glass on his desk that he drank from that afternoon. Picking it up with my handkerchief, I took it out to Brett.

"Meluso drank from the glass earlier," I said. "It will undoubtedly have his fingerprints on it to compare with those on the knife."

"Good work, Nick," she said, and called an officer over to put the glass with the other material we'd found at the scene.

Brett turned to me and said she was going to the police station with the two detectives to oversee the paperwork. I offered to drive her to the station, and she accepted. As I followed the police cars, Brett said she would try to have Dr. Largo of the Forensics Laboratory do a preliminary analysis of the blood on the knife in the morning. I could check on his progress if I wanted.

When I dropped her off, she kissed me on the cheek. "Things have been pretty exciting around here since you arrived," she joked, getting out of the car. She went into the station to begin the long process of checking in the evidence and making the necessary reports.

I drove to Antaglia's house and rang the bell. In a few minutes, Stella opened the door and told me that Antaglia was in bed. "I need to examine some of Antaglia's files," I explained, and she led me to his office and pointed to the wooden file cabinets I had notice earlier. Both were locked. "Where are the keys?" I asked, and she looked in the desk and took out a small box with a set of keys that opened the cabinets.

"Are you sure Coach wants you to look through his files?" she asked.

I assured her I had Antaglia's best interests at heart, and I believed that was the case. "Getting at the truth of the Antaglia family would help Antaglia," I asserted. Stella nodded and walked out of the office.

I looked through the folders, most of which concerned his book and brokerage accounts, found an old one labeled "Becker, Linda," and sat at Antaglia's desk to read it. In it was a long personal letter written by Linda's older sister by five years, Vala, to Antaglia dated 1986. The letter was written in broken English filled with German expressions, but I easily got the gist of it. It warned Antaglia not to marry Linda, the Americanized form of Adalinda, because she suffered from a dangerous personality disorder.

Vala told the story of Linda's childhood. Her mother, a society matron, paid little attention to Linda and died young, when Linda was thirteen. Linda suffered a mental collapse. Their father, Wilhelm, a wealthy industrialist, sent her to the best psychiatrists, who diagnosed her as suffering from an antisocial personality disorder, then called a sociopathic disorder, with a particular hatred of her deceased mother, whom she felt had deserted her. Four years later, Wilhelm remarried a much younger women, a German actress named Raina Lange. Linda was ecstatic to have a mother again. But Raina also rejected Linda. Raina was primarily interested in her film career and married the wealthy Becker because he could help her advance in it. The marriage ended in divorce in three years but not before Linda, then nineteen, had suffered a second breakdown.

Vala continued her story by describing what Linda did soon after Vala herself married in her mid-twenties and got pregnant. That summer, Linda invited her sister to the Becker family's chalet near the ski resort of Garmisch-Partenkirchen to talk over some private family issues. Once Vala was there, Linda attacked her and locked her in the cellar to starve to death. Vala survived only because one of the handymen working for the family arrived unannounced to complete some repairs. He released Vala and the incident became notorious in Germany. Linda became known in the popular press as the sister killer. She escaped a prison sentence only because of her family's wealth and connections.

Becker was a proud man deeply embarrassed by Linda's bizarre behavior. He decided, Vala wrote, to remove Linda from Germany after her trial. He was planning a business trip to the US to open Markardial, a plant to produce veterinary medicines, to be built near either Lawrence, Kansas, or Ithaca, Georgia. He brought along Linda to marry her off to an American husband so that Becker could be done with her.

I remembered from the Worshing files that Becker was a well-known Olympic athlete who had specialized in the decathlon. He easily associated during his visit with various American athletes, including college coaches. At a KU athletic dinner, he met the unmarried Antaglia, a minor coach from nearby Aurora College, and Linda, with considerable prodding from her father, found the much older man acceptable as a fiancée.

"That American husband will be you, Mr. Antaglia," Vala concluded her letter. "My sister is a sick woman, a woman who hates mothers and is determined to destroy them as she tried to destroy me and my baby. Do not trust this monster, do not marry her no matter how much money my father offers to you."

Antaglia did not take Vala's advice, and I saw why. In that same file was a signed contract between Antaglia and Wilhelm Becker. Although complicated, it in essence made Antaglia an offer he couldn't refuse. Upon his marrying Linda, she would receive a substantial share of the Becker estate. This amount was 3.5 million dollars. While Antaglia could not touch the principal, which remained in Linda's name, he would have access to its significant interest income. In addition, Antaglia was to receive regular sums to continue Linda's psychiatric treatments in the hope of curing her aggressive sociopathic tendencies. He was required to remain married to her or the contract would be voided and the money returned to Becker or his estate. Antaglia was also required to prevent his wife from returning to Germany without Wilhelm's permission.

The information in Antaglia's Linda Becker file made clear to me two points that were not clear earlier. It explained why Linda married Antaglia, an unlikely suitor for a young European heiress, and it explained why Linda would murder the two women that Mitch considered his mothers.

I left the office, found Stella, and told her I'd be back tomorrow to check on Antaglia, who she said was awake but quiet.

Chapter 20

The next morning I went to Ithaca's police station but didn't go in because Brett had told me not to disturb the interrogation of Adalinda Antaglia, which would be taking place there. Adalinda had spent the night in the city jail and was undoubtedly in a foul mood. No telling what she would say, I thought to myself, but I had a feeling she would try to protect herself. She might well give over to the police Herman Meluso/Schultz, her longtime lover.

I followed Brett's directions to the crime laboratory, which was located behind the station, and entered the cinder-block building. A secretary greeted me, and I identified myself.

"Oh, yes, Mr. Stirling," she said. "Detective Snow said you would be coming by for some information on our two most recent murder cases."

She picked up her phone, punched a number, and spoke to Dr. Largo, the forensics specialist. She put down the phone and sent me down a long corridor to the right.

"Go to the end, and Dr. Largo's office is on the left," she said pleasantly.

I thanked her and soon found myself at Largo's door. I knocked and he yelled for me to enter.

The office was small and cluttered, filled with shelved books on the science of forensics. Dr. Largo was a small man sitting behind a large desk piled high with papers. He wore a lab coat and had a pair of thick wire-rim glasses perched on his pug nose.

"Detective Snow said you'd probably stop by this morning," he said.

I explained my interest in the two murder cases.

"Brett said that you've been very helpful in investigating the two murders," he said, "and I think I have some good news for you."

He picked up a printed paper from his desk and handed it over. I looked through it quickly to find what I needed to know. Largo had run a number of preliminary analyses of the blood on the butcher knife and drew the following conclusions. First, the knife had some remnants of swine blood on it. Second, the visible blood was human.

I asked about fingerprints, and Largo said that the only prints found were Meluso's.

"I did an initial comparison of a thumb print on Meluso's glass that you gave me and a thumb print on the knife's handle. Looked like a match to me, but I wouldn't bet my life on it. I'll send the prints to the Georgia Bureau of Investigation for further analysis. I'll have to send the knife and the blood samples of the two victims there for DNA tests to see if they match. I could have the results back in about a week if all goes well," Largo explained.

Thanking him, I left his office and decided to check on young Mitch to see how he was doing. I felt some responsibility for his knee and wanted to see how much damage my body block had done. I had a feeling he might be wherever Rachel was, and I was right. When I called her cell, she seemed excited to hear from me and told me that she and Mitch, who she had gotten from the hospital, were at the Café All Day having breakfast. She invited me over, and I went.

The two of them were sitting at a back table with their heads together. They looked like any young lovers you would find talking in a campus coffee shop. Mitch had a pair of crutches leaning against the wall behind him.

Rachel saw me first, and her face broke into a huge smile. She said something to Mitch, who looked in my direction, and then she ran toward me and gave me a hug.

"Thank you, thank you, thank you for getting Mitch back!" she squealed.

The other people in Café All Day looked up from their newspapers and laptops and smiled when they saw Rachel hopping about in glee.

"I was happy to help," I said and guided her back toward Mitch, who was trying unsuccessfully to stand up.

"Keep your seat, Mitch," I said, feeling even worse about his knee.

After buying a cup of coffee and sitting down, I looked at both of them.

"Mr. Stirling," Mitch said, "I'm sorry for all the trouble I caused you."

"And I'm sorry I tackled you so hard," I responded. "And call me Nick."

"Don't worry about it, Mr. Stirling," he said, ignoring my invitation. "I was so crazy last night that I might have done anything with that gun. It was only later in the hospital that I got myself together and realized how far gone I'd been."

He explained he had damaged the meniscus in his left knee and would need minor surgery and some rehab to get his knee functioning again.

"Too bad," I said. "What about basketball this season?"

Mitch looked at Rachel, who smiled back at him. "Basketball is over for me," he said. "I'm going to switch my major to English and become a teacher. To tell you the truth, I was never good enough to play beyond college anyhow."

"And you'll be a poet," Rachel said. "Right now we're planning our first chapbook. We're going to write it together. The poems will be kinda like Marlowe and Raleigh's poems about a shepherd and his love, except we're poets who are really in love." She reached across the table to take his hand.

"You'll have to send me a copy," I said.

After sipping my coffee, I asked Mitch how he was handling the revelation that Schultz was his father.

"I was not as surprised as you might think," he said. "I saw Meluso—I can't call him Schultz—around a lot. In fact, I'm surprised it didn't occur to Antaglia that Adalinda was having an affair with him."

"Schultz really got around," I said. "He impregnated your mother—Cynthia Barnes, I mean—and he was the father of your sister with your adoptive mother, Adalinda. How does all this make you feel?"

"I haven't sorted it out yet," he said, "but what bothers me the most is how Meluso bred me like one of his pigs."

"Swine," I corrected him.

Mitch looked at me blankly. "Whatever," he continued. "But I was just a kind of experiment for him. And then he shot me full of steroids and Human Growth Hormone and who knows what else for most of my life." His face reddened as he thought about how he was treated. "To make matters worse, that bastard had done the same thing to my mother, only worse. Her face was ruined by his heavy HGH treatments."

"I understand how you feel, Mitch," I said. "You and your mother got raw deals from both Meluso and Antaglia."

"I'm just glad to know that my mother really loved me all those years," Mitch said. He hesitated, and then continued: "I guess almost every adopted child wants to find his birth mother. It's just too bad that she died so soon after I found her." He hung his head and wept. Rachel scooted her chair around the table and put her arm over his large shoulders.

After a few moments, Mitch looked up, and I asked if he'd answer some questions about the case.

"Certainly," he said.

I asked him why he ran away from Professor Connolly's house.

"I had gone to see the professor to apologize for getting angry at her," he said. "She had rejected my poems for the *Ithaca Review*, and I reacted badly, probably because of the steroids I was on at the time."

"So she was dead when you got there?" I asked.

"Yes," he responded. "It was horrible. The back door was unlocked, and I found her in a pool of blood with her little dog going crazy. I had just got him calmed down when I heard you ring the front doorbell. I know I should have waited, but I panicked, hiding outside in the bushes and then running into you when you came down the sidewalk."

"You told Jineral that you were involved in two murders in Ithaca," I said. "Were you connected with your mother's murder?"

"Not really connected," he said, "but I assumed I'd be a suspect when I heard she was dead."

"Why?"

"Because I had been seen about town with her," he replied. "I assumed I'd be one of the first suspects."

"I guess that makes sense," I said.

We chatted a bit about their immediate plans, and Rachel said that they were going to spend part of the holidays with Mitch's grandparents. This was her idea, I could see.

"You mean the Barneses?" I asked.

"Yes," Mitch said. He told me that he had visited them when he was in Kansas, after I had talked to them. They really made him feel welcome, and accepted him as part of the family. He planned to change his name to Barnes legally and thought that he might be able to develop a relationship with them. "I've never known any of my grandparents," he said.

"Are you going to see Roy?" I asked.

"I sure am if I can," Mitch said. "I don't know if he's in jail or not. Roy was a big help to me on the trip to Kansas. He explained a lot about what my mother was like as a girl and made her come to life for me—come to life just after she had been murdered."

"Did he tell you why he was arrested and imprisoned in Kansas?" I asked.

"Yes," Mitch said. "He was arrested for breaking into Meluso's apartment in Lawrence."

"Meluso lived in Lawrence? I thought he taught at Aurora College."

Mitch explained that Meluso taught at both colleges. He taught during the day at Aurora and then taught a freshman chemistry course in KU's night school and hoped eventually to be hired by the Chemistry Department there.

That might explain the Jay Hawk pin that the coroner found clutched in Connolly's hand, I thought, remembering that Meluso wore on his lab coat a Central Lions pin. If he taught at KU, he might still have had a pin from there.

"Why did he break into Meluso's apartment?" I asked.

"He often was the go-between who transported my mother's drugs from Meluso to her," Mitch explained. "Meluso didn't want to carry them himself, so he gave Roy a key to his house. That way he could pick up the vials and carry them to Aurora for Cynthia. But Roy began to see how the drugs were affecting her and wanted her to stop taking them. One day, instead of transporting the drugs, he threw them away. When Meluso discovered that, he had Roy arrested for breaking and entering."

"Sounds like flimsy evidence to convict him on," I said.

Mitch nodded. "The way Roy explained it was that he had a long record of petty crimes from when he was younger. His record made him appear to be a hardened criminal. He also couldn't tell the full story about the drugs without implicating Cynthia. He refused to do that and got two years in prison."

Roy certainly has had his share of bad luck, I thought.

"Do you know who murdered Mitch's mother and the professor?" Rachel asked me.

"I don't know for certain and don't want to say any more right now," I said.

I wished the young couple good luck and walked back to the Accord. When I got there, my phone buzzed. It was Brett, who sounded spent.

"I've never been so exhausted in my life," she said. She explained that the interrogations had gone well, and she had a lot to tell me. "I think the case is pretty much wrapped up, Nick. How about some lunch?"

"Great!" I exclaimed. "I'll pay to make up for our interrupted dinner last night."

I met her at Sherman's March. We were shown to the same table as last time. When Brett sat down and got settled, she smiled at me. "Largo said you stopped by the lab and got the basics on the preliminary blood analysis," she said. "That the fresh blood on the knife is human points to Meluso as a prime suspect."

"I have some additional information," I said and told her about Antaglia's files and what they revealed about Adalinda's past.

"So Adalinda had a personality disorder that made her attack the women she considered Mitch's mothers," she said. "That explains her murdering Cynthia but not Professor Connolly."

"Mitch had taken to calling the Professor his spiritual mother," I said, "and that, I suspect, was enough to set Adalinda off."

"She's one crazy woman," she said.

We looked at the menu and ordered when the waitress came over.

"How did it all go down in the interrogations?" I asked.

"Well, we started with Adalinda. She had met early with her lawyer, who explained the potential punishment she faced—life in prison, maybe even the death penalty—and she very quickly threw Meluso to the wolves," she said.

"Maybe you should say she threw him to the swine," I said.

She gave me her mock frown again, as if I had said something off color.

"Whatever," she said. "But Adalinda was very clear that the murders were Meluso's idea and she had tried to talk him out of them."

"But what motive did Meluso have to murder the two women?" I asked.

"I wondered about that, too," Brett said. "Adalinda claimed that Meluso had some long-simmering hatred toward Cynthia Barnes, but I didn't believe that. Under her lawyer's direction, Adalinda signed a confession that she knew of Meluso's plan to murder the two women and tried unsuccessfully to dissuade him from carrying it out."

"What did Meluso think of all this?" I asked.

Brett explained that the interrogation team went to the regional hospital after finishing with Adalinda and found Meluso weak but awake and ready to protect Adalinda. "He first claimed that he had planned the murders himself, but he couldn't produce a credible motive for murdering the two women, especially Professor Connolly, who he didn't even know," Brett said. This stance lasted only a few minutes. When Brett reviewed Adalinda's statement that the murders were his idea, Meluso changed his position quickly. "He realized that Adalinda was throwing him over to protect herself, and he explained how the murders really occurred."

"And how was that?" I asked.

Brett thought for a moment, to organize her answer. She

said that, as my evidence suggested, Adalinda had long been angry that Mitch had gotten close to two other women and considered them more like mothers than he considered Adalinda herself. She didn't much like Mitch and left most of his care to Stella, the family maid, but she was a proud woman and a jealous one. She decided to do away with both Mitch's natural mother, Cynthia Barnes, and his spiritual mother, Professor Connolly. She didn't want to dirty her own hands, so she turned to Meluso, who had been in love with her for years. She promised him that if he killed the two women, she would divorce Antaglia and marry him.

"A quid pro quo," I interrupted.

"That's right," she responded. She continued: "Meluso admitted in the interrogation that he would have done practically anything to marry Adalinda."

"Why was he obsessed with her?" I asked.

"The two of them had begun their affair soon after the Antaglias had moved to Ithaca," Brett explained. "Meluso had been a colleague of Antaglia's at Aurora College, where they had developed methods for doping athletes. Meluso knew of Adalinda but didn't meet her until he followed Antaglia here, where he was to continue his doping program. He couldn't work for the Athletic Program for obvious reasons so he took the position in the Ag School. It was a perfect cover for him since he gave many of the same steroids and hormones to his swine. Meluso and Adalinda immediately fell in love, and Adalinda had long promised Meluso that she would marry him. He wanted that for several reasons. They were both Germans, they had had Christa together, and Meluso wanted access to Adalinda's fortune. He was tired of being an impoverished lab technician."

"If they both wanted to marry, why didn't it happen?" I asked.

"Adalinda was afraid that she would have to pay Antaglia alimony," Brett said. "She was afraid of that until recently, when Antaglia's coaching book became a best seller. Then he had money of his own, and Adalinda was willing to begin divorce proceedings."

I explained what I had discovered in Antaglia's Linda Becker file. If Meluso had hoped to partake in Adalinda's wealth, he would have been disappointed. Contractually, Adalinda's money would revert back to her father or his estate if she were to divorce Antaglia. I told Brett again where to find the files.

"So how did the murders go down?" I asked

"Meluso explained what happened," Brett said. "He and Adalinda went to Professor Connolly's house and waited until she got home. They followed her in the back door, and said they wanted to talk to her about Mitch. She was willing to do so with Mitch's mother. While the two women talked, Meluso came up behind the professor with his butcher knife and slit her throat."

"And Adalinda watched that?" I exclaimed.

"Meluso claimed that she enjoyed it," Brett said. "Meluso's description of the murder supports the forensics from the scene. The coroner said that the perp was a tall man who used a sharp knife to cut the throat upwards."

"I have some additional information that you might find useful," I said.

"What is it?"

I told her that Mitch had admitted that he had gone to see Professor Connolly soon after she was murdered to apologize for getting angry at her for rejecting his poems for the *Ithaca Review*. He had found her dead, in a pool of blood, just as I had a few minutes later.

"That explains the tall man who knocked you down as he ran to a large black car," she said.

"Yes, the Cadillac Roy borrowed from his half-brother," I said.

"I'll have to talk to Mitch about what he saw," Brett said, and I told her I had already advised him to contact the police.

We sat for a moment thinking about Connolly's murder. From everything I knew about the professor, she was a good poet and teacher. I was sorry to see her murdered by a jealous woman who considered her in some crazy way a rival.

"What did Meluso say about Cynthia Barnes's murder?" I asked.

"It was similar to Connolly's," Brett said. The next evening, Adalinda had talked Meluso into going with her to the Lions Den. They watched Roy drop Cynthia off and drive away to set up the money exchange with Antaglia.

"At the golf course in Comfort," I added.

"That's correct," she responded and then continued:

"The two of them parked in front of Cynthia's room and then knocked on the door. Cynthia let them in, and Adalinda asked her where Mitch was. Meluso said the two women argued and came to blows over who was Mitch's real mother, and while the altercation went on, he slipped behind Cynthia and slashed her throat with the butcher knife. Then Meluso took Adalinda back to her house where you met her and Antaglia later in the evening before the trip to Comfort."

I remembered Adalinda had looked a little disheveled when I arrived that night. Now I knew why.

"But before meeting the Antaglias, I arrived on the scene at the Lions Den a few minutes after the murder," I said, "and found the body."

"And then left the scene," Brett said, accusingly.

"I should have stayed," I admitted, "but I didn't like the idea of being found at two similar murder scenes in two days. The police might have gotten the wrong idea about me," I continued, grinning at Brett. "Plus I was on my way to assist Antaglia with the money drop for the phony kidnapping," I added as an afterthought.

"And we know how well that went, Mr. Stirling," she said, as she leaned over the table and stroked my cheek.

"So what's going to happen now?" I asked.

"I've communicated with Ithaca's DA, and he has decided

to indict Meluso and Adalinda for murder one. He'll do that later today if he hasn't already."

"I don't think he had much choice on that, given the evidence of premeditation against the two," I said. "But what about Mitch?"

"What about him?" Brett asked.

"Will he be prosecuted for his involvement in two kidnappings?"

"I doubt it," she said. "All of these people, the two Antaglias and Meluso, are in some sense his parents. I don't think they'll testify against their own son. Meluso and Adalinda told me as much. I'm not sure about Antaglia."

We agreed to have dinner at her condo, and I assured her I had nowhere else to be that evening..

But I had one more visit to make that morning. I drove to Antaglia's house, identifying it a block away by the distinctive turret, and parked in the long circular driveway, removed the brown paper bag from my evidence box, and took it to the front seat. I carefully counted the money, which came to a total of $95,800. Roy had probably given his half-brother his $10,000, and Mitch and he had spent the rest on the trip to and from Kansas. I wrote down the total on a sheet torn from my pocket notebook and then took the $1475 I had left from Antaglia's $4000 retainer and added it to the total. I kept only my normal fee plus the travel expenses back and forth to Kansas. I didn't want to keep extra money so tainted with blood and misery.

When I rang the front bell, Stella opened the door immediately, as if she had been waiting for me.

"How are you, Mr. Nick?" she asked.

"Fine, Stella. Is Coach Antaglia awake? I need to see him one last time," I said.

"He's awake but talking crazy," Stella said. "He keeps talking about his book."

"What about his book?" I asked.

"He says that nobody's gonna want to buy it if Mitch

doesn't make it to the pros," she said.

"That might be true, Stella," I explained. "Coach promised fathers a lot in that book if they followed his advice. If it doesn't work for his main example, Mitch, why would anyone believe it would work for their sons?"

"He's also talking about losing everyone important in his life," Stella said. "Like you said last night."

"I think he has," I said.

She led me through the hallways to Antaglia's bedroom in the second story of the turret.

"Is Mrs. Antaglia coming back soon?" she asked.

"I don't think so," I said, and told her about her arrest and impending indictment.

Stella began to weep.

"Who's going to take care of Coach?" she moaned.

I told her Antaglia probably had a good insurance plan and enough money to hire the best home medical care in the region if he needed it.

We arrived at Antaglia's bedroom door, and Stella knocked lightly. When Antaglia didn't respond, she went in, and I followed. He was sitting up in his bed staring blankly in front of him.

I walked over to him and called his name. He looked wearily in my direction.

"Where have you been, Stirling?" he demanded. "I've been waiting for you."

"I've been tying up loose ends on the case," I said. I informed him that Mitch was now O.K. but needed a knee operation that would prevent him from playing basketball this year. I didn't mention his son's decision to give up the game completely. I asked him if he was going to press charges or testify against Mitch for kidnapping, and he said he wouldn't. "It would just be more bad publicity for the book," he complained.

I also informed him that Adalinda and Meluso would be indicted for the murders of Professor Connolly and Cynthia

Barnes.

"Is Linda in jail?" he asked.

"Yes."

"That's a good place for her," he growled.

I held up the brown bag and told him how much of his $110,000 was left. He pointed to the corner: "Toss it there," he directed me.

"Can I do anything else for you?" I asked.

"No, you've done enough," he muttered. He then turned his face to the wall and closed his eyes. In my line of work, I've seen more than a few people die, and I realized Antaglia had that far away look of those preparing to leave this world for the next.

I instructed Stella to call an ambulance to take Antaglia to the hospital. Then I said goodbye, walked out of the house, and started for Brett's condo. She wouldn't be there, but she had given me a key.

Michael G. Moran

Michael G. Moran is a Professor of English at the University of Georgia, Athens, where he teaches courses in rhetoric, writing, and 18th-century British literature. He has published nine scholarly books on rhetorical theory, technical communication, and composition studies. *That Far Away Look* is his first novel. He is married to Molly Hurley Moran, and has a daughter, Alison Moran.